ESCAPE *from*
AMSTERDAM

Center Point
Large Print

**This Large Print Book carries the
Seal of Approval of N.A.V.H.**

ESCAPE
from
AMSTERDAM
HEROINES OF WWII

Lauralee Bliss

CENTER POINT LARGE PRINT
THORNDIKE, MAINE

This Center Point Large Print edition
is published in the year 2022 by arrangement with
Barbour Publishing, Inc.

All scripture quotations are taken from the
King James Version of the Bible.

The text of this Large Print edition is unabridged.
In other aspects, this book may vary
from the original edition.
Printed in the United States of America
on permanent paper sourced using
environmentally responsible foresting methods.
Set in 16-point Times New Roman type.

ISBN: 978-1-63808-485-3

The Library of Congress has cataloged this record
under Library of Congress Control Number: 2022940817

DEDICATION

To those who sacrifice everything to help and rescue children through fostering, adoption, youth groups, crisis pregnancy centers, teaching, ministering, giving, and more. God sees it all. Thank you.

ACKNOWLEDGMENTS

I wish to give my heartfelt thanks to my reviewers Steve, Sherry, and Johnnie for their advice and careful perusal of this work. I especially thank Becky, Ellen, and the staff of Barbour Publishing for the opportunity and the labor of love in helping me share the lives of those who gave everything to rescue Jewish children from the horrors of the Holocaust. May we never forget.

PART ONE

The Netherlands
1939–40

CHAPTER 1

Pop, pop, pop.

What was that?

Sharp prickles of fear raced through Helen Smit's fingertips. She gripped the handlebars, her feet jostling on the pedals, forcing the bicycle to a screeching stop. Dirt spit up from the front wheel, splattering her white cotton bobby socks and bare calves.

Boom!

Her head jerked to the left and the right as she steadied the bicycle with her feet on the ground. Fields of waving emerald grass wanted to calm her anxious heart, but she'd have none of it. Instead, she sucked in a sharp breath, murmured a prayer, and forced her feet back onto the pedals, pushing the bike as fast as she could.

Boom!

What is that noise? her mind cried again.

Her hands shook the handlebars. The bicycle wobbled, and the front wheel caught on some rocks. Suddenly a scream rose from her throat, and she stared at the ground. For an instant her arms and legs froze, even as she spit out grainy sands of dirt. When she finally did move, she felt a pain in her leg. *I've fallen,* her mind finally realized.

"*Gaat het?*" A gentle voice asking if she was okay floated over her head along with a tapping on her shoulder. Slowly she rolled onto her back, squinting at the piercing rays of sunshine. Then a dark form blocked the rays, and a strong hand reached down to help her up. Once on her feet, she tugged down her soiled dress and smoothed back strands of blond hair from her face. "I'm all right. I must have hit a patch of rocks after I heard something. A boom coming from somewhere. And a popping sound."

"Maybe you heard noise from the windmills or boats on the Markermeer."

The explanation eased Helen's mind as she gazed at her benefactor. She then analyzed her current predicament—a fine stream of blood trickling from a small cut on her leg, dirt smudged on her dress and socks, and, to her dismay, the handlebars of her bike bent at a thirty-degree angle.

The man now stepped into full view, lean and tall, wearing a dark cap over a head of sandy-colored hair. He gave her a handkerchief to dab the blood from her leg and then righted the bicycle to study the misshapen handlebars. "I think I can fix this," he declared.

"Can you?" She thanked him. "*Dank je wel!*"

Helen watched his every move as he returned to his bicycle. Only then did she notice the cart he pulled and the small boy sitting inside. The boy clambered out, holding a toy boat in his hands. "What's the matter, Erik?" he asked in a high-pitched voice.

"The lady fell," Erik answered. He took a small bag from the cart and found a wrench.

Helen smiled in the boy's direction, but her attention remained riveted on this man with the tool he twirled in one hand, returning to fix her mangled bike. "You certainly are well prepared."

"I have to be whenever I take Hans anywhere. Remember when we had trouble with my bicycle, Hans?"

Hans immediately launched into a story of riding along one of the dikes. The chain on the bicycle broke, sending the bike nearly careening off the dike and into the water. Erik tried to maintain control until they had gotten clear of the dike. "Mother said we could've drowned!" Hans exclaimed, his eyes growing large.

"Mother tends to exaggerate," Erik corrected, taking hold of Helen's bicycle and locking the front wheel between his knees. He blew out a sharp breath and used the wrench to twist the metal lug nut holding the bars in place. Once he had the bars loosened, he repositioned them and retightened the nut. "That should ride well now."

Helen stared in awe before realizing she ought to try out the man's handiwork before he left. She climbed onto the bike and rode it fifty yards

11

down the road and back again. "It's perfect. *Echt heel erg bedankt*!"

Erik returned the tool to the bag and stowed the bag in the cart. "You're welcome. We need to get going. We're heading to a children's boat race in Durgerdam."

"Is that the boat you will race?" she asked Hans.

He nodded as his fingers gently caressed the gleam of the polished hull. Erik interjected that three generations of his family worked on the small boat. "Grandfather designed it. Mother sewed the sail for it. Hans and I built it."

"How wonderful. *Succes*!" Helen bid them farewell and watched, albeit wistfully, as they returned to their bike to continue the journey. She enjoyed their companionship, especially after hearing the strange noises she was certain came from the air and not from the lake, which had sent anxiety washing over her like waves on the North Sea. Not that she wanted to crash into the dirt and nearly wreck her bike and soil her clothes just to meet a man. But the Lord always worked in mysterious ways, and He had done it again with this pleasant encounter.

Mounting the bike, Helen willed her feet to pedal strong and sound as she watched the fading forms of Erik and Hans in the distance. She decided the idea of watching happy children race boats on a fine summer day would do her good after all the recent mishaps and misgivings. But hearing another *boom!* in the air, her hands once more jiggled the handlebars. Despite what Erik suggested, could the noise be forecasting what Papa had spoken about at dinner last night? She could still see Papa's face—lines of worry crisscrossing his lean cheekbones, his blue eyes narrowing, as he clutched his hands together with elbows planted on the table. For as long as she could remember, Papa rarely showed fear or any other sign of weakness. His muscular arms had carried many large boxes over the years, toiling in the work of a warehouse laborer. He always proved the picture of strength and confidence, both physically and in his words. But last night he couldn't mask the emotional tide. He'd inhaled a deep breath and told them the news. Germany was readying its forces to invade Poland soon. Everyone looked at one another, wondering what it meant for them and the world. From the worry on Papa's face, Helen knew it couldn't be good. Would there be another world war? Would it affect the Netherlands, or would they remain neutral?

The quaint fishing village of Durgerdam appeared on the distant horizon, squelching the fearful thoughts of war. Helen liked to venture here when her heart yearned for peace, away from the congested suburbs of northern Amsterdam or Noord to quieter places beside the fresh waters of the Markermeer. Once, long ago, she found a fisherman willing to take her and her brothers on an excursion out on the waters. The peace of that time filled her heart, as did the wonder of seeing the Dutch coast from a watery perspective. How she wished she could capture the scenes rising before her—of the fishing village dotting the shoreline, children at play, and farther east along the coast, windmills that kept waters from a lake called the Zuiderzee out of the rich farmlands. Perhaps one day she would have the money to buy a camera. The desire to relish fine memories rose steadily with each passing moment. All of this was too precious to forget, and one day she must have photos of the scenery to remind her of happier times.

Helen cycled through the town to where the children gathered for the race. Suddenly she heard a voice from behind.

"*Hallo*! We never did introduce ourselves out on the road. I'm Erik Minger."

Helen whirled to face her benefactor once again. This time she studied more of Erik's appearance—shallow cheekbones, a triangular chin, bright blue eyes igniting his face, shocks of hair poking out from beneath a wool cap, and his tall frame outfitted in a simple cotton shirt and trousers. Warmth invaded her cheeks when he caught her staring at him, and his lips curved into a slight smile. She looked off in the direction of the boat race where the children crowded together, each clutching their prized handmade boats, before turning to face him. "I'm Helen Smit. I came to watch the boat race after you mentioned it. I would love to see my brothers race, but they are too old for such things."

"Hans is the perfect age. He was a surprise for our family eight years ago. God has His plans, eh?"

Erik now gazed at Hans, his body straightening, as if finding strength in the words he spoke. It moved her heart to hear him speak reverently of God. Not many did these days, including her family. She wished things were different. For her part, Helen kept a small Bible under her pillow, and she would read it early in the morning before a neighboring rooster crowed *Goedmorgen*. At night the comforting words of scripture—like waiting on the Lord to renew one's strength and make one fly like an eagle—would give her peace.

Just then a booming voice called the next group of children to the race. Helen saw Erik motion for her to join him and Hans. Warmth flowed through her. They stood with Hans, who jumped up and down, ready to race his boat. The small fleet of boats from the first group were already making their way, bobbing on the gentle ripples of water in the canal. Helen watched the gleeful smiles and wide eyes of the children. She wished they could be like this forever—enjoying the beautiful day with new friends and the excitement of the race.

Hans carefully placed his boat in the water. He clapped his hands, urging his boat onward. Helen watched Erik walk over to another little boy who hadn't yet placed his boat in the water. The boy's large eyes and trembling lips tugged on her heart.

"It's okay," Erik assured him. He then helped the boy put the boat in the water. When Erik returned to Helen's side, he murmured, "His boat won't go far with that small sail. But sometimes it's the act of doing, like putting the boat in the water anyway, that matters most."

The children laughed and pointed at their boats until a humble craft floated across the finish line. And then Helen heard a wail.

"I didn't win!" Hans cried, running to Erik. "You said I'd win!" The boy's face turned pink like a tulip, and his lips formed a scowl.

"Did your brother really promise you'd win?" Helen asked, looking from Erik to Hans. "How could he?"

"But—"

"I said your boat *could* win," Erik reminded him. "But the other child had a better sail. You should go over there and congratulate him on winning the race."

Clutching the dripping boat to his chest, Hans

stared at the grinning face of the victor, and his pink cheeks turned red. *"Nee,"* he muttered under his breath.

"Hans . . ."

He shook his head, his feet shuffling. Helen knelt before the boy and looked him in the eye. "Did you make this boat?" she asked.

"Not all of it. I helped Erik put the glue on it. I painted it red too."

Helen pointed to the other boys. "You know that only one can win. But we can win in other ways too. Like by helping each other. Many loving hands went into making your boat. Three generations of your family, from what your brother said. So don't you think that a family who makes a beautiful boat together wins, no matter what?"

Hans crinkled his small face and rubbed his eye with his fist. "But I didn't win the race."

"There will be other races. You can see what went wrong and correct it. But there are other good things to think about. How you worked together with your family to make the boat. And being here with your older brother, who has helped you in many ways. I know I'm thankful you both came to the race today, or else your brother would not have been there to fix my bicycle. I would still be stranded at the side of the road. Instead, I'm here."

Hans said nothing but only stared at his boat.

When she stood, Erik was gazing at her with a grin as if he liked the scene. "Dank je wel," he said softly.

"I learned from you," Helen said with a smile.

"I don't understand."

"When you helped that scared little boy put his boat in the water and told me about true winning . . . in the doing." His gaze remained fixed on her, increasing the warmth radiating within. She found herself sidestepping toward her bicycle. "It's getting late. I'd better be going."

"Will we see each other again?"

Helen thought on it then nodded and shared her phone number and address in Noord should he have an opportunity to visit. Inwardly, she hoped he would. "*Tot zien.*"

He lifted his cap.

Helen could barely contain the tremors of excitement as she furiously pedaled back toward Amsterdam, the wind blowing in her face. Her insides mimicked the fluttering of the birds overhead. Not that she hadn't had the attention of men in the past. But there was something interesting about Erik Minger that drew her. Like the way he interacted with his little brother and the children around him. They did have one thing in common. Helen wanted to share everything she knew with the eager minds of children. When she once told her parents her interest in becoming a teacher, Mama encouraged her to learn about running a household. It was difficult trying to convince her that there was more to life. God intended for women to use the gifts given to them and do good. Isn't that what the Bible admonished? Do good and share with others? And who was needier than the children she and Erik taught the lessons of life to today?

Helen straightened on the bicycle, and her pedaling feet slowed. *She and Erik?* Where did that thought come from?

She biked on with vigor, waving at passersby she knew until she came within sight of the homes clustered along the narrow street in Amsterdam Noord. The blue sky framed the gabled roofs, with several of the dwellings painted the cheerful colors of red and blue. Pausing before her home, Helen dismounted and pushed the bike up the walkway to be greeted by an array of blooming flowers. Mama loved her flower bed, and the posies displayed in the window boxes added to the brightness of the day. Mama's gardens held so many tulips that when they blossomed in the spring, one could not walk from one end of the house to the other without passing by colorful petals.

Helen propped the bike against the stately oak tree with a wooden swing hanging from a thick branch that had given her hours of enjoyment as a youngster, and hurried into the house. She found her parents in the sitting room, gazing at a piece of paper. They looked up as she approached, surprise on their faces. Helen stared, wondering what they could be looking at.

"*Hartelijk gefeliciteer*!" Papa exclaimed. Helen continued to stare. Why would Papa be offering profound congratulations, unless . . .

She hurried to his side to see the large words, *Teacher's College of Amsterdam.* Her heart skipped a beat. Dare she even think? "Did I . . . ?"

"You did!" Papa announced, his eyes wide and bright. He patted her shoulder. "They have accepted you."

Helen could hardly believe it. She had applied many months ago, and after time went by without a word, she thought for certain she'd been rejected. Papa rejoiced, but Mama said little. Helen knew what she was thinking—that her only daughter would be thrown into an institution filled with strange ideas. For Helen, this day had seen several dreams come true. And now with the icing spread on this luscious cake—an acceptance into the Teacher's College of Amsterdam to begin her journey of becoming a teacher—the day could not have ended more perfectly.

Helen turned and hugged her father close, inhaling the scent of tobacco from his once-a-day pipe he smoked most evenings. "I'm so proud," he murmured. "You will do well."

"Will she?" Mama wondered aloud. "It's getting more and more dangerous these days,

Hendrick. How can you be happy that our daughter is going away from us?"

"She's hardly going away to another country," he told her. "Only to Amsterdam Center. And you, my darling Helen, will excel above them all. I have great confidence."

Helen would have danced around the room to match the joy radiating in her heart if not for Mama's glassy-eyed look and reddened cheeks. And then Mama took an embroidered handkerchief from the pocket of her apron and began dabbing her eyes. Helen's cheer dissipated and she felt her mouth droop into a frown of dismay. "Oh Mama, why are you crying? Can't you be happy for me?"

"I don't know. I'm afraid for you, Helen. I'm afraid for all of us. There's danger coming. I know it. And I don't know what to do."

Helen refused to worry about the unknown or the sounds she heard earlier today near the Markermeer or anything about war or invasions. Everything faded under the news of a fresh start in college, and that's all that mattered to her joy-filled heart.

CHAPTER 2

As the days passed into autumn, Erik's thoughts buzzed with images of Helen Smit after the meeting in Durgerdam. Everything had been orchestrated perfectly—from the meeting after the bicycle accident, to the way they interacted with the children during the boat race, to her compliment given under a set of large blue eyes. After she'd left that day of the boat race, he'd found someone with a spare scrap of paper and a pencil to scribble down the address and number she had given him to her family home in Noord. But the busyness of his job kept him occupied. He called her a few times, and she shared her excitement over her college acceptance. In the last few weeks, he had ridden his bike from central Amsterdam and stopped across the street from the Smit home, watching for signs of her. The house, painted white, showed off its gabled roof and the prominent scalloped patterning. The large black hook near the upper-floor windows served as a reminder of Holland's past and the pulley system most houses had to move goods from the attic to the street below. He tried to summon the courage to knock on the door and offer a greeting, but his nerves got the better of him. For now, he remained content to stand across the street and murmur prayers for the ones that resided there. Especially for Helen Smit.

Today he decided to return to the pretty home, unsure what he would do, but certain plans had a way of working out if he took a step of faith. After all, her college term would be starting in a matter of days, and he should wish her well on her endeavors. Life was a continuous walk of faith, but especially now on the heels of the German invasion of Poland and nations declaring war. Newspapers and radio programs daily blared the news and what it could mean. Anxiety lay thick in the air as he passed by people on the street. He could see the lines of worry etched into the faces of the frail and hear the loud chatter of the younger population trying to make sense out of it all. A visit with Helen was what he needed to transport him away from all the doom and gloom and focus on better things, like each other.

Erik arrived at the home with its window boxes of faded blooms to find an older man instructing his teenage son in handling an axe. Erik smiled, remembering the times his father instructed him, from fixing broken items to rethreading his fishing pole to fixing his bicycle—which came in handy with Helen's predicament—to learning how to drive an automobile. When Papa arranged for Erik's job at the grocery store owned by his friend, Mr. Baas, he dutifully accepted and had worked there ever since. Papa always told him to give life his very best in whatever situation he found himself in. Erik did what he could, even if the job proved tedious and sent his thoughts drifting to doing something more significant with his life. What, exactly, he didn't know.

When the father went into the house, the young teen turned and saw him. He waved. "Hallo. Are you here to deliver something?"

Flustered, Erik backed away. "Nee. I . . . uh . . . I was wondering if Helen Smit is here?"

"*Ja*, she's my sister. *Ik ben* Simon." Before Erik could utter another word, the boy spun about and ran into the house. Erik glanced at his bicycle where he had left it propped against a tree by the sidewalk, contemplating pedaling off before she appeared. Instead, he stood his ground and waited until Helen emerged, dressed in a pretty floral-print dress, her honey-colored hair brilliant in the sun's rays. She looked more beautiful than he remembered, but her windblown and dusty appearance that day in Durgerdam still remained an attractive memory.

"Hallo! I was hoping you'd visit," she said with a smile. "Please come in."

Erik whipped off his cap and followed her inside. He shuffled across creaky wooden floors to the sitting room. A thick red and blue rug covered the floor. Satin sheen armchairs rested in corners opposite a long sofa where he took a seat.

"I can make us some coffee," she suggested.

Erik would rather whisk her away from here—perhaps to a nearby café where they might talk until the late hours and he could learn everything about her. With siblings and parents lurking about, their gazes probing him in curiosity, the atmosphere made his throat tighten. He swallowed and asked, "Is there a café nearby? I don't want to be a bother."

Helen stepped back. Her eyes widened before a smile crept across her face. "Ja."

At least any bashfulness did not rule him to the point that he couldn't suggest another place to meet. She ran to get her pocketbook, and soon they were on their way, quiet for a time as they walked past many homes and over a small bridge crossing a canal. Finally, they spoke.

"It's so nice . . ."

"So what happened with . . ."

They laughed, and each glanced away. How he wished he had taken her to the café weeks earlier rather than engaging in a few simple phone calls. "Please, you first."

"Dank je wel. I was just going to say how nice it is for you to come. I was wondering when we would see each other, especially with college starting. But I know you've been busy."

"It's not my first time visiting," he confessed. Helen paused in her walking and turned to him. "I came here a few other times. Prayed a little.

Watched." He felt the warmth creep into his face. "But I should have come right to the door."

"Well, I'm glad you came back and announced yourself this time." She giggled and then turned serious. "I leave in a few days for college, and with everything going on, it's difficult to prepare."

They began walking again. "You will do fine. I knew you should be a teacher the first time we met. The way you talked to Hans and your excitement . . . you have a gift."

"Do you think so?"

"Of course. Never doubt it for a minute. And I know we will be able to see each other more often. The Plantage Middenlaan where the college is located is close to where I work."

"Yes, and I will be boarding near the college." She talked then of renting a room from a family called the Cohens to avoid the long trip from Noord every day. "And there's a *schouwburg* across the street from the college." Her face tilted up toward the sky, and her eyes seemed to take on a faraway look. "I've never been inside that theater, but it would be wonderful sometime to see a concert or play, don't you think?"

He liked the idea very much. It would be wonderful to see her in a fancy dress, one hand in the crook of his elbow with a pocketbook dangling from the other. They would enjoy a candlelight dinner at a restaurant, followed by the theater to hear a fine orchestra. He stored the idea away for another time. "So have you always wanted to be a teacher?"

Helen laughed, a joyful sound that went well with the bird singing from a nearby fencepost. "It was a part of me even as a child. When we were growing up, we often played school. I would put out a big board and play the teacher because I was the oldest. I would make up lessons for my brothers. We did arithmetic and learned how to write. We even put on a play for Papa and Mama."

Erik tried to imagine Helen as a young girl, her golden hair fashioned into two long braids that fell below her shoulders, standing before the eager pupils of her family, ready to teach them all she knew in her youthful age. "What play did you perform?"

"*The Golden Helmet*." She paused. "It was very emotional. You probably heard of it, since it's a folktale, but it recreates the crown of thorns *Jezus* wore and how that crown of thorns is replaced by a crown of gold. In fact, I think we still have the gold crown we made somewhere around. We made it out of flour paste and paper and painted it. We were always making things in our school. We even carved our own wooden shoes. We gave a pair to Mama once for her birthday, but they were too small." She laughed at the memory.

Erik marveled at her creativity and the way her face shone when she laughed. He took up her hand then, soft and inviting in his. He hoped she didn't think him too forward. After all, this was only their second meeting, even if they had shared a few phone calls. At least she did not draw back. Everything about her sent his mind into a whirlwind of thoughts and his heart pounding in his chest. "I would like to see what you made in your family school."

"If you had stayed for coffee, you could have seen everything," she teased. "But this is better, especially with my family's curiosity."

"Maybe when you return to visit your family during the term, I can come too. And if the holiday season isn't busy, perhaps then."

Helen smiled. After arriving at the café, they found a table overlooking a canal, and Erik went to buy the coffee and pastries. Boats slowly chugged on the water, with eager passengers enjoying the fine day. Others took walks or sped by on bicycles, the cheery ringing of bells alerting the pedestrians at the many intersections. For a time, she and Erik said nothing as they drank coffee, delved into the pastries, and watched life in Amsterdam.

"So will you attend a university one day?" Helen asked.

The question took Erik by surprise. He shook his head. "My family invested in the grocery business, so it was natural for me to work there. One day I will own a part of it."

"You could do other things also. For instance, I think you would make a fine teacher."

"Owning a business is fine work too. I help people every day."

"Of course. You meet many people. I only thought, when I saw you with Hans at the races and then talking to that shy boy . . ."

"I teach Sunday school," he said. "And I've been like a father to Hans in many ways. He looks up to me for most things in life. For instance, I taught him how to read."

"Ja, that's what I mean. Why don't you apply to the teacher's college?" She laughed. "It would be so much fun to take classes together."

Erik sighed. He did not wish to contradict her in any way, but college was not to be his lot in life. Like teaching was to her, business management seemed his call. Though the idea Helen wanted him to be with her made him happy. "I will visit you whenever I can, since the store is close by."

"It will be nice to see a familiar face. I'm nervous about going away. But it's a fine college with a good reputation. They believe in serving the Lord with our work, and that makes me happy."

"There's no better work than teaching children. I want to hear all the news. And if you ever need help . . ."

"Hopefully I won't fall off my bicycle again," she said with a laugh. "But if I do, I know who will come to the rescue."

"*Always.*" He wanted to add *and forever* but bit his lip. It was far too early in their friendship to comment on the future. Helen would be attending college, and he would work at the store and take each day as it came. He wondered if she also had reservations about the future, especially with the news of war on everyone's mind. He let that go for now when he observed her lift a napkin to pat her lips free of crumbs and sit back in her seat with a sigh of contentment.

"This is so pleasant and peaceful. I wish it would never end." She straightened. "Mama is concerned about me leaving with all this talk of war. What do you think will happen now that the Germans have invaded Poland?"

Her question made him glad to hear that similar things concerned them both. But the reality of the German invasion and declarations of war made by France and Great Britain sobered the moment. "I've heard rumors the Germans may come here."

Helen jerked, and her napkin floated to the ground. She bent and snatched it up. "Where did you hear that?"

"From some customers. I don't trust the enemy. I know we escaped invasion during the last war. But it's different this time, even if we have declared neutrality. The enemy is different, with different plans. Most do not think any declaration will stop an invasion." He paused. "Our best hope is that the Americans will also declare war. Their participation in the last conflict helped us greatly. I think it's the only way to stop this before it escalates." His voice drifted off. Watching Helen shift in her seat, her blue eyes staring straight ahead as if in another realm, her lips silent, he knew he'd lost her to sudden fear and uncertainty.

"I—I should be going," she said, her gaze turned aside as if looking in his eyes would conjure up thoughts of dread. He chastised himself for letting their time together drift to talk of war. The Germans had done more than just invade Poland. They were invading everyday lives and relationships, bringing fear and uncertainty. And it made him angry.

The walk back to Helen's home was cloaked in a quiet stillness. Even the cheery people they had seen occupying the streets appeared to have wandered off, leaving empty bridges spanning the canals. He heard Helen sigh, her hand brushing back a lock of hair that had fallen forward.

"*Alles komt goed*," Erik said.

She glanced his way, and he wondered if she could believe that everything would be fine. "You know things are not goed. In fact, they could turn bad quickly."

31

"We need to look for things we can't see. To look to God, no matter what happens here." He picked up her hand and gave it a gentle squeeze.

Helen nodded, and Erik sensed relief wash over him. He released her hand, and they walked along until they spied two children running toward them. Perched on the girl's head was a paper hat painted bright yellow.

"Esmee! Karl! What's wrong?" She turned to Erik to explain. "These are our neighbor's twins. Sometimes we care for them while their parents are working. My brother Simon loves having a boy younger than him to play with."

Esmee curtsied and said, "*Mevrouw* Smit wanted to know where you are, Helen. She is sewing a dress for you and needs you. The dress was too big on me."

Karl crinkled up his nose. "*Ja, ja*, I told you. You can't let her sew a dress on you!"

Esmee, wearing the makeshift hat, snickered loudly. Erik heard Helen chuckle then—a delightful sound after the discomfort that ended their visit at the café. "So you're wearing the golden crown," Helen said. "Simon must have found it." She looked at Erik with a gleam in her eye. "That is the crown I was telling you about— the one we made for the play many years ago." They walked together the short distance back to the Smit house.

When they arrived, Erik knelt before Esmee,

who held the hat in place on her head with both hands. "Did you know we will receive special crowns in heaven when we see God?"

Esmee's blue eyes widened, and her small hand patted the paper and paste helmet. "Like this one?"

Erik laughed. "Well, it will be much sturdier than this one. But ja, it will be expensive and beautiful, made of fine gold and embedded with many jewels." He picked up a small branch, fallen from the oak tree in the Smit front yard. "But while we are here on earth, we wear the helmet of salvation. Think of the crown as a helmet for a brave warrior. And this branch can be your sword of the Spirit. It represents the Word of God. So now you have the helmet and the sword to battle against the enemy."

Esmee shouted with joy and raced around, waving the branch while trying to keep the helmet from being tossed about in the breeze. Karl realized how much fun his twin was having and demanded he be allowed to wear the helmet.

"What a great Bible lesson," Helen said.

"We must wear our helmets and take up our swords. The days are evil."

She patted his hand. "Dank je wel," she whispered to him. "You've done more than you know." Then she called for the children to walk them back home.

Erik wondered about that comment as he

watched the threesome head down the street. He was not just preaching to them but to himself. The days *were* growing evil, and he prayed for the strength to face whatever came.

CHAPTER 3

For the next several months, Helen relished every moment she spent in study at college. Each morning the students gathered in a large room where the chaplain led them in prayer. Lectures teemed with eager students scribbling in notebooks as professors shared their wealth of knowledge. But as time passed from winter to spring, there seemed to be a growing apprehension both in the chaplain's daily prayer and in the atmosphere of the place. The professors gathered in small groups, whispering to each other. Drills of various forms, including for enemy attack, interrupted the classes. Students practiced taking cover under desks or in back rooms.

In the middle of a history lecture taught by Professor van Hulst, the president of the college opened the door to the classroom and motioned for him. Helen watched with both curiosity and concern, even as she tried to focus her attention on the lesson in the textbook. When the professor returned, lines of tension crisscrossed his face, and his mustache quivered. He removed his glasses to rub his eyes. Watching him write in slanted sentences on the blackboard while his gaze darted to the windows overlooking the street made her wonder what was afoot.

Helen then chastised herself for reading every situation and emotion as doom and gloom. At these confusing times, she recalled Erik's words of keeping one's thoughts focused on heavenly things and not on this world. Whenever he had the chance, Erik visited her during breaks between classes and came calling at the Cohens' where she had rented a room. His reassurance proved more costly than gold, especially in those times when the horn blared and the announcement came that they would again conduct a drill in case of enemy attack. Standing shoulder to shoulder with classmates, huddled in an interior room, she took comfort in picturing his handsome face and confident ways.

Thankful for the end of classes this day, Helen pedaled her bicycle along the nearly empty street to the grocery store. The smiling face of Erik Minger from his elevated position on a ladder where he stacked canned goods calmed her frayed nerves. He looked down with a knowing gleam in his eye. "Ah, my dear *Juffrouw* Smit, what can I get for you today? Perhaps a wheel of the finest smoked cheddar?"

Helen couldn't help but smile at the greeting he always gave her when she stopped by, suggesting a variety of foodstuffs, from fine herring to candies. Although it was a bit of a ride from the Cohens' home where she stayed, she liked coming here to buy food and spend time gazing at Erik's handsome face as he made small talk while checking out her purchases. The owner, Mr. Baas, allowed him breaks to sit with her on the bench outside the store. At times he would visit her at the Cohens' where he always asked about her classes and what she was learning. On a few weekends, he ventured with her to Noord to visit the family and even played ball with Lars and Simon. Within the last few weeks though, the talk of war escalated. When she told him one day about the whispering in tight circles and the constant air raid drills conducted at the college, Erik sighed.

"It seems the way of things right now," he said. "Rumors are everywhere that Germany has set their sights on our country. We share a common border, after all."

"They can't come here!" Helen said in distress, wishing her voice didn't betray her anxiety. "We are remaining neutral just like in the Great War. Queen Wilhelmina has assured the Germans that we want no part of this."

"Helen, other things are at work here. There are politics involved, and even if they were explained, we still wouldn't understand it. But you know the danger is growing. Think about the dark clouds you see from the northwest and how the wind picks up as the storm approaches. We must be ready for whatever comes and pray hard."

Helen put away their past conversations to concentrate on the smile on Erik's face. He glanced over at Mr. Baas, who waved at him. "You don't get in trouble for taking these breaks when I come by, do you?" she wondered as he descended the ladder.

"If so, I will gladly take the punishment. But don't worry. Mr. Baas understands, and he is happy to hear you are becoming a teacher."

Erik fetched some cold bottled drinks and gestured to the outdoors on this warm May afternoon. They headed for their favorite bench overlooking the canal. Helen listened as he shared the story of one customer who had a lengthy list of groceries and wanted it delivered. "And the dog wouldn't let me anywhere near the door. I stood with a box full of groceries and no way to deliver them."

"What did you do?"

"I gave the dog a bit of the customer's beef and slipped past. The woman wasn't too happy, but I had little choice. It was either that or my leg."

Helen realized her mouth had fallen open and quickly shut it. "That's awful. I'm just glad the dog didn't bite you. Have you ever had a dog attack you?"

He shook his head. "No, but I've had unfriendly people who claimed they never ordered the food I was sent to deliver. A miscommunication of addresses."

She took a sip of her drink, watching a young mother toting a bag while trying to control a rambunctious toddler who wanted to run ahead. "I think a lot about the boat race in Durgerdam. The children were so happy and carefree that day. A perfectly peaceful time. Except maybe for your brother."

"Hans still complains about losing the race. He insists I said he'd win. We studied the boat afterward, and I suggested some changes to help it sail better. I told him it should do well in the next race but reminded him that doesn't mean he'll win. He wasn't happy about that either."

"Lars and Simon were the same way at that age. Only with them it was their kites and who could fly his the highest." Helen took another sip of the refreshing drink. Above them came the sound of engines. She glanced upward to see several low-flying planes.

Erik shared in her gaze of the sky, shielding his eyes with his hand and wishing out loud he had a pair of binoculars. "They might be British. I don't know."

A man walking by suddenly stopped and pointed at the planes. "Do you see them? It's the Luftwaffe!"

"Are you sure?" Erik asked as he and Helen lurched to their feet. Several more planes roared across the skies.

Helen took hold of Erik's arm, the reassurance

of his strength giving her comfort. "Where are they going?"

"They could be reconnaissance aircraft," Erik said. "I learned about that from a friend. They send out planes to scout for enemy activity. They might be observing the land for enemy positions."

The man who identified the planes joined the conversation. "They may be heading to bomb England."

Helen gasped. "If they are bombers, why are they flying so low over us?"

No one said anything as they watched the planes flying across their beloved country. One began to dive, and Helen tried to make out the black cross on the wing. She swallowed hard, fighting back the fear. Erik said he should go back to work, that it might get busy with this new activity. After quietly following him to the store where she purchased some food, Helen bid him a quick farewell and headed for her bicycle. Everywhere she looked, the faces of her countrymen boasted wide eyes with lips pressed tight, hurrying along with their parcels, uncertain of what was happening. Helen tried not to dwell on the anxiety she witnessed around her as she pedaled swiftly to the Cohen residence, praying that the planes would soon be gone.

In the middle of the night, a strange noise jolted Helen awake. At first she thought it was part of some maddening dream until a light glared in her face. She sat up to find Mrs. Cohen standing in the doorway, shining a flashlight. Helen threw off the covers, grabbed her robe, and went to her.

"We are under attack." Mrs. Cohen's voice quivered.

Mr. Cohen came up behind them, dressed in his long nightshirt and cap. She followed them into the dark sitting room where Mr. Cohen switched on the radio.

"Repeating our news bulletin, the Netherlands have come under attack by the German Luftwaffe. Several areas have been badly damaged by bombing raids. There are an untold number of casualties. Please remain where you are and take shelter immediately. Stay tuned for further bulletins."

Mrs. Cohen swept back a strand of her black hair sprinkled with gray. "Dear God, please help us! What will happen to us?"

Helen glanced out the front window, wondering if she would see flashes light up the normally indigo sky and hear the boom of exploding ordnance. She paced about, wiping her hand across her forehead. Her first thought was to climb on her bicycle and head across the river to Amsterdam Noord to see Papa, Mama, and her brothers. Until she realized it was still the middle of the night. "I must . . . I must call my parents," she told Mrs. Cohen.

"We can't telephone anyone right now," the woman said softly. "The lines are busy. I tried to reach my friend Martha."

Tears of fear gathered in the corners of Helen's eyes. She quickly wiped them away. Now was not the time to be swept away by emotion. She must ask God for clear thinking. What if the Germans began bombing Amsterdam? What could they do to survive?

"We must prepare," she told the Cohens. "Take the cushions off the chairs, and I'll get blankets from the closet. We can pad the interior part of the room where the small study is to shield us."

"Surely you don't think . . ." Mrs. Cohen's voice drifted away.

"There is no need," said Mr. Cohen, though the high-pitched lilt in his voice betrayed his doubt.

"Do you really want to take that chance? We must be ready for whatever happens. I will get water and food."

Mrs. Cohen only stared. "I don't understand. We want nothing to do with the war. We are a quiet and kind people who never bother anyone." She began to cry.

Helen came forward and held the woman close. "It will be all right. God has us in His hands. Please, let's get ready."

She sniffed and, along with Helen, prepared the small study with chair cushions placed against the walls, fortified with pillows, blankets—anything they could think of to shield them from a blast should bombs fall from the skies. Helen filled a bucket of water in case of fire and found some canned provisions. Mr. Cohen tried to gather any further information from the radio, but it only repeated the same bulletin. No one knew what might happen next, and the mere thought proved unnerving.

"This makes no sense," Mr. Cohen muttered. "We have done nothing to irritate the Germans' cause. In fact, we've helped them in many ways. It must be some misunderstanding."

Helen could not comprehend why the man did not understand what was happening after the dire news repeated over the radio. This was no misunderstanding but deliberate actions to overrun a sovereign nation. War had come to their beloved country.

They spent a restless night in the study, waiting for more bulletins and wondering if the bombs would fall on them. During the long hours, Mrs. Cohen tried to calm her jitters by singing a Jewish hymn while Mr. Cohen claimed he would find out more information at his work in the government come morning. Helen only prayed with all her might.

With classes canceled the next day, Helen stayed at the Cohens' and, like everyone, watched more German planes flying in formation over

Dutch airspace. Once she ventured outside for some air and noticed a bald-headed man pacing back and forth in agitation.

"I hear they are dropping nuns all over the land," he muttered. "What's next? We're done for!"

Helen looked at him in puzzlement. *Nuns? What kind of outlandish thing is that to say?* Until she heard another say it and then wondered if it was possible to have black-clad figures in their habits parachuting down as a method of deception. But rumors ran wild and so too did the mass confusion. If only Erik were here to lend some common sense to the chaos.

Helen stole away to her room at the Cohens' and reached for her Bible. In troubling times, the solace given in the words of scripture soothed her. The Bible talked a great deal about wars and rumors of wars. But God promised not to forsake them. He was with them, despite the planes roaring and bombs falling and an enemy bearing down in great strength. She must remain steadfast and sure and not give way to fear, even if it seemed impossible.

Erik fought to concentrate on his work, with the store inundated by the hordes of people frantically laying in provisions. Every day the news grew more dire. For some reason unknown to them, German forces had laid siege to their humble country. The Netherlands had always avoided political dissent. Though their country shared a border with Germany, nothing significant had ever materialized between them. No disagreements, and certainly never any talk of war. Until now.

Several days after news of the first bombardment kept everyone awake in the dead of night, bewildered customers still streamed into the store, their eyes wide, lips parted in anxiety, the worry bursting from their lips.

"Have you heard?" a man said loudly. "The queen has fled to England. We have no government."

"We are finished," said another.

"Why did the government abandon us?" moaned a woman, dabbing her eyes with a handkerchief. "What will happen to us? Dear God, help us!"

Erik's hands froze around the block of cheese he had been packing into a bag for a customer. People all around turned to each other and questioned what the queen's departure meant. Erik understood, and the mere thought numbed him. The Netherlands had surrendered. What it meant for the future of their country, he had no idea. But he feared the worst.

German occupation and annexation.

Now all he could think of was Helen. He imagined her like the woman before him, shedding tears of fear and confusion, and his arms enfolding her as he whispered prayers for safety and comfort. He had to go find her and make certain she was all right.

Erik loaded a wooden box with canned goods for a customer who paced before him, raking his fingers through shocks of dark hair. "They bombed Rotterdam, you know." The man's voice shook. "Destroyed it. They say more cities could be next. Like Amsterdam. Wait and see."

"I haven't heard they'll do such a thing here," Erik managed to say, though the trembling of his voice betrayed his mistrust. "We've surrendered." But he knew what the Germans had done and feared the worst.

"What am I supposed to do?" the man cried. "I have six children. I better buy another box of food."

"I'm sorry, but Mr. Baas has instructed that families may only purchase two of each canned good so everyone can buy what they need."

The frazzled man stared at Erik. "I will pay double."

"I'm sorry, but—"

"I'm offering to pay twice what the food is worth, and you won't sell it to me?"

"Sir, you'll have to speak to Mr. Baas about that. This is all I can do. There are many like you with families who need food, and we must make sure there's enough for everyone."

The man grumbled and lifted the heavy box after slapping down the guilders to pay for it. Erik sighed, sensing his nerves close to the breaking point. No doubt the rumor he'd heard from Mr. Baas would soon become reality. They would have to ration to handle the hoarding. Despite all this, the most difficult part of the emergency for him was not seeing Helen. He had not laid eyes on her since the day the first planes were sighted in the skies over their country. On a normal day, she would have come by to say hello, but there'd been no sign of her. And he worried.

When the frenzy of customers began to wane, Erik saw his opportunity. He tore off his apron and told Mr. Baas he must run a critical errand to check on the safety of a loved one.

"But you can't leave now!" the man protested. "We're far too busy. Look at us."

"I'm sorry, sir, but I must do this one errand. I'll return as quickly as possible." Erik ignored further pleading from the man as he hastened out the door. The scene on the streets made his feet jerk to a stop. People scurried about like frightened mice trying to avoid the claws of a cat. Some had carts laden with possessions. Others transported loads strapped to bicycles. All wore the same appearance—faces creased in terror, lips mumbling unheard words, hands rattling bags. They had no idea where to go or what to do, only that they must go somewhere. Anywhere. The picture was much like sheep ready to be pounced on by wolves. Erik wondered if Helen was also scared and caught up in the melee. He had tried calling her both at the Cohens' and her home in Noord, but the lines remained busy. What would happen if bombs fell or tanks began rumbling down the city streets? Where would they go? What would they do?

Deciding to check at the college, he went straight to the building, ducking around the many bicycles and people wandering the streets. The sight of such panic wrenched his heart. *God, we are in the middle of terror. Help us all.*

When he arrived at the brick building, an older man with a set of keys was locking the doors. "Sir? Is the college closed?"

The man turned to face him, his eyebrows drawn low over his eyes, his mustache twitching. "There will be no more classes until next term." He pulled a handkerchief from his pocket and wiped his face, sighing as he did. "If there is a next term."

"I'm looking for a student. Perhaps you know her. Helen Smit."

"Ja, an excellent and inquisitive student. She's in my history class. Always ready to answer any question I pose. She is fearless, and in these uncertain times, that's good."

Erik was happy to hear how well Helen was doing but still wondered how he would find her in all this confusion. "I don't suppose you would know where she might have gone?"

"I'm sure she is safe at home with her family by now. The students were instructed to return home immediately." He paused. "Please excuse me, but I'm troubled by many things, as we all are. And now we have no president for the college. Everyone has run away."

Erik gestured toward the locked doors. "Are you leaving also? Is that why the college is closed?"

"Nee, young man. I will not leave." The strength in his words made Erik straighten. "I've been offered the position of vice president, and I plan to accept. No matter what the enemy does, the college will reopen."

"How will anything be the same with the Germans as our new masters?"

The smile that appeared on the man's worn face sent shock radiating through Erik. "There is only one Master of all. Our Lord, Jesus Christ. And to Him every knee will bow. Even the German knee. It may appear they're victorious, but man's victory is fleeting. God will give us victory over our enemies."

The words were like a soothing balm, easing the pain of the fresh wounds suffered by their country. Erik thanked the man and hurried to the Cohen home to see if Helen might still be there. When he arrived, Mrs. Cohen greeted him. "Miss

Smit returned to Amsterdam Noord today. I tried to get her to go sooner, but she wanted to help me here."

"Dank je wel." Erik placed his cap on his head. At least she was safe . . . for now.

CHAPTER 4

Helen wished she knew what to do with her long and boring days, absent the lively existence of college. Professor van Hulst ordered all students home from college for an extended leave, halting the interesting days filled with knowledge and friendship. Too much uncertainty remained after the German attack and subsequent surrender of their country. From what Papa heard from refugees fleeing the West, Rotterdam had been reduced to rubble. Helen once visited the sweet city not far from the coast and the happy people who lived there. She couldn't imagine a landscape of shattered, smoldering homes. What if they bombed Amsterdam next? Occasionally she braved the uncertainty and the unknown to step outside the house and peer skyward to check for planes. Since the day she and Erik observed the German Luftwaffe moving across the skies, she dreaded seeing them again and the thought of other cities being destroyed. God's Word said to look to things above, but how could she when bombs destroyed their land? Instead, she must do the second part of the verse—focus her attention on the unseen. And to remember the golden helmet and God's protection.

Helen tried to keep busy with menial tasks around the house, but tension was ever present within her family. Her two brothers were eager to defend their country from the enemy. The older of them, Lars, two years younger than Helen but opinionated even as a child, informed the family he would find those standing against this invasion and do whatever he could to stop the destruction of their country. His defiant talk shattered the dinner table conversation one evening.

Mama stared aghast as Papa declared, "You'll do no such thing, Lars. It's reckless."

Mama dropped her fork on the plate with a resounding clink. "I won't have my sons doing something foolish like joining a war. I'm grateful we're here together and safe."

"But we're doing nothing!" Lars complained. "We must stop this now! My friend Dietrich came from Germany. He told me what's happening there. The German government thinks they are a pure race that should take over everything. He said they want the Netherlands to become a part of it."

Helen sensed her mounting confusion over all this. "Become a part of what?"

"A new Germany. They say that we need to become what we were born to be. Part of the new master race. They believe that the Jews and other races and the sick and disabled are evil and destroying the German way of life. Dietrich says they use the radio and newspapers to share the message and make people believe it."

"And they want to do that kind of nonsense here?" Papa asked, his eyes narrowing.

Lars nodded. "My friend said they made it happen in Germany, and now they want to spread it to other countries. They want a perfect people to make a perfect society and a perfect life."

Helen thought of the scripture where Jesus said that no one was perfect but God alone. Just the idea that people wanted to play God and choose who was good and who was bad made her angry. "I hate them."

"Helen!" Mama cried, her eyes flashing wide. "How can you say that?"

"Because it's true. I hate anyone who would do this to others—who destroy homes and lives because of their evil ideas."

Mama shook her head. "Enough. No more of this now. We are frightened enough as it is."

No one said anything more about the invasion at the dinner table. But Helen couldn't help but think about it, and when she did, her heart grew heavy. She couldn't bear that her beloved country had been overwhelmed by men who planned to root out the so-called inferior in their midst and change all that they knew and loved. How she wished she had the explanations of her godly history professor, Professor van Hulst, to make sense out of this. He would reason them out of the terror they found themselves in and would supply understanding through scripture. And she would dwell on the peace that passes all understanding rather than the fear of the unknown.

A few days later as Helen was tidying up the kitchen, Lars came in to fetch a cookie out of the jar. "Is it true what you heard from your friend?" she asked. "That the German people are being forced to accept their government's supremacy and get rid of others they dislike?"

Lars took a huge bite of the sweet and munched it while staring at her. How he could calmly indulge in a confection at a time like this went beyond her sense of reasoning. He swallowed and said, "Ja. That's why Dietrich left Germany to come here. We have always welcomed the persecuted. He is Jewish and was being mistreated. The German government said that inferior races as well as those with handicaps were like a disease, destroying everything. They were blamed for Germany's difficulties. Every day the news stated that Germany was doing right by cleansing the country of the disease, and now they want their neighboring countries to do the same. They tell the public they can live in peace with good lives if the diseased masses are dealt with." He continued eating the cookie until it disappeared.

"But why did they invade us? Why don't they stay in their country?"

"They want to spread their so-called perfect society."

Helen clenched her hands and felt warmth invade her face. "So their idea of a perfect society is dropping bombs and destroying homes and lives? That makes no sense." The irony of it nearly made her laugh in a despairing sort of way.

He blinked. "To them it does. Conquer and spread perfection according to their beliefs. That's what they did in Germany, Dietrich said. It's important to understand the enemy's way of thinking so you can make plans to defeat it."

Helen worried that the spread of this propaganda to tickling ears could be used to change who they were as a country. The Dutch once embraced everyone. They should never accept a doctrine that ends up hurting others. "How do we stop them from doing this here?"

Lars cocked a small grin and reached for another cookie. "A revolutionary idea, Helen. Don't let Mama hear you say that. Remember what she said at the dinner table the other night. She said it was foolish to get involved."

"We can't let them kill more people, Lars. Think of Rotterdam."

Lars suddenly took her arm and led her into the hallway. He stared at her with large, thoughtful eyes and said in a quiet voice, "I have something I want to say, but you can't tell anyone. Especially Papa and Mama. Promise?"

"Oh no, Lars!" She could not bear to see something happen to him. He had been known for his outspoken ways in school where he sometimes ended up in the office and once was even sent home. "Don't tell me you're in trouble. I can't take any more bad news."

"Do you promise?" he repeated.

"Ja. I promise. But—"

"I was talking to Dietrich. There is a group, a resistance group, that is meeting to decide what to do to fight the German occupation." He glanced down the hall. "You can't tell Mama though. Or Papa. Or Simon, who can't keep a secret."

Helen agreed that their younger brother liked nothing better than to share a secret. She gazed directly at Lars and received a fixed stare in return, with narrowed eyes and pressed lips marked in determination. "You're only seventeen, you know. Do you really want to become involved in something as dangerous as a resistance group?"

"After what Dietrich told me about people being taken away and killed, do we want that for us here? It's just like you said. We must stop it from happening."

A chill swept over her, and she hugged her arms close. "I don't know."

"Swear to me again you won't tell anyone what I've said."

"You know I won't." She put one hand to her

chest and held up the other. "But what about you? Will you go to these meetings?"

"I've already been to one meeting. There will be more."

"Lars, if you're caught, they'll kill you." She looked at his youthful face and remembered the paper crown he had made for their play. Tears gathered in her eyes at the thought of the fragile crown tearing to bits and him thrown into prison or worse. A tear escaped down her cheek. "I couldn't bear it if something were to happen to you. You're young and—"

"War makes everyone old, Helen. No one can be young when the enemy is here. We must all fight to survive or live a life of nothing, run by the powerful who don't care if we live or die."

Helen kissed him lightly on his cheek. "Can I share this with Erik?"

"That man you like? I don't know."

"He is trustworthy, and right now I need someone who can pray with me for your safety."

Lars was silent for a minute. "You don't have to tell him everything I'm doing. Just that I'm trying to help our country. And not a word to anyone else."

"All right." Helen watched him spin about on one foot and stride off with his head held high, much like a young soldier newly commissioned for military duty. In a way, he had been, but so had they all once their country became embroiled in war. Helen ventured to a back room that used to be their playroom and found the torn crown the two neighborhood children had been wearing. She went into the kitchen and made some flour paste to repair the paper crown, thinking of the good times they had growing up. How hard it must be for children like Karl and Esmee, and even Erik's brother Hans, frightened by war, not knowing if they would be safe. When the flour paste dried, she gently placed the helmet on her head and stood before the hallway mirror. "Oh God, keep Lars safe in Your hands. Keep us all safe in Your hands. We have nobody but You."

"Why are you praying for Lars?"

Helen spun about, the crown fluttering to the floor, to see Mama with a basket of damp clothes in her hands. "I need help putting up the wash," she added, her face scrunched as if trying to study the thoughts circulating in Helen's mind.

Helen dutifully followed Mama to the backyard and the lines of rope where they hung the cotton underthings, pants, shirts, and dresses in rows to dry.

"You haven't answered my question," Mama said, casting her a sharp glance.

"Oh, you know what he shared at the dinner table the other night. I worry about him. He has his own ideas about things."

To her relief, Mama nodded. "I worry about

him too. I'll ask your father to speak to him again. I don't want him getting into trouble. If there's one thing I'm happy about, it's that we're all together."

"We don't know the future though, Mama. You heard what Lars said. In Germany they separate out those they believe don't belong in their perfect society. What if they do that here? What if they start telling us what to do, where to go, what to think?"

Mama hurriedly pushed the clothespins onto the clothesline, making it shake. She let out a loud sigh. "Helen, like you said, we don't know the future. We must pray that soon this will be over and our country restored. But it's not for us to know. We can only do what's before us."

Helen remembered Lars and the solemn look on his face when he mentioned being involved with the resistance. "I think sometimes you want us to stay children and do what *you* think should be done. It's all right for us to make our own decisions and decide what's right."

Mama turned and stared at Helen through the slits of her eyes, her features marred by a rising ire. "I want my children safe. There is no crime in that."

"The mothers in Rotterdam wanted their children safe too. And look what happened to them. They could no more prevent the bombs from falling than order the rain to stop."

Mama's hand jerked and a sock fell from the line. She snatched the sock up with a loud sigh. "Please. I—I can't think about this anymore."

"You have to, Mama. And you have to believe that wherever we feel led to go, your prayers will help us. Please keep praying. That's how we stay together, in God's care."

Mama said nothing but only pinned up the remaining clothing in haste, her lips pressed tight as she worked. When the clothing had all been hung, she took up the basket. "Please don't encourage Lars to do anything foolish."

"I've never been able to tell him what to do. I'm just the nagging older sister." But now she wished she could, seeing the distress in her mother and the way her hands clenched the basket. Maybe she ought to tell Lars how Mama felt. He was still young and needed here. But recalling the look in her brother's eye and the determination in his voice, she knew such a gesture would be useless. The Dutch had a way of independence in thought and action, and Lars was no exception. Nor was she.

Now Helen felt a bond with a certain man who might help her understand things and keep her from acting heedlessly. Despite knowing each other just a short time, with everything going on, she felt closer to Erik than anyone. Which seemed strange at times. Maybe because she'd never had a close relationship with any man before. But

Erik was kind. Always looking out for her. He'd called a few times to make sure she was all right. Sometimes she would walk the street near her house—she didn't venture far these days with the newness of the occupation—and wonder when he would visit again. She recalled with pleasure the times he had come by after their meeting during the boat races, despite being unaware he did so, to pray and hope for an encounter.

Helen wandered out of the house to steal a quick walk down the street, the same path she had taken with Erik when they went to the café. How she wished they were heading there right now and she could talk to him about Lars. Picking up a stick, she drew some raindrops in the soft earth, more a childish act than anything, even if it mirrored her heart. She felt like a child sometimes—wanting someone older and wiser to take away the strangeness and fear of the unknown and replace it with beauty and calm. Maybe she ought to ride out sometime to Durgerdam and see again that quaint fishing village on the Markermeer, or even farther to the north shore bordering the sea and dwell in the peace of the countryside. If the Germans hadn't destroyed it too.

Helen tossed the stick aside and continued on her way until an earth-shaking rumble made her stop short. Chills coursed through her. She had never heard a noise like that around here.

The rumbling strengthened, followed by a loud creaking. Suddenly she was staring at a strange vehicle made of heavy steel with an elongated gun rolling up the street on large wheels. Behind the gun stood a soldier, dressed in gray, wearing a matching gray helmet. Ducking behind a nearby tree, she peeked out to see the outline of a black cross painted on the vehicle's side. She stepped out for a better look when a passerby approached.

"It's them." He answered her unspoken question. "They have arrived in Amsterdam." And just as he said the words, a contingent of armed personnel marched down the street, dressed in uniforms, carrying rifles. The images of war sent Helen stumbling backward. She tried to find the breath that seemed to have left her. Never had she seen soldiers of any kind, even among their Dutch brethren. Talk of the Dutch army putting up a brave front against the invaders was on every tongue early in the invasion. Now strange men speaking a foreign language and carrying weapons had invaded their streets, and no one could stop them.

She thought back to the conversation with Erik. There must be a way to drive them out. Maybe England would invade. Or America, as he suggested. They were strong. They could overwhelm the enemy and restore order. Just then another armed contingent wearing green uniforms marched down the sidewalk, directly by the spot where she stood. Her knees knocked in trepidation. Suddenly one of soldiers paused before her.

"*Nach Hause gehen!*" he ordered in German and pointed down the street. "Nach Hause gehen!"

She managed to comprehend the word *house*. Likely he was ordering her to go home and stay there. "I—I am running an errand," she replied in Dutch, trying not to quake.

"*Beeil dich.*" He whirled and continued on.

A slow rage began to build. Who was he to tell her what to do and where to go in her own country? She wanted to lash out and say she would go where she pleased and stay out as long as she wanted. She sensed the similar streak of rebellion she had witnessed in Lars. She wanted to fight back against the tyranny but had no idea how. Germany possessed many soldiers, weapons of war, planes, and armored vehicles. They had sent bombs raining down and taken over the whole country in a matter of days. They could do whatever they wished.

Helen whirled and walked swiftly down the street toward her home, her heart a mess of mixed emotions. She noticed a familiar figure standing in front of her house, holding a bunch of flowers. He might as well have been an angel descended from on high. She ran and threw her arms around him, pressing her face into the soft comfort of his shirt. When she stepped back, his hand wavered, nearly dropping the bouquet.

"I never expected such a greeting!" Erik exclaimed.

"I'm sorry. I'm just so happy to see you, I can hardly speak. It was awful, just awful."

"Here. These are for you." Erik gave her the bouquet and then led her to a place by the oak tree. They sat down under the shade of its wide branches. "What happened that's made you so upset?"

"I saw them. Th–the Germans. They are marching toward our neighborhood. One of them told me to go home. Can they do that now? Order us around?"

"They have conquered our country, Helen. Our government has fled. They can do whatever they wish."

Helen reached out to stroke the soft petals of the flowers. "Wherever did you find these beautiful things?"

"Mr. Baas obtained some from the coast. It seems the enemy wants life to continue to keep the public calm. Flowers have been brought in. Music, theaters, cafés—they want them all open and serving the public as if nothing has changed."

"I'm not a fool. Everything has changed. We are now prisoners in our own country."

Erik sighed. "I only pray our people don't forget who we are and that we stand strong.

There's so much fear right now. When fear becomes normal behavior, thoughts and feelings conform to it. Complacency takes its place. And then the enemy can strike with something bolder, a new edict or punishment, to strengthen the prison walls."

"Will you fight what's happening? I know some who are." She nearly told him about Lars' involvement in a secret resistance group but did not. At least not yet.

"I don't know what to do," he confessed. "In times like this, we need wisdom from above and not earthly wisdom."

"I wish I was back at college. We would talk about it, pray, and help each other understand."

"I met one of your professors not too long ago, when I was trying to find you. He spoke highly of you. He's the history professor and said he'll be the new vice president of the college."

Helen laughed and, for the first time since the invasion began, felt joy over the kind words. "That's Professor van Hulst. I'm surprised he would know me. I'm one of the many students he teaches."

"I can tell he's a brilliant man. Hopefully the school will reopen soon, for all your sakes." He gestured at the flowers in her lap. "In the meantime, enjoy the flowers. You can one day thank Mr. Baas."

"If I'm ever allowed to walk down the street

again," she said glumly, still wrestling with her ire over the German soldier ordering her home.

"I'm sure you will soon. But even if we can't or something else happens, I'll find a way to see you. Don't ever doubt it." Erik stood to his feet. "Now I should get back to work. I only had a bit of time from the store. It's been very busy."

She climbed to her feet as well. "I'm sure it is. Dank je wel for the flowers." She watched his feet shift. He stood before her for what was only a moment but felt like many minutes. Then he turned swiftly on his heel and left. Helen looked down at the flowers in her hands. How she would love to feel his lips on hers in a sweet kiss. They were so close to such a moment. She could feel it with every part of her. But when she looked back and saw Mama peering out between the parted curtains, she realized why the opportunity had fled. Just like the German officer did a short time ago, some in her family might also try to keep her from walking where she wanted to go. Where Erik was concerned, she would not hesitate to follow where her heart led.

CHAPTER 5

Erik wished he could wipe away the despondent look on Helen's face with a gentle embrace as they sat opposite each other at an outdoor café on this late summer day. These were times of uncertainty and helplessness. Gone were the smiles and cheer from days past. Sometimes he wished he had met her much sooner, before the Germans bombed their country and sent officials to rule over them in military and civilian affairs. How beautiful it would be to enjoy their growing attraction for each other unhindered by fear and control. He'd heard, just as Helen had, of the German plan to hasten the acceptance of the Dutch into the Reich and make it a strong influence for other countries reluctant to embrace Nazi rule. But he prayed for ways their country might rise up against the new totalitarianism, that the will of his fellow Dutchmen would remain strong despite the adversity, with the wisdom of serpents and the gentleness of doves.

Right now, he cast any concept of gentleness aside when he saw several German soldiers walk by. They were a common sight these days in the city proper. Not too long ago Erik had seen the busyness of Dutch workers engaged in everyday tasks, children smiling broadly while clasping the hands of their parents, and people enjoying lazy boat rides on the canals. These days folks walked with shoulders hunched and heads bent, hurrying their children along, avoiding the occupying soldiers, or the green police, so named for their green-colored uniforms. An occasional armored vehicle or truck would rumble along the narrow streets. In other parts of the country, the Germans were building airfields as bases for attacks on neighboring nations. A wall along the North Sea was being planned. While Erik liked to visit the countryside outside the city, he could not bear to see it all changed with barracks and airstrips, patrol shacks, barricades, and walls—their country converted into a veritable military compound.

"I wish they would all leave," Helen muttered under her breath, noting the same patrol as he did. She sipped her coffee, diluted with plenty of milk. The fruit-filled pastry she normally devoured on their outings remained untouched. It was hard to eat sweets these days when all seemed sour to the taste and smell.

Erik remembered when the air was filled with the scents of summer—flowers on carts mixed with the aroma of freshly baked goods sold by street vendors. Now he thought at times he could detect the odor of war in the air. The only smells he noted these days were steel, smoke, and defeat that made his throat close over and his fingers curl.

"We have no choice but to trust in God," Erik declared. He picked up his tart and took a healthy bite, hoping she would let her distress over the situation go and take a brief moment to savor some sweetness, both in the tart and in his presence.

"God left His people in captivity for years. Generations passed." Helen stared past him to the people meandering about with the green police scattered among them. "What if God decides to do that to us and make us part of a unified Germany? They could force you to wear their green uniform."

Erik set the tart down on his plate. "I will never put on that uniform."

"What if they put a gun to your head?" He must have worn the look of shock he felt on the inside as Helen lowered her head and apologized. "I'm sorry. I'm not myself."

"No one is. We try hard to be normal, but it's like living in a world that's not our own. We've had an idyllic existence for so long, living in peace with our boats and our flowers, our windmills and our gardens. We said no to the Great War and stayed at peace within our borders. But not anymore."

A fire ignited in Helen's blue eyes. She straightened in her seat and leaned forward. "But all the things you mentioned are not evil, prideful things. What is happening to us is evil."

"I think God wants to be our refuge and strength, no matter what. To keep us strong even with the challenges ahead. To give us peace even if we're afraid. To trust Him."

Helen thought for a moment then picked up a pastry and took a delicate bite. He liked watching her enjoy the sweet and tangy goodness. "Yes. I understand what you're saying. I've been reading my Bible more than ever. Along with my textbooks. I think I'll be even better prepared when the term begins."

"Have you heard any news?"

Helen nodded. "I received a telegram that classes are starting in a week. My history professor, Professor van Hulst, is now the new vice president of the college. He's a brilliant and godly man and an excellent choice for the job."

"That's good news about your college. Maybe all is not lost after all." He scolded himself for the moment of doubt after challenging each of them to remain strong.

"I'm glad too. But you've heard the other news, I'm sure. The new edict requiring teachers to sign pledges of obedience and agreement to German philosophy. Curfews might soon be put in place. People are talking about it, and some are very angry. I know Lars is, and he wants to stop it. He's been going to some meetings of the resistance. He has a friend who left Germany and talks about the terrible things that are happening there—about people being persecuted for who they are. Lars wants to do something about it. Though he's only seventeen." She sighed and spun the coffee mug slowly on the table.

Erik listened until he noticed several German soldiers making their way toward the building opposite the café. They rushed in, shouting in German, weapons at the ready. Helen watched along with him, her mouth gaping in surprise as a young man, not much older than Lars, was dragged out, cuffed, and led away. An older woman cried, begging them not to take her only son. Erik turned back to see that Helen had sprung to her feet, her large eyes glistening, her face red. He didn't dare tell her he had seen this on several occasions, especially with her concern over Lars—the Germans rounding up certain individuals, mostly young men, and taking them away. Erik reached for her hand and gestured for her to sit down. "Pretend you've seen nothing," he whispered as several soldiers passed by. One stopped to help himself to the pastry from a customer's plate. The customer, a young man, said nothing about the stolen pastry. The soldier's gaze drifted to Erik and then back to the young man.

Erik inhaled a deep breath. He suddenly scraped his chair across the stone floor and pounded the table with his fist. "You always were a tease," he shouted at Helen. "First you say yes. Then you bring me here and say it's over." He sat back and folded his arms. "Enough of the games."

Helen stared at him, shaking her head, her eyes growing even wider. "Erik, what are you doing?"

"Well, if you don't know, how am I supposed to explain it?" He gestured with a slight nod at the soldier observing them while munching on the pastry.

Wiping his hands, the soldier approached their table and stood stiffly over it. "*Guten tag. Worüber streiten Sie sich?*"

"Does anyone know what he's saying?" Erik inquired of the surrounding customers who sat frozen in place, watching the scene with wide eyes.

"He asks what you two are arguing about," translated a customer seated at a nearby table.

"Dank je wel." Erik pointed at Helen. "Tell him she's decided on my birthday of all days to break up with me, and I'm very upset. Maybe he can talk some sense into her. There's nothing wrong with me." He folded his arms and huffed in contempt.

Helen sat frozen, shaking her head. After the translation, the German soldier burst out laughing and said if she didn't want Erik, she could have him instead. He then walked off, snickering.

Erik mopped off the beads of sweat that had gathered across his forehead and managed a small smile with trembling lips. "Sorry I had to do that," he murmured.

"I don't understand. Why did you draw his attention like that? It nearly caused a scene!"

"It was supposed to. The enemy is looking for certain things, Helen. And people. But we only appeared to be a couple caught in a lovers' quarrel, and he found it funny enough to leave us and the other man alone. He could have well sent his squad to take any of us without reason or care, as we have already witnessed." Erik hoped she might marvel at the way it ended, but he only saw a woman with a red face and tears in her eyes.

"I want to go home," Helen said, sniffing. She glanced over to see the German still staring at them with a toothy grin on his face. She turned back and opened the clasp on her purse for a handkerchief. She then squared her shoulders and said, "You may walk me home, but that is all. And you owe me a guilder."

Erik picked a coin out of his pocket and tossed it her direction. "Little good it will do you now." She grabbed it up, stuffed it into her pocketbook, and marched off, her head high.

Erik sauntered behind, scuffing his feet. When they were at a safe distance, he stole a glance behind him and sighed. "We're safe, Helen. The soldier didn't follow but is continuing on with his patrol."

Helen blew out a troubled sigh. "I was never more scared in my life. How can we live like this, Erik?"

"We can do all things through Christ who gives us strength. It's all we have." He smiled at her. "And you, my sweet lady, are an excellent actress."

"It comes from those plays we did as children." She chuckled. For a moment, he saw a flicker of joy cross her eyes, but only for a moment. Then her eyes narrowed and her eyebrows drew together in concern. He wanted her to remain firm in her faith. Many in the past had lived through turbulent times and survived. So would they, with God's help.

When they parted company at her house, Erik took up the bicycle he had propped against the oak tree, offered her a farewell, and pedaled back to central Amsterdam. He thought about the encounter and wondered how he had the presence of mind to engage the soldier and still keep his wits about him. He tried to lift his spirits after encouraging Helen to lift hers with thoughts of scripture, but suddenly he felt his own mortality. It made him feel vulnerable and weak. At times he wrestled with the situation just like everyone else. While he put on an air of confidence for Helen's sake, deep inside he felt no older than

Hans, asking simple questions that poured out of a burdened heart. *How long will this go on? How will it end? Will we be all right?*

Erik passed another group of soldiers standing in the middle of the pavement, smoking cigarettes and conversing in rapid German. They gave him a passing glance before returning to their conversation. He wondered what they were talking about. Probably discussing how puny and insignificant Erik's fellow countrymen were compared to their might. And mapping out their future plans of domination. It angered him, but he continued on until he arrived at the store and a frantic Mr. Baas.

"Where have you been?" he complained. "It's been so busy I cannot keep up."

Erik hastily put on his apron and immediately began serving the customers. It made no sense to remind the older man that he had been given time away to spend with Helen. All manner of reasoning seemed at a loss these days.

Erik caught sight of a young child with a big smile on her wee face, holding a stick of candy before her frenzied mother. The mother snatched it out of the child's hand. "Nee. We have no money for that." The little girl burst into tears. Erik scurried over and asked if he could help. The woman shook her head. "I don't know what to do," she confessed. "My husband who served so many years in the health department was suddenly let go. No reason was given."

"I'm sorry to hear this. We need a good health department, especially with what's happening."

The woman drew close, and her voice dropped to a near whisper. "There are rumors going around, you know. They're saying certain people will have to leave their jobs."

"What kind of people?"

"They say the Germans don't like Jews. We're Jewish, you see. I can't help but worry that might have had something to do with my husband losing his job."

Erik blinked. "I can't believe they fired your husband just because he's Jewish. In the Bible you are a chosen people. It's inhuman, indecent, and plain wrong." The comment sparked a small smile on her face, much to his relief. Erik fumbled in his pocket for a guilder. "Buy your little girl the candy. And I will say a prayer that whatever happened with your husband was only an error and he will be reinstated soon."

"Thank you very much. But I don't think they will let him back." Her voice trailed away as she took up the little girl's hand and moved on to select a few grocery items. The words she spoke burdened him, and he wondered if it could be true—that people were being forced out of work or turned away because of who they were. Then the words came back to him. Helen had said her brother knew of a certain population of German people being persecuted and how they escaped it by coming here. Now German soldiers were rushing about arresting young men. For what, he didn't know. Was it because they were Jewish? Or some other reason?

"Erik!" came Mr. Baas's stern voice.

Erik pushed away the contemplation to concentrate on his job. But even the simplest tasks became more difficult under the innumerable distractions that seemed to mount each day. He vowed to do something cheerful. Perhaps he and Helen could escape for a day of fun. Maybe they could return to Durgerdam where they first met and rent a boat on the Markermeer. Even take a drive in the country. Anything would be better than being here in Amsterdam, and it would give them precious time to enjoy the sunshine and each other.

The more he thought about it, the more cheerful he became—to the point that he started whistling. Maybe it was true that if one concentrated on the good, the bad had no power over life. And right now, he needed good news to prevail. He would borrow Papa's car for the outing, roll down the windows, and let the warm summer breeze blow across their faces. Helen would wear a pretty dress with a smile to match. Maybe he could steal her away to a meadow of flowing emerald grass, watch the wind blow her blond hair across her face, and kiss her. He'd thought about kissing Helen for a while now, a thought much more pleasant than their current circumstances. Maybe this was the way to make it happen. She would enjoy the moment as much as he, responding with enthusiasm and happily accepting him in her heart. Then everything would be perfect.

"Erik, I need help!" Again came the voice of Mr. Baas. Erik hurried over to the cash register to check out a customer's purchases. Giddiness and song filled his soul like a lovesick schoolboy as he wished everyone a pleasant day, even the ones he knew were plagued with worry or sadness. He hoped they came up with a plan as he had, to escape this evil for a time of peace. If only for a day.

Erik returned home that night to find Hans waiting for him with a new project in hand, a small unidentified animal he had carved out of wood. Erik hugged him, told him how good the animal looked, then asked about his boat. "We need to see what we can do to fix it so it sails better."

Hans shook his head. "You can't. It's a bad boat, so I bombed it."

Erik's cheerfulness evaporated like wet pavement to hot sun. "I don't understand. What do you mean, you bombed the boat?"

Hans trudged outside to the tiny backyard and pointed to a corner of the fencing. The boat lay in pieces, shattered by stones strewn across the ground. "See? The angry men in green came and bombed Durgerdam and the boats. These are the bombs." He picked up a nearby rock and threw it as hard as he could at the boat.

Erik stared in utter shock as the rock splintered the keel of the boat. "Stop it! What have you done? You destroyed everything we worked so hard to make! How could you do this?"

His brother's lower lip trembled. "It was no good anyways."

"It was very good. Many in the family had worked on it. Mother helped and so did Grand-father. What will they say when they hear what you've done? How you destroyed all their hard work?"

Hans ran away with a wail. Erik picked up the pieces of the smashed boat. Inwardly he wanted to cry too. Not even thoughts of a holiday in the countryside with Helen could calm the sudden distress raging like a storm within him.

He returned to the house, uncertain what Mother would say if she saw the boat. After all, she crafted the sails on her sewing machine. He would conceal it in the garbage and hope that somehow this would work out for good, as sad as it was.

Just then his fourteen-year-old sister, Greta, burst into the back room where Erik stood still holding the pieces of the boat. "What happened?"

"Hans decided he didn't want his boat anymore. He threw rocks at it."

"I saw him crying in his room. Is that the reason?"

Erik was prepared to say more when his other sister, Mary, hurried onto the scene. Erik showed her the splintered remains. "Oh no. Poor Hans," mourned Mary. "Can it be fixed?"

Erik shook his head and threw the pieces in the garbage. "Please don't tell Mother right now. She worked hard on the sails. I'm glad Grandfather isn't here to see this."

Erik buried his disappointment over the boat and worked his way up the stairs to Hans's room. Opening the door, he found Hans prostrate on his bed, whimpering. "Hans, I'm sorry for what I said. It was your boat to do with as you want. I only wish . . ." He paused. "I only wish I could've talked with you about it first. The boat meant a lot to everyone and—"

"I don't want to sail a boat anymore." Hans sat upright, wiping the tears from his face with a fist. "I'm going to be a soldier."

Erik stared, his lips parting in astonishment. "Hans, you don't want to be a soldier. Trust me."

"Yes, I do." He stood to his feet and began marching about, to Erik's dismay. How could this be happening to their family? The war had invaded even the sanctuary of their home. He sighed and realized what he needed to do. It wasn't just he and Helen who needed an escape. So did Hans. He needed a day away to remind him what it meant to be a Dutch boy without a thought of the war that tried to overtake his young mind. The more he watched his young brother, the more he realized God would have to help if there was any hope of surviving this devastation.

CHAPTER 6

Helen felt like a young woman on her first date as she looked out the window through the parted curtains, waiting for Erik's car to appear. Just the thought of a trip to the north, along with a picnic and exploring the pretty countryside, made her all bubbly inside. It would have been better if it were just the two of them on a picnic, gazing at each other while resting on a blanket spread on the grass. But when Erik told her how Hans had destroyed the boat he had used in the canal races by crushing it with rocks, her heart ached. She knew how much time Erik and his family had put into making the boat for Hans to sail and couldn't imagine why the little boy would react in such a violent way.

But children had to be affected by the invasion, she reasoned. She hadn't given it much thought until now. Then Erik described the boy's determination to become a soldier. Helen quickly agreed with Erik that Hans must have a day of fun away from all the turmoil. She also decided to invite the neighbors' twins, Esmee and Karl, to join them. Hans would no doubt like the companionship of playmates his age, and while it would cause more work for her and Erik, it could give them precious time together with the children distracted by play. She hoped and prayed.

Helen sighed and stole another glance out the window. Esmee and Karl burst into the sitting room and showed her the kite they planned to bring. "Your mama packed us a yummy picnic," Esmee announced. "When are we gonna leave, huh? I hope it's soon."

"I'm sure Mr. Erik will be along anytime," she told them, her heart pounding with excitement. Then she heard an engine noise and, looking out the front window, saw an automobile pull up before the house. "He's here!"

The children whooped and hollered, dashing for the door while Helen picked up the basket of goodies Mama had put together. The twins displayed their kite to Erik, who sat in the driver's seat. In the back seat sat Hans, looking on with large eyes. Helen greeted the quiet boy and introduced her two charges to him. Instantly Karl showed Hans the kite and asked if he had brought one.

"No," Hans said and looked out the window.

Helen glanced questioningly at Erik, but he said nothing as she occupied the passenger seat. "What a perfect day for a picnic!" she declared, gazing at the clear blue skies. She said little else while Erik concentrated on negotiating the narrow streets. Soon they were out of the city and driving on the broad highway, heading into the country. The chatter of the children in the back seat proved refreshing, and to her relief, she heard Hans adding to the conversation.

"I'm glad you decided to bring your neighbor's children," Erik told her quietly.

"I didn't want Hans bored with us. Adults aren't much fun."

Erik nodded, keeping his eyes trained on the road, but she could see his tense hands relax around the wheel. She dearly wanted to tell him how much she thought about him. They had already shared a part in this evolving conflict, watching aircraft cross the skies, heralding the arrival of the enemy, and then the situation at the café with the green police. The kinship felt real. If only they didn't have these difficult situations casting a pall over life. It made her angry to think that nothing could be enjoyed. She hoped this trip would prove her wrong as she settled in the passenger seat and watched the unfolding scenery of the distant shoreline bordering the waters of the Markermeer. Bright emerald farmland showed off the rich soil that once existed beneath the waters of the former Zuiderzee. The construction of the dam shrank the waters and allowed farmland to appear, maintained by many windmills dotting the landscape. It made no sense why Germany felt they must invade their country. They had enough land of their own. What could they possibly hope to gain? She remembered what Lars said about his German friend and his native country and how the German government controlled people's lives to bring about their version of a perfect society.

Erik's calm voice interrupted her disturbing thoughts. "Are you looking forward to returning to class?" She turned to him and saw concern in his face.

"Of course. I miss my classmates and professors. We won't allow what's happened to keep us from becoming teachers and helping students learn." She glanced over her shoulder at the children who were playing a game with the paper and pencils Hans had brought along. "Think of what this is doing to the children. We need to help them any way we can."

Erik's fingers tightened around the steering wheel. "I agree," he said and lowered his voice as the twins and Hans chattered behind them. "When I saw Hans throwing those rocks, saying they were bombs, I felt sick inside. It isn't right. None of this is."

Helen inhaled a sharp sigh, feeling the angst within Erik and wishing she could soothe it. She reached out and touched his hand, feeling it jump in hers before relaxing. "I understand. Though my brothers are much older than Hans, all this is hurting everyone. Who knows how it will change us?"

Neither of them spoke for a time until houses

began to appear on the outskirts of a town called Edam, strong and stately, with stair-step brick patterning and finely painted gables. A few of the homes boasted brightly colored fronts, giving the area a distinct cheer. Helen didn't realize how much she'd missed the feeling of joy until now. Villagers in Edam roamed the streets. Children raced after a ball thrown about in a game, and at once the twins and Hans wanted to join in the fun. Erik parked the car and agreed to their request but warned them not to go far. Like birds sprung from a cage, the threesome took to their heels and hurried over to ask if they might join the other children in their game.

"Look at Hans," Erik said with a grin. "I haven't seen him this happy since before the boat race."

"This was a wonderful idea." Helen gave in to the urge to tuck her hand in the crook of his elbow. Erik patted her hand as they strolled along the brick walkway. The quiet town with its fine canal running through the center square and leaves on the trees rustling in the wind added to the peacefulness. They came to a cheese shop with a young man standing before it, holding out slices of fragrant cheese carved from a large wheel to passersby. Erik and Helen ate a few of the samples offered.

"Zeer goede kaas," Erik said, commenting on the excellent taste of the cheese. He inquired

about the price for a small wheel. When the man quoted it, Erik nodded. "Much cheaper than the store where I work."

Helen looked longingly at the cheese through the store window and thought how delicious it would be with the fresh bread Mama had packed for their midday meal. "The children will be hungry," she reminded him.

Erik took out some guilders. "I can't say no to you," he said with a smirk. "Go buy some cheese, and I'll keep watch on the children." With a smile accompanying the pink tinge to his face, Erik handed her the money.

She slipped into the store to see a portly man wearing a wide grin. At her request, he selected a nice round wheel from the many displayed on the shelves. "Did you come far this fine day?" he inquired, wrapping the purchase in brown paper.

"Amsterdam. We needed this trip to the country." She glanced out the open door to see the neighborhood children still laughing and kicking at the ball.

"I hope you are safe in Amsterdam with everything going on."

"As safe as one can expect, with enemy soldiers and trucks in our streets. It seems quieter here. Almost as if you don't know there's an occupation."

"We've seen little evidence. A few military vehicles a week ago, heading north. Most everyone here goes about their business. The children still play in the streets, as you can see. But of course, no one knows the future. And we're not far from Amsterdam. I've heard from others there's been a good deal of trouble there."

Helen stiffened and couldn't help but blurt out the news. She told him about the Germans who accosted young men and even arrested them in broad daylight. "Patrols walk the streets, especially in the city center," she continued. "I go to college there. We had to close temporarily because of the annexation, but the college is set to open on Monday."

"Then I will say a prayer all goes well. We must always keep careful watch and pray."

Helen gave the man a small smile before putting the wrapped purchase into her wide rectangular basket and returning to Erik. He had rounded up the children, windblown and dusty but excited from their romp in Edam's homey streets. Seeing the cheese and bread, they settled down on a bench and devoured the food. Between bites, the twins announced their next adventure would be flying their kite.

Helen exchanged glances with Erik, who bit into the cheese with a satisfied hum. "I think if I didn't have my classes in the teacher's college, I would like to stay here awhile," she mused. "See how happy everyone is? It's not like Amsterdam."

Erik nodded.

"And seeing the peace in the shopkeeper's face. He's so happy. The people live their lives like there's no invasion at all." Suddenly a cloud of depression descended on her, and maybe even jealousy for what they had. "I want that same peace."

"We all do, Helen. But I believe we won't be given any more trouble than we can handle. We have to trust God just for today. Not for tomorrow, but for each day as it comes. So let's enjoy our trip."

Helen wanted to soak his words into her troubled soul. If it weren't for her studies at the college, she would ask the shopkeeper if anyone needed a worker around here. Maybe a nanny to care for a family's children. It wasn't just the happiness of the people who lived here, but the freedom of not having to watch neighborhoods overrun by the enemy or lives changed because of edicts or brutal practices.

Just then she heard laughter and saw children skipping by, their guardian clutching a wheel of cheese, no doubt another happy customer of the shopkeeper. She thought how much her family would enjoy such provision when food could be difficult to find. She told Erik she would be back and made her way once more to the cheese maker's shop to buy another wheel of sharp goodness to bring home to her family.

"I was telling my friend how I wouldn't mind staying here," she said to the jolly man, who wrapped up another wheel of cheese.

"Is it because of the trouble you've seen?"

Helen nodded. "Seeing young men arrested for no reason. Hearing a mother crying for her son. The worst part is, everyone ignores it. No one helps or does anything about it."

The shopkeeper shook his head. "I'm very sad to hear this. We never close our doors or our hearts to anyone in need." He stared at her with a piercing look that offered determination and strength. "You are always welcome here in Edam, miss. Always. I am Ephraim Visser. Remember my name."

Helen managed a smile and picked up the brown paper package. "Thank you for everything." She shuffled along, thinking how much her heart felt a kinship to this place. Coming here was like enjoying the air of springtime with the vibrant color of blooming tulips, without a care in the world. Perfect happiness. She glanced up and saw a dark cloud over the sea, reminding her that happiness was also fleeting with sudden storms that blew up.

But Helen refused to consider storms right now as they headed for a pleasant place close to the water. When they arrived at the beach, Erik opened the trunk to show Hans the surprise he had stowed away—a kite he had bought. Hans clapped his hands in glee, bringing a smile of satisfaction to Erik's face. Helen shared in Erik's laughter as the children juggled for space, seeing their kites flying high in the crystal-blue skies. "Turn the kite a little more toward the sea, Hans!" Erik called out. "There you go. See how the wind takes it higher?" He glanced back at Helen. "I've never seen him so happy. You're right. It will be difficult leaving here. Like you said, there's a peace in the country you don't have in the big city."

"I talked to the shopkeeper. He welcomed us to visit anytime we want to get away from Amsterdam. This place is like our dear Holland just a few weeks ago, with open arms to anyone who feels depressed."

"We have to also remain that way, Helen. Even if it's hard. We need to stand strong and help anyone we can." His arms curled around her, his eyes searching her face. For an instant she felt shy and looked away, giggling as Esmee and Karl struggled with their kite in the rising wind. "Oh look! Now Hans has the higher kite!"

Before she realized what was happening, a sweet warmth came calling on her lips, along with the feel of hands drawing her close. She couldn't help but settle into the kiss, eager for comfort and love to wipe away all the distresses of life.

"Hey Erik, I have the best kite!" Hans suddenly

shouted, rushing over to them, the kite following behind on a leash of string.

They disengaged, and Helen saw the look of dismay on Erik's face. She giggled. "Your brother has an interesting way of stealing the attention," she whispered.

Erik tried to push Hans back to the field with the other children, but he didn't budge. Instead, he plopped himself down and asked for another bread and cheese sandwich. "I guess that's the end of that," Erik muttered. "Thank you, Hans."

"For what?" Hans asked, his innocent blue eyes staring in wonder while his cheeks bulged with food. Helen couldn't help but chuckle. She could guess the thoughts swirling in Erik's mind and watched his mouth open, hoping he wouldn't confess what had transpired before the boy's untimely arrival.

He said with a wink, "For having the most impeccable timing ever." The boy shrugged, forced down the rest of his sandwich, then took to his feet to fly his kite once more. "Just a few more minutes, Hans," Erik called. "We need to leave soon. Could be a storm coming." He pointed to a bank of clouds gathering in the west.

"Oh!" Hans whined in disgruntlement.

Helen packed the food into the wicker basket, thinking about the kiss. When she looked up, Erik was gazing at her intently, and she wondered, with a catch in her breath and increase in the beating of her heart, if he would kiss her again. She made up her mind that if he did, she would eagerly accept with all her heart. After all, when would they be alone again? School was about to start, and Erik would no doubt be caught up in the workings of the store that had turned busy ever since the German occupation. She pondered the next session of college. Would they be allowed to study without interference? Would there be guards in the classrooms and halls? What about the edicts? Helen stiffened. The only one she would give her loyalty to was God above. And maybe one day to Erik . . .

Helen shook her head and couldn't help but smile. Where on earth did that last thought come from? Maybe because he was the one seeing her through these turbulent times. Erik wasn't the first man she'd ever kissed, but he was the only one she cared about. The first one she'd sensed a growing affection and love for. The first one she'd dared to consider in a lasting commitment.

"Looks like we're ready," Erik said. "I'll go get the children."

Helen nodded, watching him move swiftly toward the sandy shore bordering the lake. Suddenly his long legs burst into a sprint, and he began shouting. Helen left the basket and blanket and ran after him. "What's wrong?"

"Hans!" he yelled.

"He left," Karl said, clutching his kite. "The

string broke, and the kite started flying away over there."

Helen followed the boy's pointing finger toward the stark gray waters of the Markermeer. A swift fear like a sweep of cold wind flew over her. Her teeth began to chatter.

Erik rushed toward the water and waded out into it. "Hans! Hans!"

Helen took out after Erik, shivers racing through her at the cold water, the dress she wore spreading on the surface of the water in a flowery arc. She grabbed hold of his arm and pulled him back toward shore.

"If the kite flew over this water and he went after it . . ." His tremulous voice drifted away. He brushed his hand through his hair. He shouted for Hans several more times, growing more desperate with each plea. Her heart pained with the weight of his despair. Her soul matched his cry for help. *God, please help us!*

Helen carefully searched the shimmering lake-front but saw no sign of the boy or the kite bobbing in the air. "The kite must have gone in a different direction, Erik," she said, but inwardly she didn't know what to think. She shivered from the encounter in the water and from fear.

Erik dashed his cap to the ground. "I will never forgive myself. Never. Oh God." His anguished words sent her groping for his hand and holding tight to his damp, trembling fingers.

CHAPTER 7

Erik could not control the panic that gripped with sharp teeth and refused to let go. Despite Helen's plea that they stay out of the water and continue searching the coastline, all he could envision was the kite flying out across the lake. Then Hans's little body going out after it, the small arms outstretched, his blue eyes wide in distress, until the water swept over him. The vision made Erik's legs wobble and his heart feel like it had stopped. This was all his fault. He should have been more attentive and watched his little brother at every turn. Hans had not been himself lately. From the day of the boat races to the terror infecting their country that ended with Hans smashing his boat with stone bombs, the toll of it all proved unimaginable. Hans had vanished in an attempt to stay with the one thing that had given him pleasure. "What am I going to do?" he asked Helen, his voice wrought with distress.

He then heard Helen's firm resolve that strengthened his spirit and soul. "Erik, we're not giving up hope. We are going to keep looking. But I must get the twins and keep them with us. Edam isn't too far away. We can get others to help in the search. Mr. Visser will help—he said he would if we ever needed it."

Erik nodded, trying in vain to tap into Helen's faith. His had disappeared under the weight of the guilt twisting like a knife deep into him. If only his thoughts and his heart hadn't been captured by the woman now trying to take control of the situation. If only he had not fallen head over heels in love. His attention should have been on Hans with his frail emotions and the children lingering so close to the water's edge. He swept back a lock of hair from his forehead. Helen had been the one bright spot in the darkness, but now none of that mattered. Erik cupped a hand to his eyes, searching the lake once more as if he expected Hans to walk on water. His faith teetered on a precipice, and the enemy laughed. *Where is your faith now? Your brother is gone. There is nothing left.*

The breathless heaving of the two children interrupted his thoughts as he witnessed their wide eyes. "I need to know exactly where you last saw Hans. And where the kite flew in the wind."

"I saw it flying over the water," Karl declared.

"No, it didn't," Esmee said, her hands on her hips. "You always get things wrong. I saw it heading that way." She pointed in the direction of the town.

"Are you sure?" Erik asked, wanting to grip the girl's shoulders to assure himself of the truth. Instead, he knelt and inquired in as gentle a voice as he could muster, "I need to know where to look, Esmee. Hans could be in big danger."

She again pointed down the road. "I saw the kite go that way."

Helen returned from scouting the shoreline, shivering from her damp clothing. "We should check for any footprints in the dirt."

Erik followed her, scanning the ground, and noticed small footprints heading first along the coast and then taking a sharp turn westward toward town. "Ja! He headed toward town! Praise God." Strengthened by the thought of Hans wandering around Edam, Erik hurried to the automobile. Helen ushered the twins into the back seat with Karl taking longer than expected as he tried to maneuver his large kite. Erik fought to remain calm with precious minutes ticking away. Hans could be wandering farther away from them if the wind continued to take his kite on some hapless journey in the skies. He felt Helen's hand come to rest on his arm—with a soothing touch as his heart beat wildly.

"We will find him," she whispered. "God has him in His hand."

"If not, I will be lost forever."

"Don't even think it, Erik. Not for an instant."

But sometimes you're brought to the cliff's edge and you're about ready to tumble off. He wanted to verbalize the feeling but knew he couldn't with young children there, realizing doubts could infect them too. But everyone struggled with faith in the unseen. They were mere mortals after all, plagued by doubt, holding on to faith by a mere thread. Except a simple thread could still be quite strong.

Arriving in Edam, Helen burst out of her seat and headed for the cheese shop. Erik wondered why she would go there of all places and instructed the twins to remain inside the car while he asked the town children still playing in the street if any of them had seen a young boy chasing a kite. No one had. The fear began to mount once more as he fought back the vision of Hans's small body caught in the lake waters, his hand reaching out, pleading for help.

Helen came running back, her face bright like the noon sun, her lips parted. "The clerk at the shop said Mr. Visser was heading out to the coast where we came from and might run into Hans. If he does, I know he will help him."

"Who is Mr. Visser?"

"The one who owns the cheese shop. He's a friendly and godly man. He will help Hans if he can. He said he would help anyone in need. If you want to keep looking around town, I will head back to the lake area with the twins and search along the road."

Helen took off in the car, and Erik began a further scout of the town. Not far from the cheese shop, he spotted a large stone wall and, sitting there, a young boy with a kite in his hands and an older man beside him, both engaged in conversation. Never in his life did he feel such relief pour over him. "Hans!" he shouted. And then the flood sparked anger when he saw his brother's large eyes. "Don't you ever do something like this again! Ever! You had me so worried."

Hans stood to his feet, clutching the broken pieces of his kite, his small face tinged in red, his lower lip trembling.

"I'd say the lad here has had enough trouble for one day," the man said. And then his face broke into a grin. "In fact, he's told me a great many things in his life have been broken. And now his kite."

"See?" Hans said, showing the kite's jagged edges where it had torn. "It got caught in a tree. When I pulled on the string, it broke." He sniffed, wiping his nose on the hem of his shirt.

Erik desperately wanted to tell them both he cared nothing about a torn kite that could easily be replaced. This young life that the lake water or something else might have stolen away was worth more than anything in the world.

The man must have noted the expression on his face. "I do understand, young man. You're happy the boy is alive. And I'm thankful to God that my feet led me here. Normally I head directly for the lake to pray before I go home. But today I took my time greeting some folks. I found the lad on the outskirts of town, crying."

Erik marveled at the man's kindness and also his perception. He sighed heavily. "I'm grateful to you. I was never so scared in my life. The thought of losing him . . ."

The smile on the man's face turned downward into a grim expression. "I understand that too. Believe me." He stood to his feet. "But now you must come with me to my home. We have a new kite for little Hans there, and we'll want you to stay for dinner. I'm Ephraim Visser, and my wife will be delighted to have you."

Erik looked at him in surprise. "Sir, there is no need—" He spied the look on Ephraim's face and the way he nodded as he gestured toward the shaken boy. "Thank you. I came with a young woman and two other neighborhood children. They were heading toward the coast in my car to look for Hans. They were also hoping to run into you."

"Then let's go find them and make this an evening of celebration." Ephraim looked down at Hans and placed a fatherly hand on his shoulder. "We must care for each other as God would have it. There is no greater calling on earth."

Thinking of his little brother safe by his side, Erik couldn't agree more.

Helen bit her lip, trying to keep her concentration focused on the countryside around her and not on her anxiety. A return to the coast provided no new clues to Hans's whereabouts, even though she searched once more for evidence. A father and son flying a kite caught her attention, and she pulled the car over and asked if they had seen a little boy running around looking for his kite. The man shook his head, and she wistfully watched the young boy slowly unraveling the string to coax the kite higher. "Dear God, you know where Hans is. Please lead us to him."

"Are you praying, Miss Smit?" came a childlike voice from the rear seat.

"Ja, Esmee. To God."

Esmee craned her neck, staring with large eyes out the window and toward the sky. "Where is God? Up there?"

"It's hard to tell you exactly. But God sent a part of Him, His Spirit, to be with us forever. His Spirit is with us right now, helping us."

Esmee turned her attention to Helen, gazing at the back of Helen's neck as Helen looked at Esmee's blue eyes and braided hair in the rearview mirror. "Does God tell you things?" Esmee asked.

"Oh yes. And He helps us too through other people and also guides us in what we do. Like helping us as we drive back here to look for Hans." Just the mention of his name renewed the anxiety over his disappearance, and she prayed silently once more.

"Did God tell you where Hans is?"

"Well, not specifically. But I believe somehow He will show us. It's called faith."

As she headed back toward town, looking for any sign of Hans along the way, another car drove by in the opposite direction. All at once there came a shriek of brakes and a loud horn. She hit the brakes, and the twins bounced about in their seats. "*Wauw!*" Karl cried, holding on to his kite.

Helen waited until the car turned around and drove back to their location. In the driver's seat sat Ephraim Visser, beside him Erik, and in the back seat, Hans with his pale face and large eyes.

"Look!" Esmee cried. "God must've heard what you said, Miss Helen! It's Hans!"

She inhaled a deep breath. Tears filled her eyes and gratefulness poured from her soul as she hurried out of the car. Erik opened the door and rose from the passenger side, smiling. She fell into his arms, filled with relief.

"Ephraim found him on the road," he told her. "And he has invited us to dinner with him and his wife."

Helen shifted her attention to the man behind the steering wheel and the pleasant smile he wore. "How can we ever thank you?"

"Just keep thanking God above, because He is deserving. And keep listening to that still, small voice. That's how I saw the boy. God knows our steps and plans it all accordingly. And I believe my next step is inviting you to our home. It's the next piece of His plan, whatever that may be."

Helen blinked, uncertain how to receive this. Never had she heard someone talk with such faith and purpose. She slid into the passenger seat while Erik took the wheel of his car and Hans joined the twins in the back seat. There was plenty of time to contemplate the mysteries of divine purpose. For now, she thought of Hans safely in the back with his new friends and enjoyed hearing him tell Esmee and Karl how Ephraim was going to give him a new kite. She considered the kindness of the man she had met earlier that day at the cheese shop and now driving the car in front of theirs. Then she thought about the man sitting beside her who had captured her heart—the one she thought about constantly and who held her in his arms as they kissed on the beach. Thinking on what Ephraim Visser said, she wondered if Erik could be part of God's big plan for her life. Or if he was a passing shadow, like a few other acquaintances who came floating in and then left

"You look deep in thought," Erik observed as they drove. "I'm sorry this has not been the day you thought it would be."

"Well, according to Ephraim, everything is working out exactly as it should."

Erik shrugged. "Maybe." He gestured toward the car leading them deep into the Dutch country-side, away from Edam and the coast. Farms began to appear, scattered among many canals and stubby forests attempting to gain a foothold in the grassy fields. "He's an interesting man. I'm glad you got to know him at his cheese shop. That was also part of the plan." He winked and smiled.

Helen nodded, relaxing for the first time since their encounter on the beach and realizing too how stiff and tired she'd become. Her eyelids grew heavy, and she had nearly drifted off to sleep when the car braked before a modest farmhouse.

"Arise, sweet one," Erik said with a grin. "We are here."

Helen smirked at the endearment and stretched her arms above her head. The children clambered out and began exploring.

A plump woman wearing a large apron and wooden clogs came out of the house, a spoon in hand. "So, who have you brought this time, Ephraim? I cooked extra."

"There, you see?" Ephraim said with a hearty laugh. "My dear Delia anticipates my plans. The two are indeed one." He then said to his wife, "I have some nice people here, Delia. One of the children got lost in Edam trying to find his kite. Thankfully he was found safe."

She nodded and smiled, greeting Erik and Helen before waving them into the house and a comfortable sitting room. A large vase of painted wooden tulips decorated the mantel, and there were plenty of chairs and a worn rug before the hearth. While the men took seats, Helen slipped away and followed Delia into the kitchen, asking if she needed help.

Delia thanked her. *"Bedankt."*

Helen arranged buns on a platter while Delia poured *gehaktballen,* meatballs floating in brown gravy, into a large porcelain bowl decorated with windmills and flowers. In another dish she served noodles. The delft pottery with its characteristic blue patterns always looked beautiful with any meal. Helen carefully set the table with more of the pretty delftware, wondering if the woman dared trust her pretty dishes to their rambunctious charges.

"I'm pleased to hear that your young boy was found," Delia commented. "It's frightening to be lost—and also for the ones who are searching."

"I was never more scared in my life," Helen admitted. "Though I didn't want Erik to know."

Delia gave her a knowing look. "God wants us to support the men in our lives. How long have you been married?"

The question sent a smear of warmth flooding Helen's cheeks as she looked at the silverware she carefully placed at each table setting. "Oh, we aren't married. The lost boy is Erik's brother, and the other two are neighborhood children my family cares for while their parents are at work."

"How nice of you to care for the little ones.

God holds children in an extra-special place in His heart, you know." She smiled and then went out to call everyone to the dinner table.

The meal was pleasant enough, and to Helen's relief the children behaved themselves and did not chip or injure any of Delia's fine delftware. But afterward Hans stood to his feet and boldly inquired about the new kite.

"Ah, he has a good memory," Ephraim acknowledged with a wink. He disappeared to a back room, and Helen heard Delia sigh.

"I'm glad he found a home for the kite. It belonged to our only son, Johan."

"Where is Johan?" Esmee wanted to know.

Delia managed a shaky smile in the girl's direction, but Helen could clearly see her gray-blue eyes tearing up. "He went to heaven to live with God, dear girl. He got sick. He was maybe your age. The doctor could do nothing."

Helen exchanged a swift glance with Erik, who sat still in his seat, his eyes large. "I'm sorry to hear this, Delia," Helen said softly.

"It was a long time ago, when the flu was happening all over the world during the last war. Some recovered. Some did not."

Helen wondered about their faith after such tragedy. Did they question God after He took away one so young, their only son? Did they question why? Did their faith fail? How did they go on?

"It was difficult," Delia admitted, her fingers twisting in her lap. "Grief always is. There are so many emotions and questions. But we learned from our grieving to trust God. And to use it for His kingdom and for Johan's memory." Her face broke out in a huge smile as if the storm clouds had lifted and sunshine arrived in its place. Ephraim returned with the kite and several other toys, including a metal truck and a yoyo. The children shouted in glee and pounced on the playthings. The couple laughed and hugged each other, exclaiming how good it was to find homes for the toys, knowing they would be loved.

Helen sat dumbfounded, watching all this unfold before her. There was a power of God here she knew so little about. Where such knowledge would take her, she didn't know. But the comfort the grieving couple gained over their son's toys finding new playmates made it all worthwhile.

"This is a day we will not forget," Erik murmured, mirroring Helen's thoughts. "Dank je wel. For everything. You saved Hans, and now you've brought him and all of us joy."

"No, you brought us joy," Delia corrected, with her husband's approval in the way his head bobbed up and down. "I've never felt such happiness in such a long time. But we know you must be going. It will be dark soon, and Ephraim has a few chores to get done."

"I'm sorry, I didn't even think about the time."

Erik glanced at Helen, then at the clock ticking on the wall.

"But I should help with the dishes . . . ," Helen began.

Delia waved her away. "No, you must be getting home. We loved having you."

Erik gathered up the children and the newly acquired toys and bid the couple farewell.

"Please come see us again soon," Ephraim said with a wink. "We will always be here, as will my cheese shop."

Helen nodded, having every intention of seeing these wonderful, godly people again. When she settled in the passenger seat and the children were once more crammed in the back seat, she blew out a sigh, thinking of all they had been through—from the beauty of the scenery to the pleasantness of Edam, the children with their kites, Erik's kiss, Hans's disappearance, and dinner with the kind Visser family. "I've never had such a day of mixed emotions." She closed her eyes.

"Nor me. In so many ways."

When she opened her eyes, Helen found Erik's face over hers, his eyes focused intently, his arms gathering her close. She straightened and felt again the familiar heat in her face. Thankfully Erik could not see it as the skies darkened on the journey back to Amsterdam.

CHAPTER 8

Helen could barely concentrate on her studies as Professor van Hulst again posed a historical question to the class, one that she would normally raise her hand high in eagerness to answer. She only stared out the window, watching raindrops stream down the glass panes. A few nights ago, the Cohens shared the news that Mr. Cohen had been let go of his position within the government. Mrs. Cohen had dabbed her eyes with her dinner napkin, confessing she didn't understand. Never had there been complaints about his work. He had just received a promotion earlier in the year. Mr. Cohen was brave about the termination, saying he would surely have no trouble finding other employment. Helen didn't know what to think and wondered if she would need to find other housing arrangements. She knew Papa would find a place for her. She appreciated the Cohens making her feel like a part of their family and prayed everything would be all right.

"Miss Smit, can you explain to the class an additional reason for our country remaining neutral in the last great conflict?"

A fellow classmate poked Helen in the arm. She straightened to see the professor staring at her through his spectacles as he repeated the question. "Because our desire here in Holland has always been and always will be for peace and a place of refuge for all who need help."

The corner of the professor's mouth quivered in a smile, even as he shook his head. "I was looking for a political explanation to the question, Miss Smit, rather than an emotional one."

Peace and not politics is what we need right now, Helen thought as she slunk down in her seat and picked up her fountain pen, willing herself to listen as the professor called on another student. After class concluded, she was packing her book and notepad into a leather book bag when she heard her name called.

"You seemed preoccupied during class, Miss Smit," the professor noted. "Hardly characteristic of you."

"I'm sorry. I just heard another person has lost his job. The husband of the family I'm staying with—the Cohens."

He sighed. "Are they Jewish?"

Helen nodded. "What does it mean, sir?"

"It seems that once again God's chosen have been sought out for punishment by evil. We must stand strong and support them any way we can. But I'm sorry to hear this, for your sake."

Helen shifted her book bag to her other shoulder. "I asked if they wanted me to leave. They said no, that they were glad I was there."

Hearing this, he smiled. "You bring them

joy, I'm sure. That's good." He peered down at a calendar on his desk before straightening to meet her gaze. "I have a favor to ask. The holiday season is coming soon, a good time for remembering the Savior's birth by spreading goodwill to others. On this occasion, I was thinking of having the students bring small gifts to give to the neighborhood crèche that cares for the little children. Maybe you would like to organize such an activity?"

Helen stared, wondering why he would select her out of the whole student population to gather gifts for the childcare center next door to the college. "You want *me* to do it, sir?"

"You have heart and spirit. That's all you need. I believe you would do well."

Helen didn't know what to think. He must be mistaking her for someone else—someone more mature with better looks and an engaging personality that could bring the students together. But by the way he was gazing at her, he apparently disagreed with her personal examination of her faults and issues. "How would I go about it, sir?"

"You can come to all my classes and share about the event. We will have a time of gathering gifts, and then you will present them to Miss Pimental, the director of the crèche. I know the parents will appreciate an eve of gifts, their own special *pakjesavond*, given by their Gentile friends."

As much as she felt herself inadequate to represent the college, Helen did hold a secret delight at having been chosen out of all the students for this special time of giving gifts to the children. Maybe it would provide a semblance of peace after months of enduring the annexation of their country and all of its changes. No doubt with families losing jobs and unable to afford gifts, this would prove a worthy and appreciated cause. Joy began to rise up within her. She couldn't wait to tell Erik about this important duty assigned by the professor, now the vice president of the college. Just the idea made her stand straighter with her head held high.

Pedaling her bike furiously along the street after leaving the college, Helen considered creative ways to encourage her fellow students to participate. Maybe she should have someone dress up as *Sinterklaas* to add spirit to the occasion.

She braked then, her feet slipping off the pedals to the road below, to find the store where Erik worked crushed with people descending on it. Parking the bicycle, she walked over and peeked in a window to see Erik surrounded by people purchasing food for the upcoming holiday season. No doubt many were buying ingredients to make cookies like *janhagel* and *pepernoten* as well as *boterkoek*, or butter cake, and other treats for the holiday season. Soon would be the *intocht*—the arrival of Sinterklaas by boat from

Spain, accompanied by his assistants, the *Zwarte Piet*. Her brother Simon would still participate in *Pakjesavond* by putting out a wooden shoe filled with carrots and hay for Sinterklaas's white horse and awaiting the presents he would bring in return. No doubt Hans, Karl, and Esmee would all be excited by the prospect of the visit. Just the idea of gleeful children enjoying some fun amid this oppressive cloud of occupation felt like a gift given from above. For once they could be happy.

Despite the happiness, Helen felt sad she couldn't steal Erik away to tell him about the important task given to her by the professor. Returning to her bicycle, she mounted it and pedaled to Amsterdam Noord to share the news of the gift giving at the college with her family. Lars and Simon were out in the front yard playing catch when she arrived. It was good seeing them play as brothers.

"Why are you so happy?" Lars wondered. "Good news, I hope? We sure need some."

"Wonderful news. I've been given an important task by my professor at college. I'm to arrange the donation of gifts for the little children at the nearby crèche. Would you like to help me plan it?"

The brothers looked at each other and, to Helen's surprise, left the ball bouncing to come talk with her about it. On a normal day a year ago, neither would have cared anything about it.

But just to focus on happy tidings and plans like gift giving was like drinking a good tonic these days. Mama came out too, curious to hear of the upcoming plans and give her opinion.

"In your speech to the students, you should tell them what the mamas and papas need for their little ones," Mama suggested. Helen retrieved a piece of paper and fountain pen out of her book bag to write down the gift ideas the family offered. Rattles and spinning tops, rag dolls and toys carved of wood—even infant items for the parents like bottles and diapers. Simon scrunched up his face, saying diapers and bottles weren't things Sinterklaas would bring, but Helen grew excited all the same.

When the boys' interest waned and they returned to their game, Helen looked to her mother with eagerness. "May I take the large woven laundry basket with me? The students could put their wrapped gifts in it, and then I can carry it to the crèche."

"You may." Mama smiled broadly. "I'm so happy for you, Helen. I thought . . ." She paused. "I thought you and Lars might be doing things that are not good and making trouble. I've heard, you know, that if you make trouble, they send you away to a labor camp. I couldn't bear it if something were to happen to any of my children."

Helen placed a hand on her mother's cool one. "Mama, I'm not involved in anything like that.

Look at this lovely project. I'm taking classes to help children learn how to read and write and know their history. And God gave me the opportunity to do this wonderful thing for the nursery next door to our college. I'm so happy."

Mama smiled. "Ja. I am too."

The rest of the evening Helen worked on the project, creating a sign to go with the basket and writing a short speech to share with the classes concerning the gift giving. She wondered if she should visit Miss Pimental, the director of the childcare program at the crèche, to see if there was anything specific the students should bring for the babies and children in her care. She would stop by tomorrow to introduce herself and inquire.

The telephone rang, and moments later she was summoned to the sitting room. Helen left the hall mirror, where she was practicing her speech, to answer the call.

"I was surprised not to find you at the Cohens'." Erik's concerned voice came over the receiver.

"There's so much to do, and I needed help from my family. I'm sorry." She knew Erik would be confused by her standoffishness, but she didn't mean it that way. She *was,* in fact, very busy.

"Are you angry with me?" he wondered.

"Of course not. Professor van Hulst gave me a special assignment. He chose me out of everyone to give a surprise pakjesavond to the neighborhood crèche through my classmates.

Oh, it will be so much fun. In just a few days is the intocht too. At last we have some wonderful things to think about."

She heard him sigh. "I wish I could help you, but the store is—"

"I don't need help. My family gave me some good ideas, and I know I can get friends and others to assist. There's so little time, but it will be fine."

"All right." Helen could hear the sadness in Erik's voice but couldn't think about it right now. There were too many things to do and a speech to give. He had his work for the holidays, and now she had hers. She said a swift prayer that, like her, Erik would find joy and peace in whatever he did.

The intocht had arrived at last. Helen stood among the eager throng of children and adults alike, dressed in a thick wool coat to ward off the cold November day, eyes fixed on the main canal, waiting for the arrival of the *stroomboot* carrying Sinterklaas. The figure of St. Nicholas arrived in a different city across the Netherlands each year, and with all the turmoil inflicted on them the last few months, the largest city in the country, Amsterdam, was chosen as his port of entry from Spain. Everyone eagerly anticipated this moment with sheer joy and excitement. Music began to play from a street band, and children pointed, rising up on tiptoes, hoping for a better view. Helen recalled the happiness the festivities brought when she was little. She realized later that the arrival of Sinterklaas symbolized the real reason of cheer during the holidays—the coming of Jezus to a humble manger in Bethlehem and His gift of salvation to the world. This year everyone hungered for happiness and peace. As the professor had said, peace and joy, with goodwill toward men, were needed in turbulent times like these.

"There he is!" shouted several children. Everyone craned their necks. The music grew louder as the boat appeared in the canal, carrying the figure of Sinterklaas, dressed in his tall forked hat with a red cross on it. His flowing white beard offset the red robe he wore, and he waved at the crowds with gloved hands. Helen knew what the children were thinking: What kind of presents did he carry in his boat? Sinterklaas would soon ride around the countryside on his beautiful white horse to reward all the good children with special packages in their wooden shoes.

"So, have you been good this year?" came a voice from behind. Helen whirled to find Erik with a grin on his face, his sandy-colored hair poking out from beneath the black wool cap he wore. "Last year at the intocht we didn't even see each other. I was too busy at the store when several workers were ill."

"Well, I hope I've been good, at least a little." She poked him playfully in the arm before looking around. "Glad you could be here. Did you come alone or with your family?"

"The family is down the street to watch the parade. Hans already has Grandfather's wooden shoe filled with carrots and hay, even though pakjesavond is still a few weeks away."

Helen surveyed the crowd as Sinterklaas made his way up the main canal into the city center. Soon he would disembark the boat for his white horse, and a great parade would begin, with his helpers tossing candy and pepernoten cookies at the excited crowd. Helen could barely keep still at the thought. If only such excitement could go on forever before the grim reality of everything came crashing down. But she pushed the troublesome thoughts aside to enjoy this moment.

"Are you ready for the special pakjesavond at the college?" he asked.

"I will be speaking to the professor's classes in a few days. The basket is ready, and I spoke with Miss Pimentel, the director of the crèche. She is very happy to hear what we are doing. I think she and the professor have exchanged words and ideas in the past. They seem to know each other."

Erik nodded. "So, I have a question for you. If St. Nicholas was to come calling at your house, what gift would you like him to bring you? Besides a poem, of course."

Helen caught her breath, uncertain what to say. Possessions seemed so out of place with all they were enduring. "That no one would ever take our joy again. Ever."

"That's a very large gift."

"I believe God can do it."

"I think He already did, when Jezus came into this world. He said to be of good cheer, for He has overcome the world. His coming is the real gift of the season."

At that moment, Helen saw a patrol of armed green police circling the perimeter of the crowd, keeping a careful eye on everything. "I would like to see them disappear as well," she muttered.

Erik said nothing, but she could read his thoughts. He too would like nothing more than to have their country at peace again. He took her hand in his and gave a gentle squeeze in confirmation. "I need to return to the store. The parents will want to buy sweets for their children after the parade is over. Please be careful."

Helen nodded, releasing his hand to see him making his way through the throng. She wondered how he managed to find her among all these people. At times he felt like her protector—always keeping watch. It gave her comfort. She looked around to see a multitude of grins and crimson cheeks on the faces of the children. Oh, to wear a smile every day like they did today, without a care in the world.

• • •

The festive air carried Helen to college on Monday where she stood before her classmates and shared the need for gifts for the little ones at the childcare center. She asked them to bring wrapped packages, marking each one with the age and whether the gift was for a boy or a girl on each one. In a matter of days, packages began to materialize in the large basket placed in the office. Each day she stopped by to see the rising mound of gifts wrapped in bright paper, sure to please weary mothers and fathers balancing the trials of the world with the care of their children.

At the end of the week, Helen went by the office to be greeted by the smiling secretary. "It seems you have a calling for good works, Miss Smit. Look at all the generosity." She waved at the stack of packages. "I had to bring a second basket from my home. The vice president is very pleased by the students' participation."

Helen couldn't believe her eyes. God had taken the loaves and fishes of the gifts and brought forth basketfuls! She took several packages out of her book bag that Mama had bought and wrapped for the cause and placed them with the others in the new basket. She could hardly wait to present the goods to Miss Pimental next week. Maybe she could even stay and watch some of the wee ones tear away the paper with giggles and exclamations to reveal the fun toys.

Just then the vice president of the college entered the office. Professor van Hulst wore a smile on his face. "And here she is! Our own St. Nicholas."

"Oh hardly, sir. I'm just happy the students have done so much for the project."

"So am I. I spoke with the director of the crèche and told her of the great response we've received. She is eager to see you with the gifts next week." He paused. "I knew when God spoke to me about you that you would be perfect for the task."

Helen marveled at his statement as he moved away. God had spoken to the professor about her? How? What did He say? Would she know when He spoke? Did it happen like an actual voice? Or more of a calming sensation or feeling of joy in her heart like when she did these projects? Maybe it happened through an idea that came to mind, or the feeling of sorrow when she spoke out of turn, or failed to show love like she should. Could that all be the voice of the Lord in her heart, mind, and soul?

Just then she saw a vision of Erik, his arms laden with packages, and an idea sprang to mind. Maybe God was speaking after all. She hurriedly left the college and pedaled swiftly to the grocery store, knowing Erik would be busy as he had been the entire holiday season. But he was not too busy to notice her out the storefront window. He hastily undid his apron and came out to greet her.

"You look like the sun determined to make a garden grow," he said with a grin.

"I saw a vision of you."

"Uh-oh." He feigned a look of surprise and added a snicker. "I hope it was something good."

"You were helping me hand out packages at the crèche. So many students have given gifts, I could use the help next week."

"I'll be there," he said without hesitation.

Helen blinked at the rapid response to the picture she had in her mind. This must be what the professor meant—the still, small voice beckoning to her heart. She nodded, gave him some encouraging words about his job, and hurried back to school. She was already late for her language class in English, but it was a good kind of tardiness. As she slipped into her seat, the professor smiled as if she knew about the good fruit gathered for the event. *Thank you, Lord.*

Helen stood in the receiving room of the crèche with Erik by her side, each of them holding a large woven basket overflowing with gifts. When they entered the main room and set the baskets on a table, several workers began singing a song to the children—

Sinterklaas kapoentje,
Leg wat in mijn schoentje,

Leg wat in mijn laarsje,
Dank je Sinterklaasje!
(Saint Nicholas, little rascal,
Throw something in my little shoe,
Throw something in my little boot,
Thank you, little Saint Nicholas!)

Helen's heart warmed. The workers gathered the wooden shoes they had scattered about the room as symbols of the occasion. She looked up at Erik, who wore a smile on his face. "I wish I could tell them the story of the Christ child," he said softly. "Even if this is a Jewish crèche."

"I think Miss Pimentel would allow it. We can try."

His face twisted in dismay. "I have no story-book to read though. Hans has a very good book. I didn't think to bring it."

"We can return another day. I'm sure they would love more visits." She didn't want this precious moment lost by disappointment of any kind. To her relief, Erik nodded and smiled in anticipation of the gift-giving event. Helen sighed. They worked so well together. From the days they spent visiting and sharing to the time they searched for Hans near Edam, Helen felt she belonged with Erik. Could this be another sign of God's voice in her heart?

Her contemplation was interrupted when a young lady dressed in a white apron, white cloth hat, and blue blouse came forward. "Children, come form a line right here." The toddlers all burst to their feet, shrieking in glee, and stood in a line with the workers instructing them, ready to receive a gift.

"Just a moment, children!" announced an older woman who stood at the rear of the room. Henriëtte Pimentel came forward, her face and mannerism matriarchal but with an air of joy in her bright eyes and warm smile. She looked at Erik and Helen. "How wonderful of you to come and give us this special pakjesavond." And then to the excited children, she said, "Children, we must thank Miss Smit and Mr. . . . ."

"Erik Minger," he said.

She nodded. "Children, Miss Smit and Mr. Minger asked students in the school next door to gather these lovely gifts for you. Let us tell them how thankful we are." She began to clap, and the children did as well, accompanied by shouts of glee.

As the children came forward, Helen gave a gift to each child, looking with happiness at their outstretched hands and smiling faces. Cheers erupted with paper thrown in an array of rainbow colors to reveal dollies and balls, small cars and storybooks. Then Helen noticed the title of one of the storybooks, and her mouth fell open. It was about Jesus' birth. She took it and approached the director. "Pardon, Miss Pimentel, but is it all right if we read this book to the children? It's a Christian story, of course, but there are animals in it and—"

The director smiled and nodded. Helen and Erik took seats while Marion, a young worker, encouraged the children to gather around and sit on the floor. Other childcare workers held gurgling babies in their laps. Helen nodded to Erik, and with a strong voice he read the story of the Christ child's birth in the animals' home and how His mother made His bed in a feeding trough. They laughed merrily as Erik gave the noises for each of the animals that visited the manger—baaing for the sheep, mooing for cows, braying for the donkey. The children responded with their own imitations of animal noises and laughed. At the conclusion of the story, the children raced about with their toys while Helen gave Miss Pimental the remainder of the gifts to distribute to other needy families.

"This was simply lovely," the director said. "How grateful I am for all your help and for your kindness. You made this such a happy time. Thank you." Helen could see and hear the appreciation, and it filled her heart.

Helen and Erik soon exchanged the cheerful, warm atmosphere of the crèche for the cold and dreary Amsterdam streets, but that did not dampen her spirits in the least. She nearly grabbed Erik up in a healthy embrace with the joy bursting in her heart. "What a wonderful time, wasn't it?"

"And I was able to share the story of Jesus' birth." He nodded. "I guess even in times of trouble, miracles can happen."

"All the time," she said a bit breathlessly as they paused on a bridge spanning a canal.

He turned to face her, his arms curling around her, and before she realized it, they were kissing. Then he straightened, brushing strands of hair away from her face. "If you had a wooden shoe sitting out, you would find a very special gift in it."

Helen stepped back, concerned about what he might be suggesting. Could it be? "Erik . . . I don't think . . . You're not speaking about an engagement, are you?"

"Why not? You see how well we work together. We belong together. You must feel it."

Helen stared at the pavement. Yes, she did feel it. Deep in her heart she wanted to accept the gift of a ring he had in mind. But the cautious part of her warned there were still too many concerns, too much vulnerability, too much unknown, and too much doubt over the future. "I can't think about it just yet. There is so much happening right now. I have my studies; you have your work. In fact, I—I should be getting back to class." She whispered farewell and left him on the bridge to make her way back to the college, trying not to imagine the crestfallen look of rejection on his face.

And just like that, the joy of the day gave way to despondency.

CHAPTER 9

The holiday season had brought a respite from all that was happening in their country, and for that Erik was thankful. He'd hoped the joy of the season would propel him and Helen into an engagement. Helen knew he was ready to give her a ring as a special present for the season. He tried to see the hesitancy from her point of view, that despite some happy times, things remained uncertain. They each had their duties to perform amid the German annexation of their country. He should have realized the timing was not right and not allowed his heart to hastily advance the longing he had for an engagement and eventual marriage. But the occasional meetings when he could break away from the store to sip coffee with Helen at the café or have a talk by the canal did little to fill the desire in his heart to share whatever life had in store, both the good and the bad. Maybe he could get away more often now as the busyness of the store had begun to subside. Mr. Baas would likely be able to spare him more time so he and Helen could nurture their relationship. He had worked the holiday season with vigor, filling bags and bags of ingredients to make sweets or other foodstuffs for feasts. Tomorrow was December 25, and Erik desperately wanted to spend the special day with Helen when their country enjoyed a nice feast with family and friends. Hans often remarked about their adventures in Edam, and his parents inquired about her. Maybe inviting Helen to dinner at his family's home would ease the doubts in her heart and pave the way to an engagement.

Erik placed his cap firmly on his head and strode through the streets of Amsterdam to the Cohen home where Helen stayed. After some knocking, Mrs. Cohen slowly opened the creaking door, peering out with one eye as if expecting the enemy to be standing on her doorstep. Erik quickly swiped off his cap and greeted her.

"Oh, it's only you. I was afraid it might be . . ." She paused. "Helen's not here. She has gone home to Noord."

Erik noticed the dampness of her cheeks and her hand clasping a handkerchief. "Are you all right?"

Mrs. Cohen sniffed and dabbed her eyes with a hankie. "I don't know what we'll do. My husband is out of work, and no one will hire him because he's Jewish. We've just been told by the landlord that we have to move. I need to tell Helen that she'll have to find another place to live."

Erik stared. "Why do you have to move?"

Again she wiped the handkerchief across her eyes. "Because we're Jewish," she repeated. "The landlord said there are specific neighborhoods now being established for Jews to live in. While it's not the law yet, we heard from the Jewish Council in Amsterdam that the move is for our safety and the safety of the entire population. But we know that's not true. My husband says money buys everything—even enemies among the people. And he would know."

Erik frowned. "I'm sorry to hear this. If you need help moving, please let me know. I will gladly assist."

She shook her head. "Thank you, but no. We don't want to get you in trouble, young man. I will ask our Jewish friends."

"Mrs. Cohen, the Bible doesn't distinguish who I can help. Nor do people around here. We're to love our neighbor as ourselves. And I will gladly help if you need it."

Mrs. Cohen managed a small smile and a nod before carefully closing the door. The distress in her face and the fear in her eyes wrenched Erik's heart in a way he did not expect. He recalled another woman at the store many weeks ago who said her husband was also out of work and could not afford extras like candy for her children. He never thought much on these decrees being forced upon the Jews. They had been minor incidents at first. But now being told that the Jews must be corralled in certain living areas, as though they were no longer human beings but animals, kindled ire within him. The more he thought on it, the angrier he became. It didn't do his mounting anger any good when he spied one of the green police aggressively questioning a Dutch citizen. The Germans had succeeded in infiltrating every part of their lives like some plague. In the Netherlands they had always lived in peace without bothering another soul. *Why, God?* he wondered as he slowly walked on, hunched over by this burden of the soul, staring at the cracks in the stark gray pavement.

Soon thoughts of Helen's predicament lessened the woes of Mrs. Cohen. Helen would need to be told she must leave the Cohens and live elsewhere. And she would not be happy about the news. He could see her marching into the office of the local council, demanding to know why the Cohens were being forced to move. She had spunk for sure, and he didn't want to see her get into trouble.

He returned to the store to fetch the parcel he had hidden behind the counter—a pretty knitted sweater he thought would look nice on Helen's slender form. More than ever in these troubling times, he felt the need to strengthen ties not only with family and friends but especially with Helen. Hans often asked about her and Esmee and Karl. Once Erik tried to have Karl and Hans meet to play and interact, but without Helen there, it never happened. Erik felt more and more they must be together even if right now she hesitated to make a commitment. Two can defend themselves where one can be overpowered. With all the trouble sprouting up around Amsterdam, they must come together to help each other and other people.

Erik arrived at the Smit house where Esmee and Karl were playing with sticks and a ball in the front yard, trying hard to outwit the other in the game. He had to admit that the sight of them drawn to the Smit house as their playground warmed his heart. "Did you have a good *Sinterklaasavond*?" Erik called out. Immediately the children rushed over to him, their faces all smiles, and gave him hugs.

"I have a new ball!" Karl declared, showing it to him. They laughed loudly and went on to tell of their presents—Esmee's tulip-print tea set, warm socks and mittens, and plenty of candy, including the initials of their names made out of chocolate.

A face appeared in the front window, veiled by a lace curtain, and then the front door opened. "I was wondering who was causing all the commotion," came a familiar voice. Standing there in a simple cotton top and plaid skirt, her blond hair cascading around her shoulders, Helen was the most beautiful vision ever. If only she would accept a ring as her gift. But Erik forced the emotion deep inside where it remained for now.

Instead, he stood ready with her alternate gift.

He peeled off his cap and wished her a happy Christmastime. "I have something Sinterklaas gave to me," he said with a wink, retrieving the package from the basket on his bicycle. The twins rushed over, pawing at the package and asking Helen if they could open it.

"You had your gifts, remember?" Helen said. They stepped back and remained content to watch Erik give the colorful package to her. "I have something for you also, but it isn't ready yet," she confessed, taking a seat on the stoop. She undid the paper to reveal the sweater colored a perfect blue to match her mesmerizing eyes, and she gave profound thanks. "How lovely. Hartelijk bedankt!"

"The sweater seemed to have your name attached," he said.

She laughed. "We must think alike," she said, turning to reenter the house. He stood by patiently as the children whispered in excitement to each other, their eyes shining. Helen returned holding a knitting needle that trailed a long black and tangerine garment. "It's a scarf," she said. "Mama taught me, but I'm a slowpoke."

"It's wonderful! I'm sure that when the real cold comes it will be ready."

She draped the scarf around his neck, checking the length left to knit. All he saw was her long fingers and then her intense blue eyes staring at him. A red tide spread into her cheeks. Her sweet, spicy scent, like the finest *speculaas* cookie, filled him. If not for the twins who stood there gawking, he would have taken her in his arms and kissed her.

"I—I see I still have a ways to go," she stammered, unwrapping the scarf from his neck. "But the black will match your cap, and orange always looks cheerful."

"It will be a wonderful scarf, dank je wel." He paused. "Have you time to take a walk?"

Helen nodded. "Let me get my camera that Mama and Papa gave to me." She dashed off to bring out the revered camera he knew she'd wanted for a long time. He held it for her, examining its fine features while she buttoned up her coat. "Isn't it wonderful? I love it."

He handed it back to her, and she took a picture of the twins playing. "Let's get you back to your home now," she told them. Karl gathered his ball and sticks, and he and Esmee walked with them down the street to their home.

"Karl and Esmee don't live far from you at all," Erik observed after the two children went inside their house. "But they seem to like playing at your house."

"Their parents work a great deal. We often look after them. It brings in a little money for Mama." She stared at the ground, and for a moment it felt like the first time they met, with some shyness—or was it aloofness?—rising up. "I–I'm glad you came," she finally said. "I was thinking how preoccupied I've been."

"You had important work for the professor. And then there was the holiday season."

"Yes, but it distracted me too much. I mean, it seems like we've drifted apart because of it."

He took her hand and gave it a gentle squeeze. "We've both been busy, Helen. But now we have some time. And I'm here to invite you to my home tomorrow for the holiday. We're having a goose with all the trimmings. I think it would be nice for you to spend some time with my parents and also my sisters, Greta and Mary. Of course, Hans knows you, but I think my sisters would enjoy having a young woman to talk to. A mother can't always satisfy young girlish curiosities in life."

"I would like that. I have brothers, so it would be nice to chat with sisters for a change."

And just like that her head lifted, the sun's rays igniting her face, and her steps quickened with a display of happiness. He didn't dare dampen her enthusiasm with news of the Cohens and her need to move. Instead, he shared about the season, telling her of the reactions of his family members to the gifts left in their wooden shoes, and Hans in particular. "I didn't know what Hans would think when he unwrapped the new boat I gave him. He looked it all over. Then he came and gave me a big hug, and I knew I'd done the right thing by giving it to him."

Helen gazed at him, and her blues eyes became even brighter. "Oh Erik, how sweet. I hope he will sail it in the next great race . . . whenever there is another race."

"I'm sure there will be more come spring. The Germans don't appear to want to stop everyday life, or they would have a revolt on their hands." He quieted on the subject when they passed a few people on the street. These days no one knew who worked with the green police or who shared secrets in inner circles. Erik had heard stories of some turning in others with opposing political viewpoints for money, and he had no intention of creating fodder for someone overhearing talk of a revolt.

"It's nice to have some happy times for a change. I'm looking forward to dinner at your home."

Erik wondered what she would say when she found out she must seek new housing for the next term. How he wished he could give her a solution to that dilemma. He would keep his eyes and ears open to possibilities. Maybe his boss would know of a place. But things changed daily, and it was hard to know what might happen next. As scripture said, there was a time and season for everything. Right now he wanted Helen's happiness to last forever. If only it could.

● ● ●

Helen could hardly wait for dinner at the Minger home. Erik would soon be here to pick her up, and she paced the hallway, trying hard not to look at the clock with its golden pendulum ticking methodically. She walked over to the mirror to check her appearance once more, admiring the pastel blue sweater he had given her, which went well with her black wool skirt and high-heeled shoes. Despite knowing him for over a year, she had only met his parents a few times. His sisters had always been off on some frolic or errand. Erik had been a frequent visitor to the Smit house. He'd had pleasant conversations with everyone but her father, who remained busy in his warehouse operations. Had she been so focused on herself that she hadn't even considered the ones who influenced Erik's life? Maybe she could change her preoccupations with kind words and a listening ear and take pictures of his family on her new camera.

She must have had a strange look on her face when Erik arrived, because he gazed at her questioningly as he opened the car door for her. "Is something wrong?" he asked. "Did you hear the news?"

"Oh, there's always news." She smoothed out her skirt after settling in the seat and looked out the window at the many brick homes lining the silent street. Why she was suddenly tongue-tied, she didn't know. Maybe her nerves were getting the better of her. Or maybe the simple conviction that he'd done so much in their relationship, and she very little. Maybe that's why she couldn't say yes to a proposal just yet. This evening could be a major step forward if everything worked out.

"The Cohens told you then," he continued. "I was very sad to hear."

Helen stared at him. A sudden wave of curiosity mixed with fear washed over her. "What do you mean? What happened?" She saw his lips press together and his hands tighten around the steering wheel.

"You mean they didn't tell you?" His face turned red. "Helen, I'm not sure if I should say anything. But . . . I saw Mrs. Cohen before I came to visit you yesterday. She told me her husband lost his job and now they have to move."

"I know Mr. Cohen lost his job. But they aren't moving."

Erik glanced in the mirror and made a turn across the bridge toward the heart of Amsterdam, passing several green police on patrol. "These people are tightening their grip on those they think are undesirable. Mrs. Cohen told me they have to find acceptable Jewish housing in established neighborhoods."

Helen sat still in her seat, stunned by the news. She had not spoken to Mrs. Cohen for several days. Why hadn't they telephoned her about this?

"Oh no. Now I will need to find another place." Then she remembered Mrs. Cohen telling her of her husband's lost job with tears in her eyes. *Listen to yourself, Helen. Don't you feel any remorse for the Cohens? Forced out of their jobs and now forced out of their home?* She slumped down in her seat and stared out the window.

A strong hand patted her arm, and she sat upright.

"I will find you a place to stay," Erik told her. "Don't worry."

"I should be more worried about the Cohens. It's terrible what's happened to them." All of it made her angry. Not only was the enemy putting out the Cohens but inconveniencing her as well.

"Everything will work out. Don't worry," Erik reassured her.

When he pulled before the Minger home, the news about the Cohens disappeared under the thought of the coming visit. The door burst open and a cheerful Hans raced out, carrying his new boat with him, eager to show Helen his present. The mixed emotions she felt faded under the happiness of childhood.

"Come see how well it floats!" Hans said, leading the way to a bathtub filled with water, with puddles on the wooden floor. He showed her the fine sails and even the tiny rudder that moved back and forth in the water. "Isn't it super?"

"Yes, it is. I'm sure it will do well in the boat

races." *If there are any more races or anything fun for the children,* she thought, not wishing to dampen the boy's spirit.

Erik appeared in the doorway. "I wondered where you'd gone. Dinner is ready."

Helen followed him to the formal dining room. Erik made brief introductions before pulling out her chair beside his sister Mary. From what Erik had told her, Mary was the closest in age to Helen's brother Lars. Greta, his other sister, was a few years younger, and Hans was the baby of the family.

"Hans, I told you not to bring the boat to the table," Mr. Minger said, tucking a linen napkin into the neckline of his shirt.

Hans stored the boat under his chair and picked up his spoon and fork, ready for dinner. Mrs. Minger shook her head at him and bowed her head with her hands folded. Mr. Minger offered a prayer for the meal. With her eyes closed, Helen listened to his grateful thanks for this great bounty and for God's peace in their country and the world. After the prayer, she opened her eyes and took in the roast goose decorated with apples at the center of the table and, surrounding it, bowls of squash and new potatoes and glass bowls of sparkling jellies and candies.

"So, Erik tells us your training to become a teacher is going well," Mr. Minger said as he took up a large knife to carve the goose.

"Yes sir. I have one term to go, and then I'll be student teaching."

"I always said that teaching is a worthwhile profession you should look into, Mary," Mrs. Minger said. "Maybe you can ask Helen about it."

Helen saw the young woman's face crinkle. "You know I'm interested in nursing, Mother."

"Yes, but dealing with men and their wounds . . ."

"Mother, this is 1940, soon to be 1941. The old days are gone. Nurses are needed more than ever."

Uh-oh, thought Helen, sensing the tension rising around the table.

Erik cleared his throat. "I think we can offer our guest here other conversation. Such as what we each received on Sinterklaasavond."

"My boat!" Hans piped up, his mouth full of food.

"Everyone knows about your boat," Mary said. She cast another eye at her mother.

Helen could see the parents' desire to mold their children to the professions of their liking. Or rather ones that didn't promote anxiety in their eyes. She remembered well Mama's objections to her going off to college. Not to mention Mama's worries after the invasion and the safety of her children.

Erik tried to ease the tension with talk of the store, but the conversation elapsed into a tense silence. After dinner he took Helen aside and apologized. "I wasn't sure if I'd said something wrong," she told him.

"Of course not. Mary had a disagreement with Mother shortly before we arrived. Mary told me about it."

"I think nursing is a fine profession. And with the war, it's needed."

"Mother worries the Germans will take Mary away to care for their injured men on the front. It's like all parents these days. They worry about their children, both young and old."

Helen sighed as she watched Mary and Greta clear the table after outright refusing her offer of assistance. Then she frowned, stood to her feet, and boldly returned to the dining area. "I know you told me you don't need help," she said to the two girls, "but I think you do."

Mary straightened, holding a dish half-filled with potatoes, and hurried into the kitchen. Helen followed.

"I just wanted to say I think it's a very noble profession, helping the sick and injured," Helen said to her.

Mary turned, and Helen saw a small smile form on the young woman's face. "Oh, thank you. It seems like everyone is against me for this decision."

"It wasn't an easy one, I'm sure. But I don't think there's a greater calling."

"I've heard of the terrible injuries the public

still suffers in Rotterdam and in other areas that were bombed. I feel useless staying here and doing silly things like sewing. You probably understand, don't you?"

"I understand very well. My mother was against me going to college. But we need to go where our gifts are best used."

Mary smiled. "Thank you. I see you're wearing the sweater I told Erik to buy. It was difficult to find, you know. They are rationing clothing."

"Dank je wel. It's beautiful. And it makes the gift extra special, knowing you helped pick it out." Suddenly they were smiling at each other and began chattering about clothes and the new bicycle Mary had received and the application process for nursing school.

"What do you think will happen in the new year?" Mary wondered. "I worry I won't be able to attend school. I've heard about the edicts, you know, about professors having to sign pledges to Germany's new society and schools closing because of their refusal."

"I don't have to worry about that, as the school I attend is a Christian institution. But you do what your heart tells you. If you give your work and your life to God's care, everything will work out and you'll do wonderfully."

Mary smiled and nodded. "Dank je wel. Now please, spend time with my brother. Erik really likes you a lot, you know." She winked and returned to the dishes. Helen left the kitchen and found Erik in the next room. He greeted her with a warm smile.

"I think you gave Mary the best present this holiday," he said.

"I did? What?"

"Understanding." He took her hand in his. "Helen, you do realize I'm growing more in love with you every day."

The sweetness of the last hour began to fade as she waited and wondered. Was it time?

He continued, "But I understand that our times are in God's hands. I just wanted you to know how I feel."

"Erik, I wish I could say 'yes,' but with college and—"

He nodded. "I understand. There's too much uncertainty, and now isn't a good time." He turned her gently to face him, his hand cupping her cheek. "But I want to make a commitment to you right now to help you and do whatever I can to see that you're safe."

His words chased her all the way home that night as she tried hard to fall asleep. She could see his blue eyes gazing into hers and feel his warm hand on her cheek. His words of love spoke more powerfully than any she had ever heard. But life was too uncertain, as he said. And she still had other cares of the world, including where she would call home for the rest of the term. Maybe the news was in error and she would return to find the Cohens remaining in their home after all. But seeing the patrols of green police and the armored vehicles and trucks with the sound of sirens that screamed from one end of the street to the other, she realized this was now the new reality.

PART TWO

1941–42

CHAPTER 10

Helen came to the large door and inhaled a breath, her hand poised around the knob. The professor would know how to help. She felt certain of it. Professor van Hulst knew many in the area and would likely have a solution to her current predicament—finding a place to stay now that the Cohens had tearfully confirmed they must move to the Jewish Quarter. She needed a solution and quick. Papa said he would take her to school and back for the time being. But with his job at the docks growing all the busier since the occupation, she knew he couldn't do it for long. Taking a streetcar every day would prove costly. Riding the bicycle back and forth from home wasn't practical either and perhaps even dangerous. With the increase in military and civilian patrols and rumors of curfews, Mama was against it. The only thing she could do was pray for a place to rest her head. God provided for the birds and animals; He would provide for her. Jezus said not to be concerned about the things of life but to trust.

Helen cracked open the door and peered in to find Professor van Hulst in the middle of a conversation with six young men. They were speaking in hushed tones, several of them pacing back and forth or running their fingers through their hair in noted distress. Her curiosity couldn't help but be piqued, and she strained to hear the news.

"Miss Smit, do you require something?"

Startled, Helen stepped back. "I'm sorry to disturb you, Professor. I will return another time."

"Come in." He addressed the wide-eyed young men before him. "This is one of my best students, Helen Smit," he introduced.

Helen smiled tentatively as one of the young men stared at her with a grin on his lean face. She stepped back under the spark of attention and looked away.

"These students had their college close because the professors refused to sign the Aryan Oath put out by the occupiers," Professor van Hulst explained. "I have informed them we don't ascribe to political oaths here except in pledge to our Savior Jesus Christ and His work in our lives. But one could hardly call that political. Isn't that right, Miss Smit?"

"Yes sir, that's correct." She held her head high as again the young man winked and smiled in her direction. Helen shifted her book bag to her other shoulder and kept her attention focused on the professor.

"I've informed these young men they are welcome to study here. We welcome all."

"Dank je wel, Professor van Hulst," piped up

the man who had smiled at Helen. "We've heard excellent things about your reputation and this institution, and they would seem accurate."

"We do what we can to help each other in times of need. Miss Smit here helped our college with a successful gift-giving mission for the crèche next door to our college. It's projects like this that will keep our country above reproach and victorious over anything the enemy wishes to do."

"What an excellent mission, Miss Smit," the man said and again gave her a perfect smile full of gleaming white teeth.

Helen cleared her throat. "Professor, I'm sorry to interrupt your meeting. I was seeking your advice about—"

"Just a moment." He nodded to the men. "Please see the secretary, who will arrange for your stay."

Helen breathed a sigh of relief when they turned and walked out the door, feeling the smiling man's attention unnerving. She cleared her throat and returned to the matter at hand. "Professor, I see you are offering these students a place to stay. I've been staying with the Cohens, but they were told they must move immediately to the Jewish Quarter. I can't live there any longer. Do you know of any housing situations?"

The professor blew out a sigh and shook his head. "It's happening already. I have Jewish friends who were just told they must register with the Jewish Council by this Friday and obtain different identification cards from the rest of the population. Have the Cohens done this?"

"I'm not sure. Mrs. Cohen didn't mention new ID cards."

"What it really means, I don't know. But without faith these days, how does one even dare face the future?" He shook his head again. "As to your need, I'm sorry, but I don't have a recommendation for you. I'm offering the young men a temporary place here at the college until they are settled in Amsterdam. It would be unseemly, of course, to extend such an invitation to you at this time."

"Of course, sir. If you hear of a couple or an older woman who wouldn't mind a boarder, please let me know."

"I will indeed." He nodded and returned to the mountain of papers and books on his desk.

Helen slowly walked out, trying hard not to feel disappointed. She stopped short in the hall to find the young man who had grinned at her lingering nearby. "I'm Peter," he said, extending his hand.

"Helen." They shook hands.

"I know."

Helen looked aside, trying to avoid the piercing blue of his eyes that stared intently at her. "So you had to come here?" she finally asked.

"The enemy put out the edict forcing our professors to sign an allegiance to Germany and its totalitarian policies. Many refused and were put out of their positions. Other universities closed. Since I'm learning to become a mathematics teacher and heard of the goodwill of this college, I decided to seek asylum here."

"I don't understand any of this. Every day there's some new decree. The professor just told me that Jews must report to get a different card—"

"I had to get a new one," he said. "I carry a yellow card with a J on it."

Helen gazed at him. "The J is for . . . ?"

"Jew." He paused, and his blue eyes narrowed. "I hope I'm not a criminal in your eyes as being of a Jewish background seems to be to others."

"Of course not! You are highly favored in God's eyes."

His smile returned, and Helen feared he might take her words as a gesture of interest rather than helpfulness. "I'm sorry, but I must be going," she said hurriedly.

"I hope to see you again."

Helen bit her lip, knowing she ought to tell him her heart belonged to another, but said nothing. Instead, she tried not to think too much about the meeting and went off to her next class in English, hoping he would not be in it. But to her dismay, Peter slipped into a seat in the back row, and she feared further emotion clouding her mind when she already had too much to think about.

When the class finished and she was stowing

her notepad in her book bag, Peter sauntered up to her, his hands in his trouser pockets. "I was wondering if you could part with your notebook for a day or two so I can catch up on the past lectures. I believe this class is similar to the one I took at the university, but I want to make sure. And my *Engels* is rather shaky."

Helen hesitated. If she said yes, would he interpret it as proof of interest? But if she said no, would she be labeled as another person who cared little for him or his heritage? "I will lend it to you. But only overnight. I must have it back for an essay we're doing later in the week."

"You're probably very good with words. Essays were never my strength. Calculations, now there's my strength."

"I can write a fairly good essay," she said with a smile.

"See? It's not hard to compliment yourself. You need to believe in yourself and the gifts you have. Like what Professor Van Hulst said when he complimented your mission to the children."

Helen fumbled for the notebook inside her book bag, sensing her rising discomfort in this conversation. She gave the notebook to him but kept her gaze averted. "I hope it helps."

"I'm sure it will." He went off whistling with her notebook tucked under his arm. What on earth was she doing? All thoughts of her dilemma in finding a new place to live diminished under this new distraction. She should not be seeking attention from this man. Or maybe she was making an inference when there was none to be had. Everyone could use a nice smile and a kind word these days. All she did was help a fellow student with his studies—a student who was Jewish and finding life increasingly limited by mandates coming down from the occupier. Kindness could only help, not harm.

Helen pushed the door open and headed out under the gray skies that were often the norm in midwinter. A few young men her age ran down the street. She looked on, wondering what kind of mischief they had found this time, only to see several of the green police in hot pursuit. Chills swept over her.

"It is the *Arbeitseinsatz*," she heard a deep voice say. She glanced up to see Peter looking down on her.

"Should we be out here then? Isn't it dangerous?" She shivered inside her wool coat.

"Maybe you shouldn't be . . . if you're afraid. But I know what the enemy is doing. They imprison people of their choosing who have committed no crimes. They force them to work for Germany. And that's why we need to rise up and do something. What's happening here is wrong, and our continued silence means we agree."

"You sound like my brother Lars. He hasn't said anything lately, but I know he's gone to a meeting with others who want to help fight this."

"You mean he works with the resistance?"

Helen gaped and stepped back. "You know about it?"

He nodded. "There aren't many like me in it. A Jew. We are the sworn enemy, as you know. But those in the resistance want to protect people and find ways to harm the enemy. I'm heading to a meeting right now."

Helen stared, uncertain what it all meant. His face remained rigid and his eyes wide in a picture of determination. "Peter, don't do anything dangerous."

He frowned. "I'm surprised you would say that. If we don't stand up now, Helen, when does it stop?" He pulled her notebook out of his bag. "Here. I don't want this with me in case something happens, as it has your personal information in it. I will get the notes from you tomorrow. If you're willing."

"Of course." Helen took back the notebook with a shaky hand. "Is this meeting worth getting yourself arrested?"

"You should ask yourself that question. The professor saw a strength in you. He said you did great things already, helping those who are weak and vulnerable. I believe you will do something even greater. But it may cost you everything you have. Even your life." He lifted his cap. "Now I have to go. Goodbye."

Peter headed down an alley, and Helen stood like a statue, dumbfounded by his words. To think she had concerned herself with girlish nonsense, thinking he had some fleshly interest in her. Heat flooded her cheeks. Then she thought of Lars, wondering if he would know what Peter meant and what this underground organization was up to. She ought to find out. But right now, she prayed silently that whatever Peter had to do, he would be well. She stared down the alleyway where he disappeared, thinking about the meeting he planned to attend. As she did, her fingers caressed the notebook nestled in her book bag, and she prayed for his safety. She thought about his final words when she spied Erik standing in the distance. Heat flooded over her. How long had he been there? Had he seen the encounter? Her heart began to thump wildly as he walked up.

"Hallo, Helen. What did that fellow want?"

"Peter? Oh, he—he was returning my notebook that I lent him." She pushed back strands of her hair and looked aside.

"So he's in your class?"

"Yes, he's new."

She felt Erik's piercing gaze, and her cheeks felt hot. She wished she could tell him everything but wasn't certain Professor van Hulst wanted it divulged what he had done for the university castaways like Peter. Nor should she mention Peter's participation in the resistance.

"Are you all right?" Erik asked, his eyebrows furrowing. "You look like something is bothering you."

Oh, he could read her like a book. "I'm fine. It's just everything is getting so twisted these days. It makes me wonder what tomorrow will bring." She bit her lip, realizing for the first time she refused to share a secret with Erik. And for the first time since that day on the road to Durgerdam long ago, they seemed to be standing far apart, though they were only a few feet away.

"Does this have anything to do with that fellow you were speaking to?"

Now her face grew hotter. "Yes, but I—I really can't say anymore. I'm sorry."

Erik opened his mouth, then closed it. The wall between them thickened, and the distance between them grew wider. Erik frowned, looked about, then declared he needed to return to work. He strode off, his head down, kicking at a few stones in his path. He knew she was hiding something, but what could she do? She hated leaving things this way. But if Peter was engaged in secretive activity to help others, she didn't dare say anything. Though inwardly she wished she could. Seeing Erik distressed upset her as well.

For days afterward Helen saw no further sign of Peter in the class. His continued absence from college stoked a concern that something bad had happened to him. She wanted to ask the professor if he knew anything but could not bring herself to inquire. She wondered how just a few hours in the man's presence could cause such concern on her part. But the idea he was doing something for the resistance both intrigued and worried her. Maybe Lars could give her some insight into what may have happened to the man.

When she arrived home to Noord for a visit, she immediately sought out Lars, hoping he may have heard about Peter or at least know what he might be doing. She glanced in his bedroom to see him preoccupied by a piece of paper with writing on it. He looked up at her. "What do you want?" he asked gruffly.

"I'm sorry. I wanted to ask you something important." She paused. "Is everything all right?"

"You weren't here. You don't know."

She tried to control a swift tremor that gripped her. "Know what, Lars?"

He shook his head and threw the paper on the bed. He stood swiftly and stared out the window—an unusual act of thoughtfulness for an active and inquisitive Lars. She wondered what the paper contained that had changed him. Compassion flowed over her as she sat down nearby. "It will be all right, whatever it is."

"No, it won't. Not ever." His pale face turned a bright shade of red, and she saw the dampness on his cheeks. "He's gone."

"Who's gone?"

He pointed at the paper. "My best friend. Dietrich. They came in the middle of the night, is what his sister told me. They said he was required to work in a factory in Germany. The only reason his sister didn't go is because she's fifteen. Those over eighteen are being told they must work for the Germans." His voice deepened with anger. "They need workers to keep their war effort going so they can bomb and kill more people."

Helen swallowed hard at this news. She stood to move beside him and share in his view of the row of houses lining the street across from their home. "At least you're still safe."

He whirled, anger contorting his face in tight lines. His hand balled into a fist. "Is that all you can say? My friend is taken away, but I'm safe? You're no different from Mama. Everyone. Can't you see what's happening, Helen? This isn't about you wanting to become a teacher or me being safe. None of that matters if there is no more Netherlands. If we don't arm ourselves right now and drive this enemy away, we'll all die."

Helen stared at her younger brother. The boy who once ruled him had turned overnight into a man. A flame of revenge lit his blue eyes. Just like Peter's. She prayed silently for the words to help ease his pain. "This is very difficult, Lars.

I'm not blind. I see what is happening, though I didn't know about your friend. I'm so sorry." She paused. "But I have to keep the faith that God understands and we are safe with Him, no matter what."

He whirled back to the window and crossed his arms. "I don't believe in God anymore. No God would do this. They say how much He loves us. This isn't love. It's hate. For everything and everyone."

Helen had no words to stop the spiritual battle raging inside him. How could she answer when bombs fell and people were dragged away, when others, like the Cohens, lost livelihood and homes. It looked as if God had turned His face from them and left them to be pecked to death by evil vultures in the dead of night. The Bible itself was filled with times of desperation and death and the appearance that God had forsaken the righteous by allowing evil to reign. "Lars, we don't understand all of God's purposes. Or the future. We can only see what is before us. But I can say that Jezus understands our pain. From the cross, He asked the Father, 'My God, my God, why have You forsaken me?' The Son of God was left to die at the hands of evil men. He suffered greatly, died, and was buried in a tomb of rock. All seemed lost. Hell was cheering."

She paused. "But then came the third day. The empty tomb. He rose from the dead, victorious over evil. This is what we have to hold on to and remember, even in the dark. It may look like we are all dead or dying. But we have to believe the third day is coming. The Resurrection. It's all we can do." She stood to her feet, still wishing she could ask him about the resistance and Peter, but she let it go for now. The pain Lars was feeling cut her to the core and made her look at all she believed. But it gave her some comfort knowing that Jesus was also tested and that He sympathized with struggle. He was looking down at them—especially those caught in a deep pit either of their own making or by others, and praying over them in love. She prayed through her tears for strength for Lars. There was nothing else she could do.

CHAPTER 11

"I've never seen you so quiet."

Erik jerked around to find Mr. Baas observing him as he stacked the canned goods on the shelf. Keeping the store stocked proved a never-ending battle. Every day people would stream in to buy as much as possible, as if expecting that soon there would be no food. But that was the least of his problems. Foremost was the lovely blond-haired, blue-eyed dove he nearly asked to marry him over the holidays, only to find her now distant and aloof. Terrible thoughts plagued his waking and sleeping moments—that their relationship had been stolen like a thief in the night and he had been too busy to see it.

"Just thinking," he said to Mr. Baas, shoving each can in its proper place on the shelf. He didn't want to ponder the awful dream he had last night where he saw his beloved Helen dragged away by German soldiers, her scream piercing the air. He awoke in a cold sweat and nearly bicycled over to see her in the dead of night to make sure she was safe. The college she attended had grown stricter, and unless one was a student or part of the faculty, visitations were no longer permitted. It appeared the way of the times these days, with new signs popping up everywhere of who could or couldn't enter certain businesses. Just the other day he had been riding his bicycle and saw for the first time a sign prominently displayed in a shop window that read *VOOR JODEN VERBODEN*. Forbidden for Jews. He'd screeched his bike to a halt and stared in shock. How could this be happening in his native Netherlands—a place that had always extended its hand to everyone, no matter their race, creed, religion, or anything else? He nearly dismounted the bicycle to face the store manager and ask him why he'd put up a sign of prejudice in his window. Then he saw the sign again at another place of business. Everyone appeared to be buckling to the evil orders of the new council within Amsterdam—which showed who controlled the decrees. Why wouldn't they fight such laws instead of turning their backs on their own citizens? Had they no sense of right and wrong? Patriotism? Or common decency? Or was it something more sinister, like power and money, or simply fear?

Erik finished the task with the cans and went to receive a shipment of freshly baked breads and biscuits. The aroma spawned memories of childhood with Mother in the kitchen baking delicious treats and him trying to sneak a cookie without her seeing. One time he consumed a dozen janhagel. Mother had said nothing when she looked inside the near-empty tin can but simply gathered the ingredients to make more.

He thanked the baker who left with his metal

trays, and then he sorted breads and other goods into their respective woven baskets. He had just arranged the final loaves when he glanced up to see a familiar face, a kerchief tied tight around her head, her eyes sunken in a pale, lean face. "Mrs. Cohen?" he asked in a low voice.

She nodded and looked swiftly around. "Are you still serving us here?"

"Are we serving who?"

"Jews. I'm hearing we may not be able to buy goods in certain places." She pushed the handle of her purse further up her arm.

"Of course we are. You may buy whatever you wish. Can I help you find something?"

She shook her head and picked up a loaf of bread. "How is Helen?"

Just the mention of her name sent a wave of distress rushing through him. "I—I haven't seen her in a while. I thought she might still be living with you."

She shook her head. "She left shortly before we moved. We found two rooms to rent in the Jewish Quarter. Though I like to shop here rather than the market there, as the prices are better." She managed a faint smile. "If you see her, tell her I still have a few of her things. We can arrange a place and a time to meet."

"I can come by and get the items today after work and take them to her. Let me know where you live."

She gave the directions but then said, "We've had some trouble there, you know."

Erik dismissed the warning and instead considered the opportunity of seeing Helen by giving her the items. "I know Helen enjoyed her stay with you. I'm sorry about what's happened and pray every day things will get better."

Mrs. Cohen managed a quivering smile. "Thank you. It can't get too much worse, I suppose." She walked off toward the dairy section as Erik watched her hunched form, thinking about her circumstances. At least now he had an excuse to see Helen, and that gave him some comfort. Maybe bringing her the few items from the Cohens would act as a peace offering and give them a chance to talk. They needed each other more than ever in these evil days. It was unwise to drift alone in a ship with a skewed sail like Hans's boat in the canal race where he and Helen met for the first time. The pain of the memory stabbed him when he thought of all they had been through. If she did have another suitor like that man Erik saw, he needed to know. The encounter would pave the way for the truth and maybe a new opportunity to prove his love to her heart.

Work progressed slowly as Erik impatiently waited for the end of the day when he could sign the time sheet and leave. The customers seemed more fretful and demanding than usual.

Erik returned to help Mr. Baas check out some customers when he overhead one man say to another, "Every day it's getting worse. They are taking away all the young men. I've seen them. When is someone going to put a stop to this madness?"

Erik wondered about that as he checked out the purchases for a small man standing before him, staring through his large spectacles. "I'm glad you still allow me to shop here," the customer said as Erik packed the food into a large bag.

The comment echoed Mrs. Cohen's earlier fear. "We serve everybody," Erik declared.

The man shook his head. "Not for long. They will soon tell us we can't come here anymore. There is already talk of ration cards. How will I eat if I have no cards or I can't shop?"

Erik bade the man a good day and then frowned at the shallow words that meant little in light of what the man shared. How could anyone offer a good day in the midst of a storm? Especially when each day appeared darker than the one before. Despite the sun shining bright in a clear blue sky, he sensed only storm clouds in their lives.

Just then a tall, lanky man appeared in the store, carrying several papers. The man glanced up and down the aisles as if searching for someone before striding up to Erik. "Are you the owner?"

"No, just a worker."

"We are calling for a citywide strike for all

the businesses here in Amsterdam as well as in transportation, the warehouses, everywhere." He pushed several papers into Erik's hands. "We must stand together against what's happening and the persecution of our Jewish neighbors and friends. Or there will be no Netherlands left."

Erik nodded and looked at the flyer with the word *Staakt!* in large black letters, announcing the strike scheduled for tomorrow. When Mr. Baas wasn't busy, Erik showed the flyer to him. The man sighed and took out a handkerchief to mop his brow. "Some shop owners told me about this a few days ago. There seems to be a great deal of interest."

"Do you plan to close the store for the day?" Erik wondered. "People will still need food, but—"

"I thought of that. The people also need their freedom, and our Jewish brethren need relief from those forcing them to leave jobs, homes, and everything else."

Erik had his doubts that any of it would work. The enemy would mount reprisals, unleashing their venom against unarmed citizens. "I'll do whatever you want, of course," Erik told Mr. Baas, noting the lines of worry crisscrossing his boss's face. The man had been a mentor to him, and one day he'd talked to Erik about taking over his business. Not that Erik wanted the responsibility now. Daily since the annexation

Erik watched in concern the wearing down of the older man, who contended with new ration mandates and mounting shortages. Then he had the difficulty of trying to help the public with their food requests while dealing with irate customers or ones who robbed the store of goods. All this could age a man well beyond his years. Erik felt old enough without the worry of a store crippling his life.

Mr. Baas shook his head. "We have so much to think about. I shouldn't keep a mother from buying food for her children. But I will support anyone who wishes to participate."

Erik understood but doubted the young revolutionary handing out the staakt flyers would. He'd seen flickers of rebellion in the people of Amsterdam—those who displayed the Dutch flag or gathered together to hear a few impromptu speeches. The Germans knew such actions would cause difficulty and detained some. Erik was forced to consider where he stood on the issues infecting his country and what he planned to do about them. He had never considered himself a revolutionary, even if he was called to resist evil as the Bible said. He needed faith to move to those places God wanted him to be. What those places were, he didn't know.

After work Erik shrugged on his wool coat and placed his cap on his head before venturing out into the cold February day. The tension lay as thick as ever. For the first time, he rode his bicycle past a few businesses with closed signs prominently displayed and thought back to the staakt poster. *Would it make any difference at all? Or would things just get worse?*

The pounding of his thoughts made him shiver as he pulled the collar of his wool cloak up around his neck and tucked in the scarf Helen had made him. The thought of her fingers knitting the black and orange scarf that now cradled his neck in warmth gave him some comfort, even if he couldn't understand what was happening in their country or in their relationship.

Erik pedaled into the Jewish Quarter along a dark and quiet street. The outdoor market had long since closed. Businesses were shuttered and wire fencing was being constructed. The whole area felt eerie. He paused, looking at the address scribbled on the piece of paper, and searched until he found the home. When Erik knocked, no one answered. He persisted. A lace curtain was pulled back, and he waved at the person. The door cracked open, and an elderly woman looked out, her hands shaking.

"What do you want?"

"I'm sorry to disturb you. I'm looking for the Cohens. Mrs. Cohen came to my store earlier today and said I could pick up a few things belonging to a friend of mine."

The woman stared beyond Erik, up and down

the street, before stepping aside. "Come in quickly. And bring your bicycle."

Erik thought it a strange request but did so carefully and propped the bike up against the wall in the hallway. The woman shook her head and wagged a finger at him. "You should never have come here. I can't believe you weren't arrested."

Erik blinked, seeing the streaks of fear racing through her worried gaze. "Why? I haven't done anything."

"You don't know why? They claimed we hurt their soldiers after an incident with one roguish character here in the quarter. The last three days they've been taking our boys to only God knows where." Her voice shook as she spoke. "Some of those boys were beaten. I can still hear their cries of innocence." She turned, her limbs shaking. "Now they want to keep us here. They're turning this place into a prison, and we've done nothing wrong. We are living in hell, young man. We need the Messiah to come."

Erik licked his lips, searching for the words to tell her that He had come and He cared. Just then Mrs. Cohen descended the stairs, carrying a small box.

"I thought that was you. I overheard the conversation." She gave him the box. "Now leave at once, young man. What Martha says is very true. I warned you at the store. I didn't think you would come. It's very dangerous to be here.

Especially for you. You are just the age they are looking for."

"They won't get away with this. Many businesses and others are rising up in protest. They are planning to strike tomorrow."

Martha and Mrs. Cohen exchanged glances and shook their heads simultaneously. "It will do nothing," Martha said. "We have no choice but to wait. Either for the Allies to drive them away or the Messiah to come. We sometimes hear the British bombing places, but the Germans have attacked them as well. They plan to take over the world."

Erik's muscles tensed before resolve rose up within him. "We will pray and do what we can to help each other. It's the only thing we can do." He gestured to Mrs. Cohen with the box. "Thank you for keeping these things. I'm sure Helen will appreciate it." Mrs. Cohen nodded and wished him well.

Erik fastened the box to the rear of his bicycle and bumped out the door to pedal away. His thoughts repeated the scenes—the words shared from the distraught women caught in a grip of fear and the transformation of their lives into a prison where no free person could walk. It sparked a determination within him to somehow participate in the coming strike, in whatever form it might take. He would ask Mr. Baas if they could at least close the store for a few hours.

They must show their disapproval over what had befallen Amsterdam and their country. Maybe, just maybe, it would help.

Helen glanced out the window to see Papa hurrying up to the house, his face flushed, his arms carrying a grocery bag. When she threw open the door, she was met with a brief smile just as Mama came out. Helen had never known Papa to come home in the middle of the day. He was too busy with the workers under his care at the warehouse. She had returned home today when rumors of the pending strike rose in the streets. Professor van Hulst thought it wise to cancel classes and informed the students to stay home rather than become involved in the melee. "There could be bloodshed," he had warned. She now sighed in relief, happy to see her father safe and sound.

"Hendrick, what is happening?" Mama asked, taking the paper bag from him and setting it on the table. He stumbled into the sitting room and collapsed in a chair as if the mere act of coming from the docks had consumed all his strength.

"It's the staakt, Alena," he told her, wiping his hand across his face. "I didn't want my men involved, but the boss agreed the warehouses should close to protest the treatment of our people by the Germans." He shook his head. "Now I wonder if I will have a job to return to."

Helen watched the strength of her father falter under the weight of all that was happening. She peeked in the bag to find several loaves of bread, vegetables, meat, and cheese—grateful he thought of their needs, as he always did.

"I was able to buy some food," Papa said rather breathlessly. "There will be severe rationing soon, and no one knows what else will happen." He sighed and looked around. "Is the family all here?"

"Lars said he had to run an errand," Mama said. "He shouldn't be long."

Papa burst to his feet and strode to the window. "Nee! Why did you let him leave on this day of all days?"

Mama stared, and Helen shrank into the background. Now Papa's weakness became magnified by fear as he stumbled about, running his hands across his face. "If he is involved in any of this, they will arrest him." His voice ended in a shrill of agony.

Helen stared in disbelief. She should have known when Lars said he was going out that he might become involved in the protest. He'd been moody for several weeks, ever since his friend was arrested. It never dawned on her to stop him. Now she wanted to throw on her coat and go find him, if only she had a clue where to look.

Suddenly a knock came at the door. Maybe it was news of Lars, though Helen dreaded facing it.

She went to open it as Mama and Papa remained in the sitting room, and found Erik standing there with a box in his hands.

"Helen, I—"

"This is not the time, Erik," she said in a low voice. She called to her parents in the sitting room. "It is only Erik."

"I just came to bring you the few things you left at the Cohens. Mrs. Cohen was keeping them for you." Erik placed the box on a nearby table.

"Thank you." She fought to control her anguish as tears sparked in her eyes. "I'm sorry. We are very worried. Lars left this morning and has not yet returned. We are worried he has gone to the protest in the downtown center."

"Did he say anything that might give you an idea where he went?"

Helen shook her head and beckoned Erik outside. She closed the door behind her and sat down on the front stoop. "It's better if my parents don't hear. Lars has been very upset for several weeks now. His best friend, Dietrich, was taken away by the Germans and sent to a labor camp."

Erik sighed. "I'm sorry to hear this."

"And then I've heard nothing about Peter for two weeks." She paused and saw him stiffen. "Peter was only a student guest of the professor. He and some other students were given a place to stay at the college when their institution closed. But he went off on some secret errand with the resistance and has not been heard from since."

"I can see he means something to you," Erik said in a quiet voice.

"Only that like every other Jew, he was being persecuted. We can't stand for this. None of us can."

"I know. I've seen it happening. Businesses are starting to refuse service to Jews. Mrs. Cohen told me a the Germans raided the Jewish Quarter. Many young men were taken away to work in their country."

Helen nearly cried, and for the first time in a while, she pressed her head against Erik's wool coat. His arms slowly curled around her and held her close.

"Helen, if it would help, I will go to Amsterdam and look for Lars."

"It would be impossible to find him. It would be like trying to find a sewing needle out in the meadow."

"With God all things are possible. We must trust and have faith." They gazed into each other's eyes as if probing for strength in their innermost souls.

"I couldn't bear it if something were to happen to you too."

"I will be fine." Erik disengaged from their embrace, stood to his feet, and placed his cap firmly on his head. Helen watched him mount his bicycle and disappear down the street. She reentered the house where her anxious family waited.

"Erik said he will try and find Lars."

Mama nodded, but Papa shook his head. "There are too many people in the streets. It would be impossible."

"But Papa, what is impossible for us is possible with God."

Papa's gaze searched hers, and to her relief he nodded.

But even with this reassurance, their faith remained tested until the late evening. Tired after waiting all day, Mama and Papa went to bed. For a fretful Helen, sleep refused to come, and she decided to keep watch, waiting for news. She glanced on occasion into the darkened street, but nothing stirred. Reports on the radio earlier had talked of the massive protests that day in Amsterdam over the persecution of their Jewish citizens. But the news branded the event unlawful and dangerous to Holland. The reporters said the instigators of the rebellion were enemies rather than countrymen defending their nation and its principles from German aggression.

The mere ideas being broadcast sent anger mixed with anxiety radiating through her. Papa had said little during the broadcast as he sat in his easy chair, smoking a pipe. His only comments were about Lars's safety and his workers returning to the job tomorrow. Mama tried to embroider but only ended up using the embroidery hoop as a makeshift fan to cool her flushed face while she stared out the window. Helen knew her mother's thoughts centered on the well-being of her oldest son. All they could do was pray and believe for the best.

Helen sighed and padded her way back to her room. She grew fatigued from lack of sleep, but the incessant worry still kept her awake. Three were now missing—Peter, Lars, and Erik. How close must she be brought to the brink of emotional collapse over everything and everyone?

Just then she heard the door creak, or so she thought. It wouldn't surprise her if her mind was playing tricks. She threw on her robe and slippers and hurried downstairs. In the foyer stood a disheveled Lars with Erik. Never in her life did she feel such relief pour over her. She ran to hug her brother. "Oh Lars! We were so afraid for you."

"I'm fine," he mumbled, though his appearance said otherwise with his dirty, torn clothes and the dirt creased on his face. A linen bandage concealed a wound on his hand. She glanced questioningly at Erik, who shook his head at her. She helped escort her tired brother up the stairs. Both Papa and Mama stood on the landing after hearing the commotion. Simon joined them as well. They rushed to greet Lars with hugs and kisses.

"I'm fine," he muttered again.

"You look terrible," Mama mourned. "Go wash up, and I will get you something to eat. I made your favorite dish for dinner, and there's plenty left."

Lars shook his head, his shoulders hunched, and stumbled to his room. The family reluctantly let him go. Papa and Mama offered their thanks to Erik for all he had done before retreating to their room.

Helen went into the kitchen to make Erik some tea. "You can sleep on the couch," she offered.

Erik slid onto a stool at the nearby kitchen nook.

"How did you ever find him?" Helen asked.

"I didn't. I searched everywhere. He and I ran into each other as I was heading back to your house. The streets in downtown Amsterdam were mobbed with angry protestors. The green police kept trying to restore order. I heard gunfire in nearby alleyways and feared the worst. I even ran into Professor van Hulst."

Helen turned and stared. "Oh no. Was he involved in the protest?"

"He was just a bystander." Erik paused. "But he gave me some sad news, Helen. Your friend Peter was shot about a week ago. He didn't survive. I'm sorry."

Helen's hand froze around the handle of the

teakettle. She began to shake as she tried to pour the hot water into a pot.

Erik stood and came to her side. "I'm sorry," he whispered again, this time in her ear.

"I knew something bad had happened to him," she said softly. "And I think he knew it would too."

"The professor heard he was part of the underground—that he was involved in some kind of disruption of communications. The Germans found out and killed him."

Helen closed her eyes, recalling the handsome man and their final conversation, his voice strong and determined, ready to die for what was right. "You know there was nothing between us, Erik. I only knew him for a day." She turned to face him. "I think you believed I loved him or something. It was never about that. He had patriotic feelings. He wanted to do good. He was given shelter by the professor when his university closed. I didn't want that fact to be known though."

Erik hesitated before reaching out his hand to take hers. "I'm sorry he died, Helen. I think it was good for us to be apart for a time to do what we each needed to do. And to think." His hand closed over hers. "But all this is too much for anyone anymore. We both need to get away from this, even for a day. In a few weeks, the tulips will be out. It will be a perfect time for a drive in the country and maybe have a picnic."

The picture of vast tulip fields in all their glorious color sent a smile to her face, and joy filled her heart. "Oh Erik, I would love that!"

"Then it's done." Slowly he brought her hand to his lips and kissed it. "Again, I'm sorry. For everything."

Helen's joy was brief as she thought once more about Peter, who gave his life for the cause. He had challenged her to consider such sacrifice in the name of rightness. Helen inhaled a sharp breath. *God, I think I'd be too afraid to ever do anything.*

CHAPTER 12

Helen yearned for the time she and Erik would make their escape, at least for a day, from all the trouble and dwell in the magnificence of blooming tulips and each other's company. She thought long on it as she passed a café and the shop owner putting up yet another of the signs that were slowly dotting the streets of Amsterdam. VOOR JODEN VERBODEN. Forbidden for Jews. She could not understand why this was happening and sometimes huddled with a few other concerned students in a classroom at college to discuss it. One had escaped Germany to come here after the rise of Germanic totalitarianism. He explained the propaganda spreading in their country, similar to what was taking place in the Netherlands, and how Jews and seeming dregs of society were seen as an infection that must be gotten rid of or the population would die. Helen stared at the young man as he explained such depravity of thinking, wondering how anyone could believe it. But he said that when the papers and radio heralded the news night and day, people eventually accepted it as truth. They were afraid their lives would be forever damaged by those now akin to a disease. If the disease was not taken care of, the German people would not be able to enjoy the life they deserved. Something had to be done, and so came the signs in the cafés, the establishment of the Jewish Quarter, the registration, the firings, the imprisonments.

Helen stopped before a shop where the owner had just finished putting up such a sign. Anger filled her, and she stepped up to him. "You don't really believe that, do you?"

The shop owner whirled. "Believe what?"

"That Jews should be excluded from enjoying a nice meal out. Why?"

The man looked anxiously to the left and the right. "What I believe doesn't matter." He nodded at a few green police walking the streets. "Some from other political and business organizations are pushing this. If I don't obey, I could be fined or arrested. What choice do I have? I have to feed my family."

Helen didn't know how to answer outright extortion. What could they do except obey? How could they fight back? They had instituted a one-day strike that yielded little but the tightening of German decrees and more arrests. The Netherlands had completely capitulated, and no one could save them but God. But these days even God seemed far away.

Erik would try to keep up her spirits by sharing good news whenever it could be found. She had some personal good news about finding a place to stay while finishing college, with a couple Papa knew from the warehouse. Her grades remained good, and a short time ago she had learned of a teacher's aide position opening up. It seemed like God smiled in certain circumstances, but the outright evil being perpetrated on the innocent made her wonder why some suffered persecution and others did not.

"*Hoi*, lovely lady." The voice made her jump, and she whirled to find Erik standing there with a grin on his face. It quickly evaporated. "What's wrong?"

"I just saw another of those terrible signs in one of the cafés. Can you imagine the Cohens walking by signs telling them they aren't allowed to eat there because of who they are? It's terrible!"

Erik sighed and thrust his hands into his trouser pockets. "As the weeks go by, things are getting worse. It makes me wonder what tomorrow will bring. But that's why we aren't supposed to worry about it. The Bible says today has enough trouble of its own."

"What if they say only certain people can eat or shop? Like those who have sworn allegiance to the Reich? What if we aren't allowed to buy anything either?"

"God feeds the sparrows. He will do the same for us, and we are worth much more."

Helen so wanted to enter the comfort of his strong arms and enduring faith but didn't want to attract attention on the street. Instead, she asked about their outing.

"What about next Thursday? Do you have classes that day?"

"Yes, but I don't care," she announced. "I need to get away. If I could, I would go far away. Some other land. Maybe even America. They are not involved in any of this."

"No place is safe," he said grimly. "The whole world is at war. I believe America will have a stake in this. We have no way of knowing what will happen or when it will end. But we will have times of peace and joy, so Thursday it is."

Helen smiled. He leaned over and gave her a quick kiss before leaving. She carried the tiny symbol of affection with her in her heart. They needed each other more than ever. When one suffered, the other could lift the one up. Thursday could not come soon enough.

As she walked back to the college for her afternoon classes, a scuffle ensued on a side street. Whistles pierced the air, and a truck came barreling down the street. Helen inhaled a sharp breath to steady herself and kept her sights on the pavement, refusing to look anymore. Suddenly she plowed headlong into two green police coming from the opposite direction. They yelled in German as Helen stepped back and issued a very ardent apology in Dutch. They continued to yell, and one of them asked for her identification card, pointing to her purse as he spoke.

Oh Lord, help me, Helen prayed, fumbling to open the clasp of the purse slung over her arm. The soldier grabbed the card out of her hand to look, then thrust it back and waved her on. Helen breathed a sigh of relief and jammed the document back into her purse. An order had recently come forth for everyone to report to their nearest registrar to obtain new IDs. Helen already had one for college, so it was a simple matter to acquire the one the new government ordered. She noticed that some of the cards were different—colored yellow and bearing a huge letter *J* as Peter had described.

Walking along and passing yet another café with the VOOR JODEN VERBODEN sign, it dawned on her why the cards had a *J* on them. No doubt if she wished to go into one of those lovely cafés she and Erik enjoyed in the past, she would have to show her ID and they would look for the *J.* What might have happened to her if the green police had seen the letter *J* on her card? Would they have taken her away under the piercing whistles as she had seen others be taken away?

Helen shuddered at the thought and hurried on to the college building, breathing a sigh of relief when she slipped behind its solid doors. There was something to be said about a place of refuge, and the college was becoming more of a safe haven from a world spinning out of control with every breath she took. But remembering her Thursday excursion with Erik, she would hold on just a few days longer for a breath of fresh air and to see the beauty of God's creation.

Helen glanced behind her at the picnic basket sitting in the rear seat and then to the side window, watching the scenery flash by. Already she felt as if she had stepped into happier times, traveling these quiet country roads with very little traffic, passing farmhouses and an occasional windmill or two used to grind grain. They headed south and then west toward Leiden, home to some of the most beautiful tulip fields in the world. The skies were a lovely blue and the sun bright. She and Erik had exchanged little conversation since the trip from Amsterdam but were content to immerse themselves in the scenery.

Stifling a yawn, Helen wished her sleep last night hadn't been disturbed. A siren had blared in Noord, sending the entire family scrambling for their robes and peeking out the windows between parted curtains as vehicles rushed by. Papa kept vigil at the stoop, but nothing happened on their street. They finally trudged back to bed, weary.

Visions of the upcoming excursion with Erik soon lulled Helen back into a dream-filled sleep despite the anxiety. That morning during breakfast, her brothers had chattered about last night's commotion, with Lars trying to convince everyone that German raids were now happening in their neighborhood with people being rounded up and taken away. Mama scolded him for stoking fear. Helen could not think any more on it but busied herself with happier things, like putting together the picnic lunch and thanking the Lord she was escaping more bad news for this time with Erik.

Now she watched Erik struggle to reach into his pocket. He pulled out a guilder. "I'll give it to you if you tell me what's on your mind. You've been very quiet."

Helen laughed and pushed his hand away. Then she drew his hand back and held it tight. His eyebrow raised before she sheepishly let go and folded her hands on her lap.

"I'm just grateful for this trip. Last night we were disturbed by the green police and a German patrol. Lars said it was a raid."

Erik's fingers gripped the steering wheel. "What were they looking for? Did they come to your house?"

"No. They were elsewhere in the neighborhood. Lars said the police are gathering up people in Noord and taking them away. It scared Mama to death." Helen glanced out the window at the passing fields of waving emerald-green grass. "I'm tired of feeling afraid. I only want to think about today." She changed the subject to brighter things. "I packed cheese sandwiches on freshly made biscuits."

"Mr. Baas told us milk is being rationed. Customers must now have cards for it. More rationing is coming soon."

Helen looked at him. "No more cheese then?"

"I don't know." He paused. "Maybe we should pay a visit to our friend Ephraim Visser, in Edam, on our way back and see what he has to say about it. And if we can, pick up some extra cheese for the families."

Helen brightened at the suggestion of seeing the friendly man who had helped them when Hans disappeared. And, of course, of savoring the delicious cheese he made on his vast farm. "I'm sure he has plenty of milk and cheese." She again watched the fields and saw long rows of pinks and reds and yellows unfold to the horizon. "Erik! Look at that!"

When they drew closer to the tulip fields, Erik pulled to the side of the road. Helen took out her camera to snap a photograph. "I wish the photos were in color," she mused. "But it's beautiful, nevertheless." She snapped a picture of Erik. "Perfect."

"Let me take one of you."

Helen shook her head and giggled, feeling like a schoolgirl as she clung to the camera. "Maybe later. The breeze is mussing my hair." She smiled and looked down with thankfulness at the camera. For so long she had wanted to take pictures, and now she could take as many as she wished on this wonderful day with the man she loved.

They returned to the car and drove on to more beautiful sightings of tulips while Helen contemplated the thoughts passing through her mind. She had refused an engagement during the holiday season, and Erik had reluctantly agreed. But did it make sense to put off something that now seemed right? No one but Erik could ever fill the places in her heart. Whenever she heard troubling news or sensed a new emotion or fear trying to cripple her, the only person she wanted to confide in was Erik. She could tell him her innermost thoughts and her deepest secrets. She cast him a glance, but he only looked in his rearview mirror, his cheeks turning red, his fingers gripping the wheel. She looked behind to see a convoy of German trucks pull up behind them. The driver honked his horn.

Erik blew out a sharp sigh and pulled over. The truck did as well, and instantly all of Helen's emotions turned to fear and uncertainty. "Erik, what could they want?"

"Don't worry. We've done nothing wrong."

A German soldier walked up, offered a good day, and asked to see Erik's identification. Erik produced it after shuffling in his pockets.

"*Wo liegt Den Haag?*" barked the soldier.

Helen heard her heart pounding in her ears, wondering what he wanted. Erik looked around the car and then reached under the seat to produce a crinkled map. He pointed to an area on the map.

"*Ich brauche das*," the soldier demanded, ripping the map from Erik's hand. He marched back to his outfit, waving the map before his comrades.

The convoy started up and pulled out with the smell of exhaust and cold metal filling her nostrils. "Erik . . . ," Helen began, wanting so much to tell him of her fear.

"We're okay, Helen. They just wanted directions to The Hauge. They're probably part of the engineers building the wall defenses. I heard about the huge wall going up along the North Sea." He appeared so matter-of-fact about the incident that Helen began to relax. But she wondered all the same how he could remain calm in the face of the enemy. It spoke of a strength she needed in times like these. "How did you do it? Stay so calm?"

"I was plenty nervous on the inside," he confessed. "But if I showed any emotion, who knows what might've happened. In everything we do, Helen, we must look and act as if we are calm, confident, and unconcerned. Fear breeds power in others. Don't give them an opportunity."

Helen straightened as Erik steered the car back onto the road. Soon the incident with the

Germans faded with more tulip fields unfolding before them. Her camera captured what she could, and she allowed the colorful sights to fill her mind. If only she could linger here forever, surrounded by colorful flowering heads like tiny teacups that nodded whenever the wind called their name. They did nothing but show off their brilliance. As scripture pointed out, they did not toil or make clothing. But God clothed them with great finery, better than any fashion. If He could bring such lasting beauty to the fields that went on as far as the eye could see, He could still do wonders in their lives. Even in the face of the enemy.

Helen snapped a few more pictures and finally allowed Erik to take one of her kneeling before a huge patch of tulips. He said it looked as if the tulips were going to swallow her whole. She laughed at the thought of such a picture, and Erik made her promise that when the film was developed, he would be given that picture as a keepsake.

She agreed, staring out over the field of color. She felt his hand on her arm, turning her to face him. "Yes, I'll marry you." The agreement to an engagement came out quicker than she realized.

Erik stepped backward in sheer surprise. "You're quite a woman. I didn't even ask you yet." He burst out laughing.

"Yes, you did. During the holidays. I wasn't

sure of the timing. But I can't imagine being with anyone else." His arms holding her close, his lips eager for hers in a kiss, and then the feel of the ring he plucked out of his pocket and placed on her finger all intertwined into a beautiful moment.

"I hope you like the ring. It's an emerald." The colorful gem glinted in the sunlight, and next to the colorful tulips, it stood out all the more.

"It's perfect. Thank you."

He took her hand in his and gave a gentle squeeze. "I know we've each had our duties right now with school and work, but the wedding date . . ."

"We'll know the right time to get married. I'm not worried."

Erik squeezed her hand once more before they returned to the automobile. "Now let's go visit some friends and share our news."

Helen gazed at the sparkling ring on her finger and knew nothing could ever take away the happiness she felt at this moment. Nothing.

"*Gefeliciteerd*! We're so happy for you!"

Helen loved the exclamation of hearty congratulations offered by Delia Visser. When Erik suggested they pay a visit to the Vissers, she was uncertain about it all. Which was a silly notion, considering how the couple had invited them to dinner, given the children gifts, and been nothing but hospitable. After a pleasant picnic, Erik drove east and was soon heading down the country lane toward the large farm. All her concern was laid to rest when Delia hurried out, waving and smiling. Erik encouraged Helen to show off her hand, gleaming green with the fine ring he had given her.

"What a lovely ring. Ephraim should be here any moment and will be so thankful to see you and hear your news. But come in now and rest. Did you drive out from Amsterdam?"

"We came from the area near Leiden," Erik said.

"I'm sure it was to see the beautiful tulips," Delia said with a wink.

Helen hurried on. "Erik took a picture of me among them. And then I proposed, surrounded by tulips." Helen caught herself. "Erik had already proposed to me earlier during the holiday season, but I only got around now to telling him yes." She flushed red, realizing how fickle it sounded.

Delia let out a hearty laugh that made her body quake. Both Vissers were portly, which only added to their friendliness. She went over to the mantel where Helen had first admired the bouquet of wooden tulips carved of wood and hand painted in bright colors. She picked out several and gave them to her. "Again, gefeliciteerd. May this serve as a reminder of your special day."

"Hartelijk bedankt!" Helen admired the pretty

colors of the tulips and nearly touched the petals, expecting to feel their softness, before remembering they were carved out of wood. Delia saw her action and laughed, which warmed the atmosphere even more. Helen couldn't help but join her until their laughter filled the room.

"What is the joke so I can laugh?" came a booming voice from the foyer. Ephraim came into the room, wearing a huge grin. "Ah, I should have known. The young couple from Amsterdam who brought us such joy the last time you came." He glanced around. "Where are your young charges?"

"We left them home," Erik said, wrapping his arm around Helen. "This day was for us."

"They got engaged, Ephraim!" Delia announced with glee. "I gave Helen some of the painted wooden tulips because it happened among the tulips in Leiden. Isn't that lovely?"

Ephraim ventured forward and slapped Erik on the back before turning to shake Helen's hand. "Gefeliciteerd! I had a feeling when I saw you both that God brought you together for a special purpose. Look at Delia and me—married thirty-eight years, and we have an excellent farm and cheese business." His voice quieted. "Except the Germans seem to know we have good cheese. They have come to our store several times since you last visited. I will say at least they do pay— not the prices I ask—but they pay."

"Which is another reason we came," Erik confessed. "We would like to buy more cheese, and we could also use some milk if you have any to spare. My brother Hans is fond of it; it's the only thing he will drink. And since they began rationing it, Mother uses the ration cards up too quickly."

Ephraim beckoned to Erik with a wave of his hand. "Say no more. Follow me, young man."

Delia moved to the kitchen with Helen following. She put a few cookies on a plate, apologizing there wasn't more.

"Where are they going?" Helen wondered, biting into a cookie as she watched out the window at the men heading for an outbuilding.

"Ephraim has a cold cellar where he keeps extra milk. He will make certain you have plenty to take back to Amsterdam."

Helen wanted to embrace the woman, feeling as though she had known her all her life. She breathed grateful thanks for how everything worked together. Despite Hans losing his way as he gave chase to his wandering kite, it led them to this interesting and godly couple.

Delia came to the sitting room with cups of steaming coffee just as the men returned with Erik toting a metal can of milk and Ephraim carrying a cheese wheel. "You won't believe the production facility they have here," Erik told Helen. "If I lose my duties at the store, I could come here and make cheese." He winked at Ephraim and helped himself to a cookie.

"You would be most welcome. We could use the help. So how is Amsterdam these days? We have not been there since the invasion."

Helen sobered at the mention of the reality she had managed to thrust aside for a day of happiness. "The cafés have put up signs forbidding Jews to eat in them. There was a huge registration of the city residents."

The Vissers exchanged glances.

"But on the bright side, I will graduate soon from the college and begin new teaching duties."

"How wonderful." Delia glowed. "I know you will do well. I saw you with the children. You have a gift. As for everything else, all we can do is pray."

"Pray and seek God's will above all else," Ephraim chimed in. "No matter what happens, stay close to Him. And we are here if you ever need us."

Helen reflected on everything as she and Erik headed back to Amsterdam. She held tight to the wooden tulips with her hand decorated by the emerald ring, thinking of the promises shared in a tulip field and with the Vissers. The pleasant thoughts tempered the knowledge of what lay ahead as they returned like expectant warriors to a raging battlefield.

CHAPTER 13

Helen found decision-making difficult as she twirled the emerald engagement ring around her finger. Weeks had passed, with Erik finally ceasing to ask about a wedding date. Early on in their engagement, he inquired when they should wed. Helen could not make such a decision until things had calmed down in life.

"How long will that take?" Erik pressed, the edginess evident in his voice. "The war could go on for years."

"I heard on the radio that the Allies are making advances in North Africa. The RAF bombs Germany constantly. The liberation has to be soon."

Erik paced before her. How she wished she could give him a definitive answer. It would be lovely to plan their big day surrounded by friends and loved ones, exchanging their vows and celebrating their love. But with each passing week, new edicts rained down with new rationing and a tightening of everything. None of it gave her confidence that this was the right time for a new marriage to take root and bloom. She hoped he did not think she was putting off their wedding date out of doubt. But as the days grew grim and no one could predict the future, it made no sense to rush to the altar. If only he would understand.

Now with college at an end, a myriad of pathways in life occupied her. Such as where her newfound teaching skills should take her. Many students had already gone off to new positions as aides or helpers in secondary schools around the city and neighboring towns. Then came the news in late August that Jewish children would no longer be welcomed in most public schools, and the need for private teachers increased.

Helen rested in her parents' sitting room, her eyes closed, reflecting on a recent meeting with Professor van Hulst at the end of the term. She had walked into his office after being summoned, wondering what he could want. He shuffled some papers before looking at her expectantly through his spectacles. "Miss Smit, I've had a request from Miss Pimentel, the director of the crèche next door. You remember her, I'm sure."

She would never forget that joyous occasion when she and Erik presented gifts to Miss Pimentel's children, and he read to the little ones. "Of course, sir."

"She is in need of a teacher's aide. I gave her your name and told her you'd be excellent at it."

"But I'm not a nursery worker," Helen said. "I have no training in childcare."

"This would be for the older children, mind you. Some of the best teaching one can give is from the heart. And you have a big heart, Miss Smit. You're always ready to help. You answer every question when most refuse to engage. You are always ready to act. You could be of great use to her and others. She's in need of someone dedicated to the children's well-being. And you know how to teach ABCs and rudimentary math and history, correct?"

"Well, yes, but . . ." Helen blew out a sigh. She had always imagined herself a stately schoolteacher in a blouse and nice wool skirt, wearing high heels, teaching eager youth Dutch history. How could she leave her dream of teaching for a nanny's uniform and crying babies?

"Think about it," the professor said simply. "That is all."

While Helen wrestled with the decision, planes roared above the house, sending the windows rattling in their frames and the dishes dancing in the cabinet. She burst to her feet and paced the room. How could she even think of her future in the midst of war? If only the RAF would bomb the Germans out of existence and end this. It may not be a good Christian thought, but scripture talked about the need to conquer evil in one's midst. The other day, Lars confided in her of the rise in underground activities. Every time he mentioned it, she worried he might be captured and sent to Mauthausen or worse—meet a similar fate as Peter's. The mere thought made her tremble. "You must stop doing this," she'd told Lars. "It's too dangerous."

But like Peter who died for what he believed, Lars simply looked at her and said, "If I don't, who will take up the fight? You?"

Helen had stepped back in astonishment. What on earth was he saying? What manner of resistance could she possibly bear in this fight? Except to teach children hope for a future, free from the oppression of an occupation. Maybe that's what he meant.

A knock came at the front door. When she opened it, Erik stood there, holding a bouquet of flowers. He set them down, swooped her into his arms, and looked for a kiss before suddenly withdrawing. He searched her face. "You've been crying. What's wrong?"

She brushed away a tear. "I didn't even realize it." She took the bouquet. "I didn't think there were flowers anywhere in the city."

"Of course there are. And love is still every-where too."

The mere suggestion made her laugh in scorn. "No, it isn't."

"Yes it is, Helen. If you look for it." He took her hand and squeezed it. "I can see you're deep in thought."

Helen sat down on the sofa with Erik following suit. "I'm trying to decide what to do with my teacher's assistant role. I think I want to teach history."

"Then teach history."

She twirled the bouquet in her hand before placing it on the table. "It's not that simple."

Erik sat still and gazed at her. "Then you must be thinking of something else."

"The professor told me I could be of great use to Miss Pimentel at the crèche. But I don't want to care for babies and toddlers. That's not why I went to college."

"But remember there are older children who come to the crèche before and after school while their parents work. And now others are finding their schools closing or their parents being sent elsewhere to work. I'm sure the professor believes you can help the older children." He paused. "The best thing to do is pray and ask God. He knows where your gifts should be used."

Helen remembered Miss Pimentel with her aides, laughing with the children. And then the older children surrounding Erik as he read the Christmas story to them. Helen straightened. "I could read to them and teach them their letters and how to read and draw and write. I've even planned a few lessons. I have the book *The Ugly Duckling*, which I think would be good to read aloud and—"

"Then maybe you have your answer?"

Helen sighed. "I'm not sure."

"It's only temporary," Erik encouraged. "Once this is over, I'm sure there will be plenty of opportunities for teachers everywhere. Think of it as a time of training for better things to come."

Helen glanced over at him, and for the first time that day, her lips turned up into a smile and her concern began to fade. "You always know the right thing to say."

"It's because we're engaged. And hopefully soon to be married . . ."

"Erik . . . ," she began.

"I know, I know. Soon though." He fingered the emerald glittering on her hand. "A reminder of a commitment, no matter what lies ahead."

Helen enjoyed his arm wrapped around her in a warm embrace and decided to accept the path laid out before her. Even if sometimes she questioned where it was leading, like most things in life. When paths became marred by traps and barricades, bullets and bombs, arrests and disappearances and death, faith had to rise above it all. To sights unseen. To where peace reigned.

Erik pulled away and searched her face. "I can see you're not happy about it though."

"There are many paths to reaching our goals and dreams. But I can be a little disappointed in the plan."

"Try it for a few months. You already have some good ideas for the older children. And you aren't going to be a wet nurse." He chuckled, but Helen did not find it amusing. His grin rapidly disappeared as he stood and held out his hands to her. Helen grasped them, using his strength to propel her to her feet. He then went over to the phonograph to put on a record.

"Mama will scold the both of us!" she warned.

"Why? I feel like dancing with my wife-to-be. Music isn't a crime these days, is it?"

Helen hid a smile behind her hand as he selected a record. The next thing she knew, he swept her up in his arms and they were dancing. She heard someone at the doorway and glanced that way, expecting to see Mama aghast at the sight. But Mama only dabbed a hankie to her eyes as she smiled.

When the song ended with the sound of the scratchy needle, Mama came over and turned it off. "That was lovely," she said.

Helen could barely contain herself. She wanted to ask Mama if she really approved of their engagement. Neither of her parents had said much when Erik and Helen announced it. Lars commented it was about time, and Simon grinned, saying he liked Erik. She often thought their silence meant they were unhappy. But Mama's reaction signaled something she had not considered—that silence could also mean a thoughtful way of looking at things.

"You make a lovely couple," Mama added.

Mama was happy. And Helen too would be happy for whatever God had in store. Like her new teaching responsibilities along this next path in life. She realized it as Erik led her by the hand to the door. "Everything's going to be all right," she said softly, pecking him on the cheek.

"It will be more than all right. If it's heaven-sent, then it has to be very good." He turned and kissed her full on the lips before heading out the door.

"So when will you be getting married?" Mama asked. "We should start making plans."

"Soon, Mama. Maybe once I settle into a new job. I hope."

Helen finished reading *The Ugly Duckling* by Hans Christian Andersen to her young audience. They gazed at her with large eyes and their lips parted in wonder. She closed the book and asked if any of them could tell her what noise a duck makes.

"A quacking sound," responded a young girl with dark brown, curly locks. Lida had been dropped off daily by her parents as they went off to their jobs, like many parents of the children at the crèche. Some, though, had no parents, with their care now relegated to relatives or good friends. All of them needed love and someone to tell them about the world God had created, even if that world right now appeared to be only sirens on roaring trucks or marching patrols. Helen knew they needed an escape into the world of the ugly duckling where no matter who they were, they were loved and accepted. She smiled big at Lida and told her that, yes, ducks do make a quacking sound.

"But the goose honks," exclaimed another boy.

"How about a cow?" Helen asked her eager charges.

Moos came loud, and the children laughed. They added other animals to the repertoire—pigs and goats, dogs and kitties, horses and chickens. The room turned into a noisy barnyard when Helen encouraged the children to become their favorite animal and make that animal's noise.

Miss Pimentel ventured in to observe the ruckus in the large room, and to Helen's relief, she smiled. "I came here to find out what's become of my children!" she exclaimed. "I see now you all have turned into farm animals! Oh, when will my children return, I wonder?"

The children giggled, and the animal noises grew louder. Helen greatly admired the older woman who held a natural rapport with the children and understood them well. Miss Pimentel insisted on fresh flowers in the classroom to make it bright and cheery, and each student had their own little desk. Helen asked them now to occupy their desks and draw or write a few words about the animals they had chosen. The morning flew by, and soon it was time for a snack, which amounted to a piece of bread and a small cup of milk for each child.

Helen retreated to a rear room for a break as

other caretakers took over for the meal. She pushed the damp white hat back from her forehead before getting some water from the sink. At that moment Miss Pimental waved her over.

"You are doing splendid work here, Miss Smit," she said, then paused. "I only wish I didn't have to call a meeting. We will be having one later this afternoon when the children are picked up, to talk about our work and the staffing needs. Unfortunately, we need to make some changes."

Helen's joyfulness disappeared. Did that mean she might need to find another teaching position? Despite her past reservations, Helen had grown to love this place, the staff, and especially the children. The little girl with curly hair, Lida, had stolen her heart, but they all held a special place within her. Life was hard for the children, coming from Jewish households. Just the other day, she overheard Miss Pimentel alert another staff member that several of the children had lost their parents. Now they must find homes for them with relatives or they would be sent to orphanages. Helen despaired, thinking how terrible it must be for children who were alone and helpless because of the occupation. The crèche provided them the only means of refuge in a war-torn world.

For the rest of the afternoon, Helen remained distracted, wondering what the meeting might entail, as she tried to concentrate on the task of helping several older children write out the Dutch words for hen, pig, and cow in big block letters. Helen had created writing paper with lines drawn across the blank sheets to offer the children guidance in forming their letters and words. Erik helped by obtaining pencils and paper that the crèche lacked. They did have toys for the little ones, and she recognized several that had come in the basket she and Erik had presented. She wished there were more materials to work with, like easy readers and other educational books.

The active day soon came to a close, and parents filed in to pick up their little ones. Helen motioned for Lida when her mother arrived. Mrs. Brinn was a young woman only a few years older than Helen, with deep black hair and dark circles under her eyes as if she had not slept in days. Her lower lip trembled when she greeted them. Helen nearly inquired what was wrong when Lida interrupted.

"I wrote about a duck, Mama! Miss Smit helped me."

The young woman smiled. "Bedankt for bringing Lida some happiness. I'm sorry to say this, but I have to tell Miss Pimentel I will not be able to bring her anymore."

Helen's cheerfulness fell, but she tried to keep her composure. "Is everything all right?"

"I was let go from my job today. I can care for her now."

"Can you find another job?"

Mrs. Brinn shook her head. "I don't know. There is no work for a Jew. My husband ran off last week. I don't know where he is."

Helen stared. "But . . . how will you live? What will you do?"

She shrugged helplessly.

Helen couldn't bear to hear this. "Just a moment." She went and fetched her pocketbook. "I have some money. Take it."

Mrs. Brinn shook her head until Helen pressed the matter with some guilders until she relented. "Echt heel erg bedankt." She whispered grateful thanks.

"I can get milk too. I know friends who have milk and cheese, and my fiancé works at a store. Let me know if I can get you anything, and I will. I love Lida. She is precious."

"I believe you do. Lida is a different child since coming here. She loves looking at books and sounding out the words. I hate for it to end, but I simply can't pay."

"I'm sure if you speak to Miss Pimentel, she can help with arrangements while you look for new work. She is very understanding."

"All right. I will see what she says and do my best to keep bringing her."

The young mother left with Lida by her side. Helen watched them, feeling as if a part of her heart was leaving with them. She turned to see Miss Pimentel looking at her from the doorway as the other workers assembled for the meeting. Helen apologized for her tardiness and entered the room, taking the seat closest to the door.

"I couldn't help but overhear," the director said to Helen. She turned to the rest of the staff. "We are seeing parents struggling to keep their jobs. Some have been taken away on false charges or forced to work at the factories. Others must go far away for work, leaving their little ones behind. Still others are struggling to make ends meet. We will do whatever we can to meet the families' needs."

She paused. "But I must tell you, I fear more drastic changes are coming. We need to be ready in both our hearts and our souls. We may find ourselves caring for even more children and some who may be fussy or sad. It is our duty to provide the best care we can no matter what happens." Her gray-blue eyes appeared to snap and sparkle as she looked at Helen. "I can see the great love you all have for our young charges. God looks down on you as you care for the least of these. What we do for them we do for God, and He will not forget."

The director lifted a paper. "Now for other news. We've been issued a decree that only Jewish workers will be allowed to be employed in a Jewish-run business. Since we are a care center for Jewish children, that includes us."

Helen froze at this announcement. A wave of

panic seized her. Suddenly she saw her job disintegrating before her eyes. Never did she think this would really happen to her—losing her job because of her religious affiliation.

"I have told the Dutch council that all here are registered and approved to work in our center," Miss Pimentel went on. She glanced at Helen briefly before going over a few other housekeeping details. When the meeting ended and everyone had filed out, Helen remained, feeling a numbness mixed with sadness. Miss Pimentel came over, and she knew her job had ended.

"I know you are a Gentile," the director said in a low voice. "Therefore, I did not mark you down as one of the employees. But I plan to keep you on, nevertheless. You will be paid of course, but from a discretionary fund that I will give you. That is . . . if you want to stay. I hope you do."

Helen inhaled a deep breath. "Ja, I want to stay. But how can I? What about the other workers? Is it safe for you and them?"

"Don't worry about the workers. I will notify each of them of my decision. No one can guarantee safety these days, as you well know. We must take everything as it comes. As for your personal safety, that is up to you." She patted Helen's arm with a warm touch that soothed her chills. "I'm grateful for all you're doing here. It means more than you can know. I won't let the injustice of heartless and evil decrees dictate the education of the children, which takes priority over everything. There is a higher calling, you know."

Helen was glad to hear this but knew what it meant. She would work undercover for the crèche from now on, in disobedience of a written decree. The mere thought worried her but also made her furious for the evil that seemed to multiply by the day with nothing to hold it back. She prayed for the strength to endure.

CHAPTER 14

Erik awoke with a start when he heard the door creak open and the padding of soft feet. Hans stood in the doorway, staring. Erik hadn't realized he'd drifted off to sleep—the book still clasped in his hands. They had just finished another Sinterklaasavond that lacked the normal semblance of happiness and joy. Every day sirens blew and trucks roared down the streets. Peace these days was nonexistent.

He stood and put the book on the nightstand. "What's the matter, Hans?" he asked, dreading the next bad news.

"Papa just said that America has been attacked! He said to come get you. It's on the radio."

Erik followed him into the sitting room where the rest of the family gathered around the radio, listening to a British broadcast relaying the news. The Japanese had bombed Pearl Harbor in Hawaii. They told of massive air strikes that destroyed a good portion of the American fleet. Despite this terrible news for the Americans, Erik's family hugged each other. For so long the Americans had stayed out of the conflict, sending occasional armaments and money but leaving Europe alone to deal with the German juggernaut.

Now that America had been attacked by the Axis country of Japan, the tide must turn. For the first time since the annexation, hope surged within him. Even though men had died and great damage had been done, America would be forced to respond in soldiers and armament. The attack would open their eyes to the suffering Europe had endured for years. The time had come for the world to unite and defeat the enemy.

Soon after the attack, country after country declared war on one another, and even their own exiled government declared war on Japan. The whole world was embroiled in conflict. What it meant, only the future would decide. Although Erik missed seeing Helen because of her work schedule and his busyness at the store, he understood more than ever why it was a good idea to wait on wedding plans or anything else. Wartime filled everyone's minds and hearts. Everywhere he went, talk circulated of the attack on Pearl Harbor and the escalating war. But for the first time, there were rays of hope that the newly formed Allied armies would come liberate them. German patrols had stepped up in the streets, as if they also expected the Allies to invade at any moment. Just the idea that the enemy might be afraid gave Erik a small sense of satisfaction.

Yet the scenes of persecution and bigotry, hate and violence, continued unabated. He missed spending time with Helen as she worked nearly constantly at the crèche these days. Some days he was able to get away to see her. When he did, he noted the respect the enemy patrols paid to anyone in a uniform as she walked the street in her caretaker dress and hat. But he dearly missed seeing her honey-colored hair and once asked when she could take off the ugly white cap she wore. When her hair flowed around her shoulders, he couldn't help but run his fingers through it. The moments of gazing at her beauty were too sporadic for his liking, but there was nothing he could do. Everyone waited and wondered what would happen next.

Erik sighed as he hastily dressed for another day at the grocery store. The job had grown more difficult with the increase in rationing. Many food items were steadily becoming scarce. Flour was in short supply, as were dairy products. He often thought of the Vissers' cheese farm and the pleasant day he and Helen had, complete with her accepting the emerald engagement ring, surrounded by tulips in all their splendor. He must be patient just a while longer. Spring would come again after the dark winter passed. When it did arrive, maybe they would find themselves able and ready to marry.

Erik hurried along, not wishing to cause more distress for Mr. Baas by being late. A commotion in an alleyway made him pause. A patrol of green police scanned the IDs of a man and his young son. They then took the man by the front of his jacket and hurled him forward to join another group of detained men. The boy stood where his father had left him, begging for the police to let his father go. The boy cried, his wails growing louder, and one of the soldiers scowled at him. Erik ran forward to the young boy with outstretched hands toward his father being forced into a large truck. Erik took the boy's arm and hurried him away, even as the boy cried to be let go and help his father.

Once safe on a side street and away from the arrest, Erik turned the boy around and knelt before him. "Papa needs you to be brave. He has to leave now, but he wants you to be strong. Can you be brave?"

The boy stared at him with large eyes. He shook his head until Erik repeated the words of strength and bravery for the sake of the boy's father. "*Hoe heet je?*" he asked.

"David," the boy mumbled, sniffing, dragging his hand across his runny nose.

"Did you know that's the name of a brave boy who fought off a giant with a slingshot and stone?" Erik pulled out his handkerchief and gave it to him. He wanted to inquire about the boy's mother and other relatives. But seeing what just happened, he couldn't trust that the boy wouldn't still be in danger with other family. Erik wondered what to do with him. He couldn't take him to work. He didn't have the time to take him to his parents' house. Then he thought of Helen. The crèche cared for children. The director would know what to do.

Erik walked along with David's hand in his, in the same way he once cared for Hans. He paused at a place of business with a sign clearly saying NO JEWS, and walked in to buy a pastry. He sat the boy down and the child gobbled it up. They said little, which was probably for the better, being in the public eye. After he finished, David looked at him with dark eyes and asked, "Will I see Papa again?"

"I'm sure you will. But I couldn't leave you alone in the street. I have to go to work now, but I will take you to a kind woman who is going to be my wife soon. She is very nice. Her name is Miss Smit."

David nodded, and Erik was amazed at how willingly he went along, as if God had given the boy peace. They walked on to Plantage Middenlaan and into the crèche where they were met by the portly director. Erik explained the situation.

"I'm sorry, but we have no room," Miss Pimentel said.

"But he was left alone after his father was arrested today. He has nowhere else to go."

She sighed. "How old are you, little boy?"

"Eight," he said quietly, looking around with large eyes.

"Where is your mother?"

He shrugged his shoulders.

"Do you have grandparents? Aunts, uncles?"

He shook his head.

She sighed again and said to Erik, "I'm sorry, but if we cannot find any relatives, he must go to an orphanage. We are full at the moment and—"

Erik opened his mouth to object when he spied Helen in the hallway and their gazes met. She came running.

"Erik!"

"Do you know this man?" the director asked.

"Oh yes, Miss Pimentel. You've met him. He is my fiancé, Erik Minger. He helped bring the pakjesavond for the children from the college and read the Bible story."

"Ja, of course. I'm sorry I didn't recognize you. So you brought in a little boy who was left alone in the street?"

"His father was arrested," Erik told Helen. Her eyes widened, and she nodded. Immediately she took charge, guiding David to a large room where other children sat at their desks. She told David they were learning how to write a simple poem. "And I'm sure you could write something very nice for your papa."

As Erik watched Helen from the doorway, his love for her grew. Despite her initial doubts over this job, she was perfect for it, and the children loved her. When their gazes met once again, he motioned to her, and when she came, he quickly murmured, "Can I see you this evening?" She nodded and returned to her charges, including a cute little girl with curly brown hair who sat by her side as she continued teaching the class.

When Erik came out of the room, Miss Pimental was standing in the hallway. She acknowledged the great room where Helen taught the children. "I cannot keep them all, you understand. I wish I could, but I don't have the staffing or the room."

"I understand. Thank you for doing what you can."

He watched as she turned for her office, thinking of the great weight of responsibility resting on her and thankful Helen intervened. If only he knew what else he could do, but at least the boy was in safe hands.

The day progressed slowly at the store despite the people who streamed in looking for food. Every day Erik had to contend with people who didn't possess the correct ration cards, those trying to exceed the amount allowed, and even those who attempted to steal goods by hiding them inside their coats or satchels. Mr. Baas decided to employ one of the Dutch police to help oversee the issue of thievery. The moment Erik met the officer, he felt an instant mistrust of the man. His instinct was confirmed when he heard the officer inform a family of three they were not permitted in the store.

"But we have always come here," the woman protested.

"Jews are only allowed to shop in stores within the Jewish Quarter."

Erik stared, sensing his own dismay. How he wished he could reprimand the man outright, but only Mr. Baas had that authority. He hurried to see his boss, who was bent over paperwork at his desk, looking as if he carried the weight of the world on his shoulders. But Erik couldn't worry about that when injustice reared its head. "Mr. Baas, a family was just denied entrance by that policeman you hired to protect the store. He said Jews were no longer allowed to shop here. He must be let go."

The man looked up at him with dark circles under his eyes. Erik drew in a deep breath. He didn't want to burden the older man with anything else, but he couldn't let this go. "I'm sorry, Erik. I wish I hadn't hired the man, but I had no choice. I was told my store can no longer serve Jewish customers."

Erik stared wide-eyed. "What? Why?"

Mr. Baas shrugged helplessly. "Why is any of this happening? Why can't everyone eat in cafés or shop or walk down the street at a certain hour? If you find out, please let me know." He returned to his paperwork, though the fountain pen trembled in his hand.

"But sir, they need food as much as anyone. The children need food. . . ."

Mr. Baas spun about in his chair, his eyes wide. "Don't you think I know that? But if I refuse the edict, they will send me to Mauthausen and take over my business. No one comes back from that place. And I will not do that to my family. No."

Erik retreated into an alcove, and for the first time since all this began, he wanted to break down in tears. A huge lump filled his throat, and he began to cough. His eyes rapidly filled. His nose grew stuffy while his soul cried, *What is the reason for this madness? Why?*

Erik tried to think of ways to restore a bit of his good humor before seeing Helen later in the day. He did not want to burden her with what was happening at the store. No doubt she was tired also, not only from the daily work but from stress coupled with the injustices that plagued each day. He ought to try and cheer her as best he could.

He stopped outside a store after work and saw the now familiar and prominent JEWS FORBIDDEN sign. He wanted to buy Helen something, but the sign sent a wave of distress over him as he remembered the encounter with the family earlier that day. How could anyone work or buy in this hate-filled environment?

How could they advocate keeping food out of children's mouths and letting them starve? Not that the Jewish people didn't have the outdoor market or stores in the Jewish Quarter to buy food. But if there were empty shelves and limited stock, not to mention ration cards, they must be hungry. He also considered what Mr. Baas had said. If the shop owners did not do what was commanded, their livelihood would be confiscated. They could be sent to the notorious camp from which many never returned.

"So what are you up to? Sneaking around?"

Erik whirled to find Helen at his side, a smile on her face. He wondered how she could be happy at a time like this. But she had no idea what had transpired at the store or of his raging thoughts. He inhaled a breath, willing himself to calm his troubled heart for her sake. "I was wondering what you might like," he said.

She laughed and tucked her arm in the crook of his elbow. He could see the hem of her uniform poking out below the wool coat she wore. "The boy you found, David, is a nice young fellow but curious. And with some opinions."

Erik began to walk with her. "I saw his father dragged away in front of him. No one cared. No one intervened. If I hadn't been there . . ."

Helen sucked in her breath. "I wondered what happened exactly. We have several like him at the crèche. Children without parents. We are trying to find relatives, but David doesn't appear to have any."

Erik bristled. "I don't want him to go to an orphanage, Helen. Can you imagine the conditions, especially under the occupation?"

"We've had several children leave with the green police. I guess they are finding homes for them." She paused. "But I do understand. I wanted Lida to stay and learn at the crèche also. And it worked out with her mother."

He glanced at her. "Was that the little girl I saw sitting next to you in the classroom?"

Helen smiled and nodded. "She doesn't leave my side. I thought for a time her mother, Mrs. Brinn, would stop sending her when she lost her job, but Miss Pimentel made an arrangement with her. I feel so sorry for Mrs. Brinn. Her husband disappeared, and she has very little money."

Erik stopped walking and threw up his hands. "What is going on here, Helen? Shops no longer serve people because they are Jewish. People are being dragged away even though they've committed no crime. Others are forced out of their jobs, or they can't be on the streets after a certain time." He pressed his lips together, regretting the words that had tumbled out. He'd gone against what he wanted to do—keep Helen out of his struggles when she had plenty of her own.

"I wish I knew. The director believes more

difficult times will come." She straightened and lifted her chin. "But I'm hopeful. The Americans are now in the war, and they have many men and money and weapons. They can no longer ignore what's happening. I know they will come soon."

"If it's not too late," he murmured, then took her hand and kissed it. "I'm glad these hands take care of the little ones. It's an excellent calling. I know it's not the job you expected, but I believe it's the job God wants you to have right now."

"Just being under the tutelage and joy of Miss Pimentel who loves the children, I can't help but love them too. Though most seem so scared. I spend a lot of time giving them hugs. I even hugged your boy, David, today."

"What will happen to him?"

"Miss Pimentel has a list of homes that might help with orphaned children. She will take care of him until then."

"All this . . . because of evil," he muttered, "and with nothing to stop it."

Helen reached for his hand and pressed it against her face. He was glad for her love, but it did little to put out the fire of anger he felt.

CHAPTER 15

Winter turned to spring, and for Helen, the change of seasons brought with it fond memories. Last year in the tulip fields, she and Erik confessed their love and sealed the promise of marriage with the beautiful emerald decorating her ring finger. But this change of season also brought sadness. Mrs. Brinn came one day and took Lida away, saying she could no longer keep her at the crèche. Helen missed the little girl and prayed for her often, wishing that something would change and that the despair she read in so many downcast faces would lift. But working near the Jewish Quarter, she sensed a new desperation that she did not understand and maybe didn't want to understand.

One day a fresh edict came like so many that had been endured for years now. Identification cards were no longer enough. The Jewish people had to be exposed for all to see. A yellow Star of David must be displayed on their clothing while in public. They were not allowed to ride trams or streetcars or even bicycles. Each day when Helen went to work, she saw the beleaguered figures walking along the street, the yellow star sewn onto their garments, their faces a mixture of sadness and exhaustion. For her part, Helen also attached a star to her uniform as part of working in a Jewish crèche. One day she took one of her fellow workers, Marion, aside and asked her about the difficulty of being Jewish under these circumstances.

"We don't know what to expect next," Marion said. "I talked with my papa and mama, and they say every day it gets worse. My brother was taken away to serve in Germany several weeks ago."

"Are you worried about him?"

She nodded. "Yes, but what can you do? Papa said it's only for a short time. Most of the German men had to go to war, he said, so they had to take people from elsewhere to help in their factories. I'm sure once the war is over, he will come back."

"Where did he go?"

"Mauthausen."

The children called for their attention, and Helen and Marion parted to perform their duties. But the conversation remained in Helen's thoughts as she helped David sound out the words in his book. She looked at his head of shiny black hair and his luminous dark eyes and wondered what he was thinking. Did he miss his father? Did he wonder if anyone in this world loved him? Did he cry himself to sleep? Just the mere thought made her want to cry too, but she kept her emotions bottled up inside for the sake of the children. Things were difficult enough without breaking down.

Later that day, Miss Pimental called an unexpected staff meeting. She closed the door and turned to face them all with moist eyes and lines of distress creasing her cheeks.

"I wanted to notify you all as soon as possible what will be happening. I have been informed by Mr. Suskind of the Jewish Council that the green police are converting the schouwburg across the street into a holding center for Jewish families and individuals."

Helen wondered what it meant. She had seen in recent weeks more activity than usual in the Jewish Quarter and at the theater. Not so much with the authorities but more with Jewish families trying to find places to stay in the area. They appeared to be migrating to Amsterdam from all parts of the Netherlands, as if the enemy wanted them all in one place.

"I have been informed that children will come here to be cared for until it's time for them to leave with their parents."

Helen couldn't help but vocalize her confusion. "Where are they going?"

The director's face tensed and her cheeks flushed. "We are not told their business. As I've said before, we must be ready to do things perhaps we've never done before. We must open our hearts and arms even more for the children's sake. I wanted you to be made aware that it will be very busy here. If you are able to spend the night, we can arrange for sleeping quarters here and at the college. Professor van Hulst has assured me the college will help in any way they can."

Helen knew the professor had a tender heart and would offer assistance. She recalled how the college had sheltered students whose universities refused to sign the decrees placed upon them. Like Peter. She caught her breath and nearly let out a groan, thinking of his death for the cause of freedom.

The caregivers stood and began to converse in soft tones with one another. Miss Pimental waved Helen over to an isolated corner. "Are you familiar with a Lars Smit?"

"Ja, he's my brother." A sudden wave of panic seized her, and her heart began to pound. "Is something wrong?"

"Come into my office."

Helen followed in trepidation, assuming the worst—that Lars had met the same fate as Peter. The Germans made it clear that any resisters who were caught would be killed. Not that she had heard much about Lars lately. The crèche had consumed all her time, and she rarely spoke to her family.

"He left a number to call him. He said it was important."

"May I use your phone?"

Miss Pimentel thought for a moment. Then she went to her desk and opened a drawer to reveal a phone tucked inside. Helen wondered about it for only a moment before her attention returned to Lars. With trembling hands, she picked up the receiver and dialed the number. A garbled voice answered before she asked for Lars. The person asked for her name, and she gave it.

"Helen!"

"Oh Lars, I was so scared you were dead!"

"No, I'm still here. But many of our countrymen are not. The Germans have been successful in capturing and torturing many. Just the other day there were several executions."

"Why do you do this? It's so dangerous." She shivered.

"Helen, we have no choice. And now you must act before it's too late. The time has come."

Helen froze. Her fingers grew numb as they gripped the receiver. "I don't understand."

"We are hearing from reliable sources that the Nazis are getting ready to conduct mass raids to deport as many Jews from Amsterdam as possible. The schouwburg across from where you're working is to be the deportation center."

"Yes, I heard. Our director told us that many children could be coming here to the crèche from the theater before being returned to their parents."

Lars blew a sigh into the receiver. "Helen, I'm working with several here who want to help save children. They have already been in touch with Juffrouw Pimentel about their intentions."

Helen inhaled a sharp breath. "What? They have talked to Miss Pimentel?"

"Yes. They are part of the secret N.V. That's all I can say about them. Others are forging paperwork, destroying other paperwork, and coming to hide children with families in the countryside, away from Amsterdam."

"I—I don't understand. Why are they hiding the children? From what?"

There came such a long pause that Helen worried their call had been disconnected. She dearly wanted to know even if she feared the answer.

Finally, she heard his low voice come over the receiver. "You've heard of Mauthausen?"

"Yes, the work camp—"

"It's not a work camp, Helen. It's a death camp. The people that go there never come back. They don't because they're dead."

Helen nearly dropped the receiver. *Death camp?* She could not repeat the words. Then she remembered that Marion said her brother had been sent to Mauthausen but she felt certain he would return after the war. She didn't know. A terrible anguish began to fill her.

"Now they've built more death camps all over

eastern Europe," he continued. "They will send all the Jewish people there. Whole families. Thousands of them. As many as they can. Empty our towns and cities of them so they can establish their new Aryan society."

"But . . . they can't kill innocent families. Women, children . . ."

"Helen, they already have. We're hearing reports from many different countries. If not in the camps, then in the ghettos. And it's coming here. Wherever the Germans have invaded."

Helen tried to steady her voice, but it came out strained. "Why are you telling me this? What can I do about it?"

"You have a big heart, Helen. I know it, even if I've been a pesky brother. You're working at a Jewish childcare center across from the central place of deportation. They will come for them like they have at the hospitals, the orphanages . . . Anyone they feel is weak and useless to their society, they will take them all away and kill them."

Helen envisioned Lida's sweet cherub face and her small hand in Helen's larger one, her dark locks bouncing on her shoulders as she skipped along. And German soldiers bursting in to take her and her mother away, throwing them into a truck covered by a huge gray canvas, their cries piercing the air. She gasped. "What can I do? I—I can't stop it."

"Helen, you can take children away from there before it's too late. Find a place to hide them. You're always telling me how God takes care of things. And people. Now is the time. I can help you with connections for ration cards and new ID papers so if you're stopped by a German patrol, you won't be arrested."

Helen couldn't believe what he was suggesting. Hide children? How? Where? Just then she heard the patter of tiny feet and turned to see a three-year-old boy, a teddy bear held tightly under one arm, his thumb tucked in his mouth. As if God Himself had sent a sign. A wave of strength poured over her. "I—I have to talk to Erik. I don't dare do anything like this without his help. Two are better than one. He must agree, Lars, or I can do nothing."

Lars sighed. "Ja, but call me as soon as you can so we can help you prepare. It will take some time."

Helen slowly replaced the receiver and sat down hard in a chair. The weight of all this came crashing down on her like boulders off a cliff. But then the little boy came over and climbed into her lap, bringing the little bear with him. She felt the warmth of his body as she buried her face in his soft hair, inhaling its fragrance. She had no choice. She had to act. But how could she take the dangerous task of hiding children to Erik? What would he say?

For a week, Helen said nothing to anyone about the phone call. While the passion to help gripped her at first, she couldn't make herself believe the Germans would outright murder little children. It went beyond all sense of reasoning. One day after work, she ventured out of the crèche and looked across the street to the busyness of the schouwburg. A large truck stood parked out front, and soldiers and police carried in many cardboard and wooden boxes, pieces of wood, rolls of wire, and more. The crèche then received the news to have the little boy with the bear report to the theater with his parents. Later, another truck drove up, and Helen watched through tearful eyes the boy and his parents be herded into the back of the truck along with many others. In that moment, the conversation with Lars came back to haunt her.

"The people that go there never come back."

The pain of this ripped through to the very pit of her stomach. She grew so nauseous that she nearly retched. This evil she could not begin to fathom in her darkest nightmare. Yet she felt totally inadequate to the task, like Moses did when he was first called to lead the people out of Egypt. How on earth could she take children away and keep them out of the hands of the Germans? *Who am I, Lord? I'm just a young Dutch woman. I'm not part of the resistance.*

I'm no warrior. I went to college to teach children. How can I take them from beneath the Germans' noses and keep them safe? Where will we go?

By now Erik must be wondering what was going on with her. They had not communicated at all this week despite the fact he called the place where she was staying several times and left messages. He tried once to call her at the crèche, but she told him she was busy. Her heart ached keeping this from him as she battled the fear, the worry, the doubt. She had no idea what to say even if she did see him. How would she bring up the idea of saving children? But how could she turn a blind eye if what Lars said was true? How could she live with herself if she knew she could have saved David or Lida and did not? The green police would sweep the children away in a truck and then to some black-filled abyss. And she would be left behind to sift through the guilt of having done nothing about it until the end of her days.

That night Helen spent time in the Bible, reading about the heroism of Deborah who led a mighty army and Jael who slayed Sisera, the commander of the enemy. God had chosen many mighty women to engage in battle and perform difficult tasks for His glory. What more of a battle did she face than this—of outwitting an invading foe and their master plan of evil by rescuing the innocent and keeping them from slaughter? *God, please help me. Help me know what to do. Help me know what to say when I talk to Erik about this. And if this is Your will, God, bring us together in this.*

Helen had never felt so nervous as she did the next day at the crèche. Especially when she watched out a window as German officials gathered on the sidewalk in front of the schouwburg, engaged in conversation and smoking their cigarettes. Another large truck pulled up, and a line of people walked out of the theater and to the truck. Some led children by the hand. They climbed up into the truck one by one, without question. She gripped the windowsill. *Oh God.*

"You seem very preoccupied today, Miss Smit."

Helen whirled. She didn't realize she had been staring so hard at the scene unfolding across the street until she saw the concern on the director's face. "Juffrouw Pimentel, I need to ask you something. I–I've heard the Germans are going to kill those people in the trucks. Even the children. They won't return." She pointed at the line of people entering a second truck. "Is that true? Have you heard anything?"

Miss Pimental stood quietly for a moment. Finally, she said in a low voice, "Where did you hear this?"

"My brother. It's rumors, I guess. But if they are, what about the children we are keeping here at the crèche? What can we do?"

Miss Pimentel gazed at her thoughtfully. "We can only keep doing what we are called to do, Miss Smit. Care for the children. Love them. Before they leave to be with their parents or elsewhere."

"But have you heard what happens? Where do the trucks go with all those people when they leave the theater?"

"They are being taken to a transit center called Westerbork."

"So, it's just temporary? They will return?"

The director took a step back and then joined Helen at the window. She said softly, "I heard they will be moved after that. To other camps far away in Poland."

"But the children. We just give them the children?"

"If their families are called up, then we must give them over."

Helen whirled. "How can we do that? What will happen then?"

Miss Pimentel hesitated. Helen could see her struggling with the words. The woman stared hard at her with gray-blue eyes. "I will tell you something, but it must not be repeated. There are rumors that the camps being constructed in Poland are killing camps. A few young women from the underground have already been here to take some babies and children to safety. To give them a home away from this barbarism. But few have left so far."

Helen inhaled a deep breath. Lars was right. The time had come. "Miss Pimentel, I want to help take some children away from here."

The director stared at her. "Have you a safe place for them to go?"

Helen knew she could not take them to her home. She had not even talked to Erik about the plan. Though she had no answer, God had the answer. She responded in faith, "God will provide it. And I am willing to do it."

"Then please, take them when you are ready, dear. We will miss you greatly, but it is God's work you are doing. May Adonai bless you."

Helen could see the desperation in the woman's eyes, and any doubt she once had disappeared, replaced by determination. But there were so many unknowns, chief of which was a safe place for children to go. And most of all . . . Erik. But she had no choice. Life or death hung in the balance.

Erik couldn't help but worry. Helen had not spoken to him for many days despite his calls. None of it made sense. They were engaged, after all. They could not stay apart like this, even if the busyness of life filled every waking hour of each day. He didn't think it was her work that was keeping her from him. But what, he had no idea. Finally, he told Mr. Baas he must take some time away to tend to a personal matter. Helen must be deeply troubled to be evading him like this. And he would find the reason why before it was too late.

He walked swiftly to the crèche, noticing a great deal of activity on the street. The green police prodded lines of people wearing the yellow Star of David on their clothing. For a moment he wondered where they were going. But he couldn't concern himself with it at the moment. His chief worry was his love, who, for some unknown reason, had chosen not to communicate with him.

When Erik came into the crèche and announced that he must see Helen, a worker stepped in front of him and shook her head. "You can't be in here. Go to the college next door, and I will tell Helen to meet you there."

Erik wondered what was so secretive but did as she said. He entered the quiet building and waited in the dark hall for what seemed like an eternity. At last the door opened and Helen came in, her hair undone from the bun she wore beneath her white cap, lying in golden strands around her neck. She gave him a wide-eyed look as if she had seen something terrible. "In here," she said, guiding him to an empty classroom. "I once had a class here," she mused and then flicked a tear from her face. "It feels like a lifetime ago."

Erik heard her sniff. "Something is very wrong. Please, Helen, whatever it is, we can face it together. Please don't shut me out."

Helen turned, and he saw fire in her blue eyes. Her face flushed a deep red. "Erik, we have no choice. We must take the children away from Amsterdam and into hiding."

Erik stared. Never in all his dreams did he expect to hear this. "What?" he choked out.

"David . . . and Lida too. If we don't, the Nazis will kill them. They are Jewish."

"Helen, wait. Where did you hear this?"

Her voice rose. "You saw the theater. They go in there, and then they are taken away in trucks. And—and they never come back. Miss Pimentel confirmed it."

The breath he had unknowingly been holding came out, the knowledge nearly knocking him backward. Dizziness overtook him. He stumbled, regained his breathing and his footing, and tried to think. "I—I don't know what to say."

She leaned toward him and stared, unblinking. "And please, please don't tell me that your job is more important. Nothing is more important than saving lives."

Never had he heard her speak with such ferocity, her face flaming. He swallowed hard and tried to gather her in his arms, hoping to arrest this frenzied emotion gripping her. Instead, she only looked at him in determination. "Helen, please think about what you're suggesting. If you're caught . . ."

"I know. But they will die if we abandon them here. They will be taken away in one of those . . . those awful trucks."

Erik released her and swiped his hand through his hair. "Helen, you can't do this on some wild emotion. It takes careful planning. These are children's lives at stake. And we are under a military occupation."

"I know it's a lot to ask. Did you ever wonder though why we have gone through what we have? Like in Edam when Hans was lost." She halted, and her face brightened. "The Vissers! Ja! Of course. We can take the children to their farm. I—I need to call them. I know they will help us. They live on a farm in the country. It's perfect."

"Helen . . ."

She rushed on in a strange euphoria. "Lars knows someone who can make new documents. I can get extra ration cards if we need them. I need to contact Ephraim and Delia. I know they will help. They have to." She paused, and a faraway look drifted over her blue eyes. "And we can't tell anyone, Erik. Not even our families. We can't come back here until this is over. They can't know what's happening. This must be done in complete secret."

Erik heard the implication behind her words ringing clearly in his mind. *Count the cost.* He stood frozen for several minutes, thinking, wondering, fighting off the raw surge of panic that tried to block what God might be calling him to do. He prayed silently, even as Helen stood before him. Without a doubt, she'd heard a call to help and felt led to embrace it. But what about him? "If . . . if this is what God wants us to do, we will both have peace about it." He faltered. "But I'm not there yet, Helen. I need time to think. To reason. To pray. What you're suggesting is a huge and dangerous undertaking . . . and with little children who are not ours. In the travel alone we could run into German patrols."

"We will have ID papers for them. Lars can arrange everything. They will be our children temporarily." She gazed at him with eyes deep blue like the sea.

He couldn't help but be mesmerized by her eyes and her soft trembling lips. "Helen . . ." They stared at each other before clasping hands, closing their eyes, and praying like never before.

CHAPTER 16

"Please, Mrs. Brinn. I beg you."

The young woman looked at her with dark circles under her eyes and deep sags beneath that matched the sagging Star of David sewn onto her clothing. Beside her, Lida played with her doll, gently dressing her in a wee dress. Tears filled the young mother's eyes at the awful decision Helen was forcing her to make. But there was no choice. Once she and Erik made the decision, Helen went straightway to the young woman's home to beg for her daughter's life.

"But she is my life," the woman said with tears gathering in her eyes.

"I have a good and loving family who is taking us in. Just until the emergency is over."

Mrs. Brinn sniffed. She stood and walked to a small table and an envelope resting there. She picked it up, returned to Helen, and gave her the contents. The words typed on the letter inside ordered Mrs. Brinn, her husband, and their daughter to report to the Hollandsche Schouwburg tomorrow. To take only one small suitcase. And to report promptly, under penalty of law.

Helen thought her insides would melt at the sight of these words. She looked up at the young woman. "You won't come back here, you know.

You are being deported to Westerbork and only God knows where else."

"B–But I heard from my neighbors. They said it was only temporary. For labor. I hear some rich folks were planning to pay the Germans off so they can return, so maybe we can find someone who can help us and . . ."

Helen shook her head as Mrs. Brinn spoke. "Even if that were true, what will they do with children like Lida at a camp? Put her to work? They will take her away from you. This way she is safe with someone you know. Someone who will love her."

Mrs. Brinn bit her lip and gazed for several long moments at her daughter before leaving for the back bedroom. Helen knelt and asked Lida about her doll. They played for a bit until her mother returned, carrying a leather knapsack. "Here are a few clothes and her coat. She—she likes to look at books, as I'm sure you know. Can she take Jane, her doll?"

"Of course. We can't go anywhere without dear Jane. Right, Lida?"

Tears rolled down the mother's face. "I can't believe I'm letting you take her."

"Mama . . ." Lida looked up at Helen questioningly and then back at her mother. She disengaged herself from Helen's hand and buried her curly hair into her mother's leg. "Mama, please don't cry."

Mrs. Brinn managed to stifle the tears. "Now, Lida, I need you to listen to me. You know Miss Smit here. Sh–She loves you. She is going to take care of you while I'm . . . I'm away on business. You'll be a good girl for her, won't you?"

Lida nodded. "For how long?"

"I'm not sure. But hopefully not long. You like Miss Smit. You will do fine." Mrs. Brinn managed a smile and then gave Lida over to Helen's care. "May God go with you," she whispered. "Thank you."

Helen inhaled a deep breath and said goodbye. Once she was on the street and wearing her caretaker hat, no one thought any different of her with a young charge in hand as she strode down the sidewalk. She walked right past several green police who nodded as if understanding her childcare duties. Inwardly her heart burned for what they were doing. She wondered when the Allies would come and wipe them out of existence. Helen gripped the girl's hand tighter to make sure she did not stray, especially as they neared the place that once housed whimsical musicals and stirring orchestras on stage, the Hollandsche Schouwburg. Now it had been converted to a place of evil. As they walked by, the authorities ordered a line of Jews into the truck. She dared not look at anyone but walked into the crèche where Erik stood with Miss Pimentel and David.

Erik offered a smile that steadied her pounding heart. "You got her."

"It—it was difficult," she murmured, trying not to think about Mrs. Brinn's tear-stained face.

Miss Pimentel looked at them with a kindness in her eyes that infused Helen with strength. "The tram will be here soon," she said.

"Good. We will take that tram, then a bus." Erik exchanged glances with Helen, and she could imagine his thoughts. *What have we gotten ourselves into? And with these children's lives in our hands? God, help us!*

Just then Marion burst into the crèche with a young boy in tow. He sniffed, his face wet with tears. "Juffrouw Pimentel, this boy's parents just arrived at the theater. I asked the parents if he could come here." She then added in a low voice, "Mr. Suskind told me he destroyed the boy's card and asked if we knew anyone who could help."

Helen understood what that meant. There would be no record of the boy for the authorities to call back to the theater. He could be saved without suspicion. She stared at the little boy who appeared to be about David's age. "Hallo, hoe heet je?"

"Josiah," he mumbled, staring at the ground.

Helen looked at Erik. "They have no record of him. They won't suspect. You know what will happen to his parents. They will be . . ." She couldn't finish her sentence.

"Helen, we planned for two," Erik began gently.

"We can take another. You know we can. David, would you like a playmate?"

David nodded with a smile and went over to show Josiah his truck—one of the gifts Helen and Erik had brought to the children from the collection at the college long ago. The boys immediately began to talk and play with the truck.

"We can do this," she whispered to Erik, searching his face. "The Vissers won't mind."

"But you don't have papers for him."

"We will make it work. We do what we can and trust God for the rest." She knelt before the little boy and removed the yellow star from his shirt.

"Helen . . . ," Erik began, then lapsed into silence.

"The tram will be here at any moment," Miss Pimentel said, pointing to the clock.

"Come, Josiah," Helen said. "Lida, don't forget your doll." She told them to put on their small leather knapsacks. Erik took David's hand and a suitcase while Helen grabbed Josiah and Lida's hands. "We have a tram to catch."

Helen looked beyond to the other room to see the children running about without a care to what was unfolding in their midst. How she wanted to take them all. Who knew what the future held for them? A sick feeling swept over her until she felt the pressure of Erik's hand on her arm and a strong whisper in her ear.

"Helen, we have the children God wants us to

care for. The others are in His hands. We have to go now."

She wiped away a tear and nodded, even if her heart ached to take just one more.

Reluctantly, she turned and stood by the door with the children as Marion kept watch. When the tram stopped, blocking the view of the guards who stood before the schouwburg across the street, they slipped onto it. Safely on board, Helen glanced back at the college next door to the crèche and saw the front door open. Professor van Hulst peered out as if sensing her departure. At that moment, she felt he knew what she had done, and he was proud.

So far everything had gone well, and Erik thanked the Lord above. Though he'd been wary of accepting a third child when two was all he ever thought they could manage, he could not say no to Helen. God would never give them more than they could handle. In matters of life and death, it shouldn't matter anyway, as Helen pointed out. While the bus rumbled north, he considered the strengths in the woman he'd asked to marry him and quietly praised his choice. If only they'd been married, he reasoned, it might have been easier to claim the children as their own. But there wasn't time, and they agreed a hasty ceremony might arouse suspicion with their families.

Erik had told his family goodbye a few days

ago without actually saying it. He spent time with Hans doing wood carving, something his brother had become quite good at. He spoke by phone to Mary, who was helping in a nearby hospital, and to Greta, who worked at a café. Finally, he spent time with Papa and Mother. Papa asked if anything was wrong, as if he could sense something afoot. Erik said little, only that he missed them with his work, and gave them an extra hug. They inquired about marriage plans, but he brushed the subject aside. Now, with Helen and two of the children seated behind him and David nestled beside him staring out the window while holding tight to his little metal truck, Erik knew he'd made the right decision to leave, as difficult as it had been.

A short time later, the bus stopped at Volendam where he and Helen departed with the children. A few passersby smiled in Helen's direction, paying respect to her role as a caregiver of a crèche. But the uniform she wore drew attention, even though she had removed the yellow star, and Erik grew wary. He didn't like being in the middle of town where police might roam about and ask questions. At the moment, though, he saw little of German authority in the small town. He tried to calm his concerns, remembering how he and Helen had arranged everything with the Vissers. He prayed they could trust the plan. They had no other.

"Ik heb honger," complained David, rubbing his tummy, with Josiah nodding in agreement. The children had had nothing to eat, and now they must find food. Erik took a few guilders out of his pocket. "Can you get some food, Helen, and I will stay with them?" He would not leave her alone with the children in the middle of a town. Thankfully, she did not argue and took the money after he told her where they would be.

Erik ushered the children into a field beyond the town, away from curious townsfolk. He wished he had asked Helen when and where the Vissers were to meet them. He tried keeping the children entertained by having them count the boats they saw in port. A soothing sea breeze blew across their faces. Once they finished that task, Erik asked the boys about boats with sails versus rowboats. Lida remained content to pick wildflowers. A sudden wave of questions gripped him as he looked at his charges. *Will Helen return safely from running the errands? Will the Vissers come as planned? Will we live to see tomorrow?*

After a fitful time of waiting, Helen finally appeared, carrying a bag of provisions, and to his relief, Ephraim Visser accompanied her. "Thank You, God," he murmured aloud.

Ephraim's once jovial disposition had been replaced with a serious expression. "I see you have a third child. Very good. Come."

He began leading them through fields thick

with tall, green grass. They trooped along in a line, the children bearing their weight with small leather knapsacks, but soon they complained of hunger and thirst. Their feet began to drag. "We must go as far as possible from town," Helen told them. "There could be bad people around. Let's pretend we're foxes looking for a place to hide in the grass."

The children didn't want to play and continued to complain, which slowed their progress. Ephraim finally stopped the group. "We are safe here. Please feed them."

The children sat in the grass and devoured the cheese and bread sandwiches Helen had made, taking turns with a bottle of milk that Mr. Visser brought. It was like a special picnic, finished off by a chocolate-filled pastry for dessert. The meal cheered the children, and when they stood to walk again, they willingly played fox-in-the-grass, laughing all the while.

"There were several patrols out on the road when I came near the outskirts of town," Ephraim quietly told Helen and Erik. "I didn't dare pick you up in Volendam with all the curious eyes about. There are always people willing to betray others for a price. That's why we are walking."

"But isn't it a long way to your home from here?" Erik asked. "I worry about the children walking that distance."

"I placed a car not far from here," he said. "I

found a field that I was able to drive into and leave it." He paused, looked about, and fished a small device from his pocket. At once the children crowded around to watch the needle bobbing about in the liquid. Each wanted to play with it. "Oh no," he admonished. "This is a magic box, you see. We must be careful."

"Magic box!" David said, his dark eyes widening. Josiah also breathed in wonder, looking over the shoulder of his new brother. "What does it do?"

"Why, this is going to tell me exactly where my automobile is parked so I can take you to my farm and let you meet the animals." Ephraim showed them how the compass worked so they could observe the direction in which to travel. Erik marveled at how the older man related to the children, recalling Ephraim's tragic loss of his young son. He watched the interaction, so much like the ones he'd once shared with Hans—satisfying a child's natural curiosity. In many ways, Erik's years of caring for Hans had prepared him for this critical time.

"Now, for the magic box to work, you must be very quiet and walk single file behind me," Ephraim instructed. "Don't make a sound. It's very important, or the box won't tell us what we need to know."

The children followed his orders as they all walked parallel to a nearby road. Just then there came a loud rumbling of several vehicles. Ephraim gestured toward the ground. "The magic box says to lie flat on the ground and be very quiet, so we must obey." He put a finger to his lips, silencing them, and kept David by his side. Erik watched from his place with Josiah nearby. Behind him, Helen was taking charge of Lida. Two large German patrol vehicles pulled to a stop opposite their hiding place in the grass. Erik thought his pounding heart would explode out of his chest. He glanced over at Ephraim who lay calmly, motioning for them not to move or make a sound. The children seemed to understand the danger of the situation. Several soldiers exited their vehicles to study a map. Erik squinted and made out a distant road sign. After several achingly long minutes, the men returned to their vehicles and rumbled off.

"You all were excellent and so quiet!" Ephraim proclaimed as they came to their feet, shaking off the grass. "And for that, the magic box rewards you with a treat." From inside his pocket, he produced candy, which the children took with glee. He offered some to Helen and Erik, who shook their heads, grateful for this godly man sent like an angel above to guide them to a safe haven.

When they reached the car parked behind a tree, Erik's sigh of relief matched Helen's. When she gave him a warm embrace, Erik felt dampness on his cheek. "Are you all right?" he asked.

"Just happy. And nervous too. But I think the hardest part is behind us."

"I hope so," he murmured. But the sight of the German patrol was a stark reminder they were still under occupation and nothing could be left to chance. Especially with three Jewish children smuggled out of Amsterdam.

PART THREE

1942–43

CHAPTER 17

Six weeks had passed since the family of five found refuge at the Visser farm in the countryside. At first excitement mixed with anxiety occupied their days. The Vissers had been generous in opening their home and seeing to their safety should neighbors, their farmworkers, or a German patrol stumble upon the farm. Erik, Helen, and the children hid out in a barn in the back of the property during uncertain times. But Helen, realizing they needed a better place should issues arise, found an old dugout on the farm, carved into a hillside of earth and protected by a layer of sod. She opened the heavy wooden door to find a room fairly empty but for a few glass jars of preserves and baskets of root vegetables. The tiny area could be made livable with some work. She would ask Delia about furnishing the place as a temporary hideout for the children. She and Delia had already put aside some of the toys the Vissers kept after the death of their son to help ease the boredom. This place would be a refuge for the children if they needed to hide for a while, and the extra toys would help. Helen wanted to find a few chairs, a rug to cover the earthen floor, and many blankets. It concerned her that the days would soon grow cold, and if they needed to stay here for longer than a short time, they would freeze. She made a mental note to ask Ephraim what they could do. Besides the blankets, perhaps they could install a tiny stove that could be lit at night to help heat the small hideaway.

None of this would matter unless the Vissers had overnight guests or some other difficulty arose. With the passing weeks and everything quiet, hopefully the children had fallen off any potential German radar and were no longer a concern. After all, the enemy had the rest of the Jewish population to concern themselves with. According to the news on the radio, raids continued unabated. But there was still the worry of betrayal by their own people, and any guests to the farm must be treated as threats to their safety.

Helen felt a warm presence draw near and an arm come around her shoulder. Erik drew her close to his side—a pleasant sensation with the autumn chill in the air. "What are you up to?" he asked.

"I found a better hiding place we can fix up. I just feel we need to be ready. You never know."

"I think if there was going to be trouble, it would have happened already."

Helen shook her head, drawing even closer to the protection of his embrace. "Nothing is sure until the Allies come. And you heard Ephraim talk the other night about several of his customers in Edam being taken away by the Germans. Edam is not far from the farm."

He rubbed circles along her back in a soothing gesture that lessened her anxiety. "So what did you find?"

She told him about the dugout. "I want this place made ready for the winter in case we need to hide. We can store the extra toys and books the children haven't yet seen in there. Bring in a rug. Some furniture and plenty of blankets. Oil lamps. And find some way to heat it."

Erik frowned. "The Vissers have already done so much. I hate for us to burden them with more."

"I understand, but we have no choice. I wish we knew if the workers are trustworthy. When they come those two days to help with the cheese making, I have to keep the children in the back barn and keep them quiet. It isn't always a good situation. At least in the dugout and away from the farm, they are more protected."

"Then we will ask Ephraim."

Tears burned her eyes at that moment, and she didn't know why. Maybe it was the stress of these thoughts occupying her mind as well as remembering all they had been through. The escape from Amsterdam. The friendly disposition of Miss Pimentel, the friendship of Marion, the laughter of the children. Mama's voice, the serious expression on Lars's face, the neighborhood children, Esmee and Karl. "I miss my family," she admitted and rested her head against his wool coat.

"I know," he said with a sigh. "I didn't want to bother you with this, but the children are also missing their families. Josiah was in a corner crying the other afternoon, and Lida said she wanted to go home."

"David seems to be the strong one," she mused.

"He saw his father taken away. I think he knows. All this is too much for any child to bear."

Helen couldn't help but agree. They must all bear it, not knowing if any of them would ever see their loved ones again. "Oh Erik, did we make the right decision?"

He released her and stepped back. "What? Why the doubt all of a sudden?"

She buried her hands in her coat pockets. "I don't know. Maybe because what we have done is so hard to live with. We could be living in comfort and without this constant fear."

"It would be a false comfort, with people being dragged away against their will or obeying whatever their masters tell them. One can't live in peace under tyranny."

Helen couldn't help but agree. With each passing day and wondering what the future held, she wrestled with her thoughts and feelings. Thankfully, Erik seemed to understand them all.

A bell sounded from the main house, summoning them to the noonday dinner. Helen dried her eyes before going to fetch the children, realizing she should have been helping Delia in the kitchen rather than wrestling with melancholy. The children were visiting the sheep, and Helen came up to the barn to find Lida sitting on the ground inside a pen with a newborn lamb cradled in her lap.

"Lida, you aren't supposed to be in there," Helen admonished, but she couldn't help smiling at the sight of the girl cuddling the lamb. At that moment, she dearly missed not having her camera to capture the sweet scene. It had been too dangerous and too cumbersome to bring it along from Amsterdam.

"This is my new baby," Lida announced and gave the lamb a kiss.

"That's not a baby," David said with a sneer. "It's a sheep."

"But it gives her comfort like her doll," Helen told him. "Just like you when you find things. It makes you happy. Like the interesting rock you found the other day."

"I'd rather shoot the Germans." He turned and marched toward the main house.

Helen sucked in her breath but let the comment go while she entered the pen and took Lida's hand. Erik found Josiah and they all went to the main house where Lida announced to Delia that the lamb was now her new baby. The woman chuckled heartily as she poured out milk for them all. Helen looked on warmly, thanking the Lord for milk and cheese when such things were rationed in Amsterdam. The fall harvest had yielded plenty of fresh vegetables. The hens were laying well. God had fulfilled their every need. But looking at David as they took their seats, still wearing an angry frown on his face, worry assailed her. The anger festering inside the boy was coming to a head, and she wondered how to handle it when her own emotions seemed to incapacitate her at times.

"I hope Ephraim is having a fine day at the shop," Delia mused. Most days Ephraim manned his cheese shop in Edam. On Monday and Tuesday he was at the farm all day and so were the workers, making cheese and readying shipments. On those days, Erik, Helen, and the children remained in the barn at the back of the property, away from the workers' attention. Delia and Ephraim thought it wise for them to stay hidden until allegiances could be determined. Too many were betraying Jews to the Dutch police for guilders. Some were paid as high as seventy guilders for information. The Vissers feared one of the workers might take advantage of such temporary wealth over the meager salary they offered for working on a cheese farm, and so kept their existence a secret.

They began to eat, the conversation turning to Lida's lamb, which Delia said she could name.

The honor sparked a sweet smile on Lida's face. "Rosie!" she declared.

The boys giggled, and David poked at Josiah, who let out a howl.

"David, don't bother Josiah," Erik reprimanded.

David threw down his fork and stood to his feet. "You're not my father," he shouted and strode off.

Helen exhaled a loud sigh. "What are we going to do with him? He's like dynamite ready to blow. It could hurt us all."

Delia placed a comforting hand on hers. "It will be all right. He has to express himself somehow. Think about what he's gone through and what he's still going through."

"We all are going through it," Helen murmured, betraying the turmoil in her soul, not unlike David's. At times she wouldn't mind shouting and screaming and asking why she and Erik had to take children away from the only homes they had ever known and on the run from evil men, leaving behind their own homes and families. But she bit her tongue and said nothing.

Just then David came running back. "Mrs. Visser, a car is coming up the road!"

Helen gasped. Delia calmly took up the plates and glasses while instructing Erik to take the children from the house by way of the fields. Helen helped Delia clear the table of dishes and food and was preparing to follow Erik when they heard a knock. She glanced at Delia, feeling the heat in her face, looked around, and slipped inside the walk-in pantry.

"Hallo, Gloria," Delia said to the caller. "How nice of you to drop in."

Helen peeked through the slit between the wall and the door to see the woman named Gloria pushing the handle of her pocketbook up her arm. "You took forever to answer the door, Delia." She looked around. "Seems like you're running a bit of an unkept house."

"Well, you really didn't expect workers to keep my house. Besides, I've not been well, you know."

"Oh my goodness, I didn't know that." The woman plunked herself in a chair while Delia spoke of her medical issues.

As Helen watched, she wondered if Delia was indeed ill or if this was only a ruse.

"I had no idea you weren't well," Gloria said.

"I'm sure it's nothing, but you never know."

They chatted a bit about illnesses and how Gloria's husband also had a bout with a cold from the changing seasons. "I will bring you a good tonic that I swear by, Delia. And maybe help you clean the house. When you feel like it, that is." She stood to her feet.

"Would you like some coffee?" Delia asked.

Gloria shook her head. "No. You should get some rest. You look pale."

"I will. Thank you for coming. Just be sure to call next time. It helps my nerves if you do that rather than coming unannounced."

"Of course. I should have called. Keep well, Delia. Goodbye." Gloria headed for the door, opened it, and walked out. Suddenly there came an "Ooof!" She picked up the culprit that tripped her, one of David's trucks. "Humph," she muttered but said nothing else and put it down before going to her car.

Helen blew out a sigh of relief, listening until the roar of the engine disappeared in the distance before she emerged from the stuffy confinement. She followed Delia into the kitchen where the dirty dishes had been hastily stacked inside the cold oven and took them out to begin washing them. "Are you really ill?" she asked.

Delia shrugged. "I get spells now and then. But who doesn't at my age? Some heart palpitations and a few tremors. Ephraim says it's nerves, and I agree."

"Well, it was an excellent idea to send your friend on her way."

Delia sighed. "Gloria is no friend of the Nazis. I think she would have been fine with you all here. But things being the way they are, we can't take any chances. At least not yet." She returned to the dining room table to see the tablecloth soiled with food spilled by the children. "We will need to have a clean tablecloth ready to put out next time. Gloria nearly had a heart issue seeing my dirty tablecloth. But this was good practice for unexpected arrivals, wasn't it?"

Helen nodded. Leave it to Delia to always find something good in any situation, no matter how troubling or dire. Helen felt it as good a time as any to ask about converting the small dugout into a hiding place. Delia quickly agreed after the afternoon's abrupt encounter and said she would speak to Ephraim about it. But Delia's ill health still concerned Helen. What if their presence here had worsened her condition? What should they do?

The weight of it carried her to the distant barn and the children wrapped in blankets, listening intently as Erik read them a story. His smile when she arrived soon turned into a frown. He followed her into an empty stall. "Something's wrong."

"Delia had a friend visit, and she noticed things. The dirty tablecloth and rug, and she tripped over one of David's toys on the porch."

A muscle twitched in Erik's cheek, and his mouth drew downward in distress. "Are we in trouble?" he asked in a low voice.

"I don't think so. During their conversation though, Delia said something quite upsetting. She's been having spells, Erik. Heart issues and tremors. She says it's nerves. But Erik, what if it's something serious? We're already putting so much stress on the Vissers by being here."

Erik sighed as he turned to see the children gather sticks and other wood and begin building a tiny house. "I don't know. It never occurred to me that if something went wrong or the Vissers became ill or worse, what our next course of action would be." He pushed a hand through his hair, making it stand on end—a motion he frequently did when faced with a trying situation. "We will talk to the Vissers tonight and see where we stand. And if we must, we will get in touch with the underground to find other options for a place to go."

Helen let out a troubled sigh. "I don't know if I can keep doing this. I truly believed the Vissers would be our answer."

"Helen, they may not be. They are not young, you know. This is a huge burden we are placing on them. They have loving, Christian hearts, but we made the decision to take these children under our care. We must continue to make plans for their safety and not injure others by it."

"I still have the phone number Lars gave me. Maybe he can help." She remembered her final conversation with Lars when she told him they would take children out of Amsterdam. A week later, she met the underground forger in a dark alleyway—a woman whose talent for artistry helped reconstruct on paper new identities they would need should they run into a German patrol. Helen's paper lay in her pocket at all times with her alias: Margaret Visser, niece of Ephraim Visser of Edam, North Holland. She had memorized information concerning the Visser family tree and her pseudo parents in case of questioning. For an instant, she wondered about Lars and if he was safe. He had told her of others who'd died for the cause, and she prayed God would watch over him and keep him and the rest of her family safe.

"We will do whatever needs to be done," Erik said. "We will talk to the Vissers, and if we must find another hiding place before the cold weather sets in, God will provide a way." He took her hand and kissed it. "He has always provided for us, Helen. He will not fail."

They returned to their young charges in the midst of constructing the miniature house, and Helen remembered God as a refuge in times of trouble. She shared with them how God would be a shelter from the storms like how a house provided for people.

"I hope Mama and Papa are safe," Josiah said.

"They're dead," David declared. "Just like my father."

Helen stepped back in horror as Josiah burst into tears. "David, what an awful thing to say. We have no idea what happened, nor should we guess. We must pray that—"

"They took my papa away," David interrupted.

"They had guns. They said he was a spy." He picked up a stick and aimed it at the barn wall. "Pow, pow, pow! The bad men are dead!"

Lida stared with wide eyes before she began to cry. Josiah cried all the louder. Erik came and took the stick from David. "We trust the Lord to fight our battles for us." He sat on the ground and motioned for them to gather around. "Now we will pray for our mamas and papas and all those in danger. That God will keep them safe until we see each other again, whether here or in His grand home of many mansions in heaven."

Rays of afternoon sun streamed through the eaves of the barn with a welcoming light. Helen knew God had heard. Whether in life or in death, God would be there, and only He could give them peace.

"You will not leave," declared Ephraim Visser, his gaze unflinching when Helen and Erik asked to speak to him and Delia after dinner that night. Delia had made another of her tasty meals, *hachee*, a beef stew with new potatoes, onions, and freshly dug carrots that Helen helped to harvest. Now they sat with the older couple in the sitting room where Helen shared her misgivings.

"I would feel terrible if I thought our staying here was contributing at all to Delia's condition," Helen said.

Ephraim exchanged glances with his wife. "If

Delia has such a condition, God used it to keep away curious eyes. Her friend Gloria knows many people. That means she will tell them Delia is sick, and they will not be coming here, snooping around. All things work together for good, don't you see?"

Helen hadn't considered this and sat amazed at the man's wisdom.

"But we do want you to know that we are willing to find another place," Erik said. "We know this is difficult."

"I would say that escaping Amsterdam under the full eye of a German occupation with three young children is much more difficult than us giving you shelter for a time until this madness is over," Delia declared. Helen saw her trembling hand overshadowed by the bright smile she wore.

"Thank you for all that you're doing," Erik said.

Ephraim smiled. "We should thank you. We'd always wanted a purpose for our lives after losing Johan. Now we have three grandchildren to care for and enjoy. How can one ever think that would be a burden?" He chuckled heartily, and joy filled the once tension-riddled room. And suddenly they were all laughing as though they had never laughed before. No one quite knew why, but it felt right to do it.

"But I do agree that we need to be careful in case we get unexpected visitors," Ephraim added.

Helen shared her ideas about fixing up the dugout. Ephraim heartily agreed, and the next thing Helen knew, she found herself with Delia, looking for extra blankets and rolling up a small rug in one of the rooms to cover the dark, damp ground of the dugout. "I will have Ephraim put in some wooden planks for flooring," Delia suggested, "or it could get cold."

"Erik can do that."

The older woman looked at her and smiled. "You told me your new papers say you're our niece. But it's fine if you want to call yourself my daughter. You are one in so many ways, you know." Tears glimmered in her gray eyes. "I never had a daughter. But if this is what it's like, I'm so grateful you came."

Helen embraced her and remembered Mama giving her a hug with the love of the Lord that sank into her very bones. Delia was like a mother to her at this time, and Helen prayed that whatever ailed her, God would heal. *Please, Lord.*

CHAPTER 18

Erik observed with a smile the three wooden shoes filled with sugar cubes and hay in anticipation of the arrival of Sinterklaas. A few snowflakes lent holiday cheer after the times of tension these past months since their escape from Amsterdam. Thankfully, the Vissers had few visitors to the farm. True to Ephraim's prediction, after Gloria heard of Delia's health, family friends stayed away and only called on occasion.

Production continued on the farm as Erik spent early mornings with Ephraim, learning how to milk cows and help with the cheese-making process. Erik talked with Helen, and they decided, along with the Vissers, that it was all right for the workers to know they were there, so long as Helen and the children were kept away while the workers were present. Erik took on the role of an additional worker for the holiday season, and Helen played the role of Ephraim's niece. It was also decided, should any of the workers inquire, that the children were Helen's and that she was a widow. Helen wondered privately to Erik if she looked old enough to have an eight-year-old son, and he assured her that what she had accomplished in such a short period of time showed her maturity far above her years.

Helen remained determined to keep the children out of the public eye and avoid inadvertent conversation slipping out about their departure from Amsterdam. When Erik was off working long days with Ephraim, she remained out of sight, teaching the children reading and math and history and trying to keep them entertained. Her creative ways always impressed Erik, and the days leading to the big holiday were no exception. When Helen announced the children would put on a play for the Vissers as their present to them for Sinterklaasavond, they crowded around her with youthful glee.

"What kind of play are we doing?" David asked.

"A special play about a special child born among the animals in the barn. And we will have it in the barn and have a few animals in it too. Like Lida's lamb, Rosie."

They laughed excitedly, and Helen immersed herself in the project. Erik rarely saw her these days as their lives filled with the responsibilities given to them. He knew the play would be excellent and couldn't wait to see what they would do.

After dinner one night, Ephraim informed Erik he needed help in the shop in Edam as one of the workers had fallen ill. Erik balked, worried about showing himself in public. "I'm not sure that's wise," he said slowly.

"Why not? You're my worker. You have papers. Don't worry so much."

Erik's papers confirmed he was a laborer, but he grew concerned that Ephraim might forget his alias of Jules Rider or inadvertently make some other error. It would also be the first time he would venture from the safety of the farm since the flight from Amsterdam, leaving Helen and the children alone. The more he thought about it, the worse his anxiety became. The lack of sleep that night, which he needed for the busy day, didn't help.

The next morning, he must have looked tired because Helen asked if he was all right. "I'll be fine," he said. What good would it do to tell her his fear? It would only concern her. More than likely she sensed it anyway. They had shared so much—from the time Hans went missing, to the edicts passed one by one in Amsterdam, to protecting the children from certain slaughter. Today's challenge was no different from any other they had endured.

Erik headed out to help load the big truck with wheels of aged cheese from the storehouse. The sight of it sent his hunger pangs soaring. He had not told Helen, but he'd tried to keep check of the food he consumed so the Vissers would have enough for everyone. Once Helen commented he was getting thin, but he didn't tell her how truly haggard he'd become, with the few clothes he possessed sagging on his scrawny form. His fellow countrymen had far less, and those caught in the suffering of the camps had nothing. It was a small price to pay so they all had enough. Erik had also taken to growing a set of whiskers that appeared more like the fuzz on a peach. Helen joked about it. To him, the whiskers spoke of how everything had changed . . . on both the inside and the out.

Ephraim got behind the wheel, and the truck chugged along the country road. Erik hoped they didn't run into any German patrols. To his relief, the ride proved uneventful, with Ephraim's cheery conversation easing his concerns. Erik thought of the man's son, Johan, who likely would have taken over the cheese business had he not died in the epidemic. Erik found satisfaction lending a hand when Ephraim needed him most.

The town of Edam still held the same charm of a thriving Dutch village it had during Erik and Helen's initial visit and the ordeal when Hans disappeared. Erik could still picture himself running through the streets looking for his brother. The gabled homes and canals sparked a homesickness for Amsterdam and his family. He hoped they were all right and not too distressed over his disappearance. He often wished he could phone his family and let them know he was safe. He couldn't imagine what they were suffering. They would think he had been taken to the Mauthausen camp or worse. But to tell them anything would make them vulnerable to questioning. And he couldn't have that.

Erik forced his concern aside to concentrate on the task at hand as he began unloading cheese wheels. The shop assistant who had opened the store early for business came out to greet them.

"Mr. Visser, some German soldiers came by the store early this morning when I was opening. They took many cheese wheels."

"I'm sure they didn't pay," Ephraim grumbled with a look of disdain.

"Ja, they did. The captain spoke perfect Engels, not so much *Nederland*, but I could understand him with the schooling I've had. When I gave him some samples, he asked who made such perfect cheese."

Erik gave Ephraim a quick glance and saw a muscle twitch in his cheek. "Surely you didn't send those soldiers knocking on my front door," the man said with a lift to his voice that Erik knew was anything but jovial. "Delia would have a fit."

When the man said he did tell the captain who made the cheese and the location of the Visser farm, Erik's worst fear was realized. The German captain and his patrol could be descending on the farm this very minute and finding the children. Ephraim must have seen him tremble as he asked Erik to check that all the cheese had been unloaded and brought into the storeroom before following him outside.

"What are we going to do?" Erik asked, trying to steady his shaky voice. "They could be at the farm right now. We must call the house and warn them."

Ephraim shook his head. "It's too late for that. And I dare not draw further attention from my assistant. We can do nothing but pray, son. Your wife-to-be has a good head on her shoulders, as has mine. They are in God's hands."

Erik swiped a hand through his hair, wondering why on earth the man would take such a chance. The lack of control over the situation nearly drove him mad. Then he saw a new patrol come down the street, and he composed himself enough to return to the storeroom to stack the cheese and avoid any further suspicion. But inwardly his heart cried out to God for protection over the ones he loved.

The young assistant then came to help Erik. "I'm sorry for telling the soldiers about the farm," he said with large eyes and downturned lips. "I never should have done it."

Erik nodded, but inwardly he wanted to take the truck and return posthaste to the farm. *And do what?* he scolded himself. *Confront the Germans?*

Any intervention could be deemed hostile, and they could all be arrested. He found his faith teetering on a precipice. Until he saw a vision of Helen, her hands on her hips, informing him they would be taking children into hiding, no matter the consequences. He knew God would guide her through yet another storm.

"It's a German military vehicle," Delia said in a strangely calm voice, peeking through the parted curtains when they heard a rumbling noise outside. "There are three soldiers. Get the children into hiding, quickly."

Raw cold swept through Helen. She hastened upstairs to where the children were looking at picture books. There was no time to move them to the dugout. She told them to hide in the closet. Some bad men were coming, and they must be as quiet as mice. "David, you're in charge. Please keep Josiah and Lida still. No talking at all. None, not even whispers. Don't leave the closet until I come for you. Understand?"

David nodded, and the three huddled in the back of the closet together. Helen inhaled a sharp sigh as she heard the front door open and Delia greet the visitors. She considered staying with them but did not want to leave Delia alone with the enemy. She inhaled a deep breath, smoothed back tendrils of blond hair flying in her face, and walked carefully down the stairs. In the hall stood a rather tall man in uniform with a weapon holstered at his side, accompanied by two other soldiers. When he saw her, he immediately removed his helmet and performed a short bow. He rattled off words in both German and English. Helen managed to understand the English parts from her schooling and told him.

"I will speak in English then," said the soldier. "I am Captain Vogt. I met your worker at the cheese shop in Edam early this morning, and he said you had a farm here."

Helen forced a smile and nodded but silently wondered how on earth they could have Germans standing here in the house with three Jewish children hiding upstairs. Thank goodness she wore a long-sleeved sweater that hid the prickles erupting on her skin and the deep red flush of her neck.

Delia said in broken English, "I get cup. Sit, sit."

The captain smiled in Helen's direction, and she felt flustered. She hurried to help Delia in the kitchen, trying to keep her hands from shaking as she plated a few biscuits from breakfast and gathered some dishes together. When she returned to the sitting area, the captain stood to his feet and took the plates and cups from her to put on the small table. She tried to avoid the gray eyes boring into her. When Delia appeared, Helen took the coffeepot and began serving. She wished her hand didn't shake, but it did, and several drops spilled on the table.

When they were all seated, the captain asked, "Will we be able to talk?" He pointed to Delia.

Helen said, "I will translate into Dutch for my aunt. I am her niece, Margaret Visser."

He nodded, picked up the teacup with fingers stained black, and began drinking. Looking at his fingers, Helen wondered if he had been responsible for the deaths of her countrymen. The mere thought made her jerk, with the heat of anger filling her cheeks. *Don't, Helen. Do not!*

The captain rested the cup on the table. "Thank you for your Dutch hospitality, which is well known. I have distant family in the Netherlands, but I never did learn the language. When I was sent here, I went to see how they fared. They love this country." He began eating a biscuit. "Delicious."

Helen translated for Delia who said, "My niece made them."

"Ah. I may need you to come and cook our rations Miss . . . What was your name again?"

Helen hesitated then realized he was looking at her. "Margaret."

Delia continued jabbering about good food and the cheese-making business and how her husband was famous all over the Netherlands and particularly North Holland. Helen translated it all as best she could.

After finishing the baked goods and coffee, the captain straightened in his seat. "We would very much like to make a business proposition to supply cheese to my unit before we depart for the north. Is your husband at home?"

Delia shook her head at Helen's translation. "Oh no, he is in Edam now. I expect him back by dinner, but you could go by the shop in Edam and talk to him. It's not far from here."

"I will then. I was there this morning." He stood to his feet. "Now I would like to see your farm."

Helen froze, remembering the far rear barn, with their possessions scattered about. Toys and books. Blankets. If he went there, he would know youngsters resided at the farm, and the questions would begin.

"There's really not much to see," Helen said hurriedly. "Cows, the cheese storage . . ."

"I would like to see that, thank you. It's not that we don't trust you, but . . ."

Delia nodded. "You want to make sure you are buying a good product. I can certainly understand that."

Helen stood and began gathering the cups and plates, hoping to check on the children while they were gone on the tour. Her heart sank when the captain waved for her to accompany them. She bit her lip, wondering if the children would grow anxious hearing the front door close. They could come out of hiding and scamper about or worse. "Let me get my coat," she said quickly and scurried upstairs.

Helen made for the closet where the children sat concealed and told them she and Delia had to show the bad men the farm. They must stay still inside the closet and not say a word until she returned. To her relief, they all nodded, and she hurried back downstairs.

"The coat?" the captain wondered, chuckling.

"Oh, where is my mind? I was too busy at the mirror." She giggled nervously, fluffed out her hair, and went to the coat closet to fetch the first coat she felt. She shrugged it on to see the cuffs falling well below her hands and the hem far below her knees. Heat rose in her cheeks.

The captain looked on in amusement before they walked outside. The cold December air nipped at their noses and cheeks. Delia shared the history of their cheese-making venture over the years, beginning with Ephraim's late father and how they inherited the farm from him. She showed them the barn with the many cows, all chewing their cud contentedly, except for an occasional moo, as if inquiring why the enemy was traipsing around their home. The captain and the other two soldiers walked with their arms behind their backs, their faces expressionless, taking everything in. They arrived at the building that housed both the cheese in various stages of the aging process, and the huge bins where the preparation and processing took place. "We have workers that come and help, of course. It's far too difficult an operation for just the three of us."

"So you live here?" the captain asked Helen.

"Of course. I can't expect my poor aunt to do everything. She isn't well, you know."

Helen watched Delia show the captain her trembling arm. "It's like it has a mind of its own," she said with a short laugh. "But don't we all these days."

The captain said nothing but continued surveying the cheese-making facility. He then stared at them, and for a minute Helen feared the worst, that he would demand to see the rest of the buildings. After a pause, he said, "I must know before we conduct business where you stand on the German occupation. And if you agree to our means of ascension to an Aryan society that will benefit all, including our fellow Dutchmen."

Helen translated what he said for Delia, but with every word, she wanted to spit on his Aryan society.

"I always thought we must be perfect," Delia said stoutly. "Which is why I believe in Jesus. He said, 'Be ye perfect as I am perfect.'" Helen translated and, when she did, found strength and peace in the words.

The captain twisted his lips then cleared his

throat. "A perfect society is the only way to avoid starvation, disease, and death."

Helen shuddered, wanting to call them liars and murderers to their faces. Delia smiled and kept a perfect if not holy composure in the enemy's presence. "Then we have more in common than you know, Captain," Delia said. "The Lord also wants to end disease. He has a perfect plan for it, in scripture. Eternity with Him."

The captain frowned. "I will not bandy religion here, but as we do agree that perfection is an important goal in life, we can proceed with the business at hand. I am satisfied that you can help us with our food requirements, and I will seek your husband in Edam to discuss the arrangements." He cast another glance in Helen's direction. "I will see that you are compensated fairly."

He turned and walked outside. Helen feared he would inquire about the other outbuildings in the distance, but they only headed back to the house. Now she prayed the children had remained in the closet as she told them. Captain Vogt bypassed the house and went to the truck where he slowly drew on a pair of black leather gloves.

"Thank you for your hospitality." He eyed Helen once more, too long for comfort, then entered the passenger front seat while one soldier took the wheel and the other the back seat. A few moments later they disappeared.

Helen broke down in tears of relief. "Oh Delia! I was so scared."

Delia sighed. "We have a lot to talk about. First, we must get the children. I'm sure they are very frightened."

Helen hurried to see how they were and was thankful to find them still in the closet, none the worse for wear. They had amused themselves by making hand animal shadows on the back wall of the closet from the light that seeped in. She gathered them in her arms and hugged them close. "You're all right. Thank You, God," she murmured, her cheeks wet and her nose stuffy.

Lida traced the tear on Helen's cheek. "Mama did that," she murmured. "She cried."

"I know. Mamas cry. Mine cries too."

"Are you now my mama?"

All three children gazed at Helen. She didn't know what to say. Finally, she took up Lida's doll and straightened out her dress before handing the doll to the little girl. "I would be happy to be your mama until this terrible time is over. If you want me to."

Lida hugged her close. Despite the fear that sought to paralyze Helen, God brought the love of a child to remind her that sacrifice was always worth it.

Later that afternoon, they heard tires crunch on the stone-laden road and worried the Germans had returned. Instead, it was Ephraim's familiar vehicle. Erik raced to the house, his eyes wide and his face red. "Did they come here?" he asked breathlessly.

Helen put up the towel she had been using to wipe her hands. "Yes. How did you know?"

Erik embraced her. "The shop assistant told the Germans about the farm."

"They were here. They took a tour of the cheese-making area but thankfully not the whole farm. They are intending to talk to Ephraim about buying cheese."

"They came shortly before we left for the day. What about the children?"

"They were safe in a closet."

"I'm so glad. I was worried to death."

"We're fine. God was with us." She watched him sift his hair with his hand. "But now the children need the assistant director to help with the play. Let's put this aside and think about the holidays. It's all we can do."

Erik nodded, sighing loudly, and went to gather the children. Helen couldn't help but smile as she thought of Lida, who had accepted her as her mama. They were still a family even if she and Erik were not yet married. But how she wished life would return to normal. Looking at all of them, bundled in their coats, making their way to the distant barn to practice the play, she knew a new day and a new future must be embraced.

Trials drew people closer to God. She now prayed the German army would soon be overcome and allow them to return to Amsterdam in peace.

The time of Sinterklaasavond arrived with the children giddy over the goodies overflowing Ephraim's and Delia's wooden shoes. Erik and Helen smiled, watching in delight as they unwrapped the colorful packages to find warm hats and clothes, games, and books to read and color. All good items to keep eyes and minds engaged and out of mischief during this difficult season.

The play was a tremendous success. Bundled in their coats but warm with excitement, the children acted out the birth of Jezus in the manger, accompanied by a real cow, a donkey, and of course Lida's lamb, Rosie. When Lida came forward to put her doll in the manger, Helen couldn't help the tear in her eye. They all stood, and Helen sang a song she often heard at this time of year, "Silent Night." When the children were finally tucked in for the night, worn out by all the excitement and laughter, Helen stood with Erik to see the multitude of stars lighting the night sky. She thought of the special star that led the magi to find the Christ child and looked heavenward for a special star this night, one shining brighter than all the rest, to give them hope amid the chaos.

"A perfect day," she said, snuggling close to the warmth of Erik's wool coat.

"Soon to be a new year. What will it bring, I wonder?"

Helen shook her head. "I don't even want to think about it. It can't get worse, can it?"

"I don't know. We can only live one day at a time." He turned and kissed her gently.

Live life one day at a time, filled with the unexpected—both the easy and the difficult. It was all they could do.

CHAPTER 19

Helen couldn't keep her hands from trembling when Delia handed her the envelope. She feared the worst when she remembered poor Mrs. Brinn, Lida's mother, handing her the ill-fated letter that ordered the family to report to the Hollandsche Schouwburg. She could barely open the seal and unfold the crisp linen paper with its fine handwriting in English.

> *Dear Margaret,*
>
> *I hope you will not find this letter inappropriate. Since the day I came to your delightful farm, I think about you often and your excellent cooking. I have a day of leave this Friday and would very much like to see you again. Perhaps in Edam or elsewhere. Please wire me your reply so I may receive it in a timely manner.*
> *Sincerely,*
> *Werner Vogt*

The letter flew out of her hand on the breath of a sudden breeze when one of the children burst into the room and shut the door. Helen snatched the letter up before Delia could and saw a look of question flicker in the older woman's eyes. "The captain wants to see me again. How can I accept? I'm engaged." Not to mention everything else, like concealing Jewish children from German threats and wondering what would happen if this captain or anyone else found out.

"Let me see the letter." Helen handed it over for Delia's inspection. "My dear, I'm afraid if you don't respond, he will come back here."

"But he could do that even if I say yes."

"Perhaps. But if you don't answer, he most definitely will. I suggest you go and trust God with the meeting. You can tell him that you are engaged, and hopefully it will end any future contact."

Helen thought on it. The news of her engagement would surely put away any further intentions. She should also ask Erik's opinion but worried he wouldn't understand. Like the episode with Peter back at college, would he think she was abandoning him and likewise their cause? Yet what else could she do?

The letter left her distracted the rest of the day. Erik looked at her strangely, appearing ready to inquire, but said nothing. For that she was thankful, especially as she had no idea how to tell him. When dinner was through and the children tucked in bed, she handed him the letter.

As he read it, his cheeks flamed and he crumpled the paper. "You're not going," he said in a low voice that sounded more like a growl. "And if that captain so much as lays a hand on you—"

"Erik, I have to go. If I don't, he will come back here. The children will be exposed to more danger."

"I don't understand why he's suddenly attracted to you, Helen. What happened the day he came here?"

Helen bristled at his insinuation. "Do you have any idea what it was like to have armed German soldiers here, knowing there were three Jewish children hiding upstairs? Or what I had to do to avoid any suspicion?"

Instantly he extended his hand. "I'm sorry. I'm sure it was terrifying for you. But I worry that if you pretend you're interested by accepting his invitation, it will only encourage him."

"Not if I use it as an excuse to tell him I'm engaged. Delia suggested it."

"Will you tell him you're engaged to Jules Rider?"

"I don't think it's wise to bring up your alias. I–I'll make up a name. Or maybe use one of the other workers that Ephraim employs here."

"You can't do that. What if this captain comes looking for the man to see if you really are engaged, and the worker denies it? Or he looks around, only to find out you gave the name of some phantom worker? At least if you use my alias, it's the truth. I can look the devil square in the eye and tell him you are mine."

Oh God, help me. Helen felt her head spin and a headache tease her temples. "Erik, I don't want you involved."

"But I'm already involved. We're engaged! What concerns you concerns me. And the intentions paid by some fiend, our enemy, concerns me greatly. More than I can say."

"Erik, we've had to trust each other through this whole awful thing. Remember how you said God brought you to the brink the other day when you found out the Germans might be coming to the farm? That you had to trust God to protect us? This is another one of those times."

Erik shook his head. "It's not the same. We have the children to think about. He could take you away. I—" His voice cracked with emotion. "I couldn't live if something were to happen to you. I couldn't."

"I couldn't live if something happened to you either. That's why I will do whatever's necessary."

They said nothing more about it, although Helen could plainly see Erik's anxiety in the way he paced about and ran his fingers through his hair. She peeked in on the children sleeping soundly. Lida clasped Jane tight, her eyes shut fast, already in dreamland. Occasionally Helen found her sucking her thumb. She once tried to get Lida to stop but gave up after a short while. The habit probably gave her comfort, and they certainly needed some of that.

For a moment, Helen wished she was Lida, safe in bed, slumbering away without a care in the world. Now she must see a German captain, and the thought made her stomach heave. The nausea became so great, she ran outside and vomited on the frozen ground. Tears came quickly, and so did a wail from her throat. The stress of the past months, years really, came crashing down, and she saw life as putridity with no remedy in sight. Every day seemed a battle for peace to win out over an avenging enemy and to trust a God she sometimes questioned even existed. But she refused to travel that road of doubt, no matter how awful she felt. She had to believe He would be with her. What else could she do?

Helen tried to settle her jitters by inhaling deep breaths. She thought about the vast fields of tulips where Erik asked for her hand in marriage, reminding her of love and a commitment made long ago. It calmed the rapid beating of her heart as she waited on a park bench near the central canal where the return wire from the captain suggested they meet. She smoothed the skirt of her dress with gloved hands and felt her hair, neatly braided and wound into a bun fastened at the back of her head. Delia had even found her lipstick to wear. She felt out of place, wondering what on earth she was doing and where it would lead her in the end.

A man approached her then, his head held high, dressed in pressed trousers, a shirt, and dark hat. She inhaled a deep breath as he paused before her. "Miss Visser?"

"Captain Vogt?"

"Werner, please." He offered his hand, and she grasped it, wondering if it was ice cold as one would expect from an enemy.

"I never would have recognized you out of uniform."

"The uniform constricts my life," he admitted.

Helen gazed at him, not expecting that kind of response as they began walking down the street. "I would think your uniform gives you a feeling of invincibility."

He smirked. "In the German army, it is the *führer* and the government that bear the appearance of invincibility. I am only a humble subordinate."

"But you follow the commands of those who believe they are invincible."

"No one is invincible, Miss Visser. We are all mortal. One cannot cheat death."

Helen grew puzzled by his responses. Last night she had tried to imagine how the conversation would go. She expected a man proud of his accomplishments in conquering a country and its people. Proud also of telling some in society that they were inferior and must be plucked out like undesirable weeds in a garden. Now those thoughts kept her sights on reality, unswayed by anything he might cleverly try to say or do or by his handsome appearance of wavy sandy-colored hair and deep-set brown eyes.

"Let's not talk about the war," he said. "Please tell me about yourself."

Thankfully, Helen had spent time with Delia, rehearsing her role as a niece of the family. She told him of her father, Ephraim Visser's brother, who was a simple fisherman. After he had passed on, she spent more time at the farm helping out. "You know, my aunt is not well."

"She seemed well when I saw her. Except for some tremors."

"Looks can be deceiving, Captain. Just as I know that despite the civilian clothes, you are a German officer who is occupying our country."

Werner turned and looked at her with a raised eyebrow. Helen realized she had overstepped her bounds and hastily looked away. They came to a café, and he opened the door for her. Helen proceeded to a small table in the back of the room where a few customers were eating and conversing in quiet voices. She watched Werner scrutinizing the customers. "Do you see something suspicious?" she asked.

"No. I'm trying to learn about your people. They are our brethren in many respects. I've heard, of course, of the Dutch willingness to help others and invite refugees to become a part of the culture."

"We've always been kind and hospitable." The waiter approached, and she gave her order, followed by Werner. "But you don't seem to like our giving ways. They annoy you."

"Please, don't link me with others who issue commands."

"Commands that you follow."

"I took an oath."

"You can always take another oath." At this, Werner sat back and looked at her, his eyebrows narrowing questioningly. Helen didn't care and pressed on. "I did that many years ago when I was lonely and confused and seeking purpose. Then I gave my oath to God and allowed Him to take control of my life."

His lips twisted in disdain. "Religion is for the weak."

"But you said yourself you're not invincible. That you are mortal. And that's where a faith in God comes in. He is immortal."

Werner stirred in his seat, clearly uncomfortable by the conversation. "I would rather return to who we are."

"All right. Who are you?"

He smiled, just as the server arrived with their sandwiches and coffee. "Pardon me, please," Helen said. She bowed her head and prayed, imagining the captain's frown as he looked on, but thanked the Lord anyway for the food and watching over their country with love. When she opened her eyes, his gaze had drifted to a couple sitting a few tables away from them. "So please, tell me about yourself. I really would like to know."

For the next fifteen minutes, Werner talked about his childhood in Germany in a small village not far from a large castle where he liked to visit. Sometimes he imagined himself a knight from the tales of old, guarding the castle's keep from invaders. Helen couldn't help but be captivated by his storytelling. She had never been anywhere outside her native Netherlands, and the idea of seeing castles overlooking the mighty Rhine intrigued her. "Why did you leave such places to come here? Your country sounds lovely."

"My father said it would honor the family to serve in the German army. He arranged my commission. And with an interest in helping our country and its citizens, it felt right for me to accept. My duty is to help oversee the northern wall defenses."

Helen dearly wanted to ask him if his duties also included rounding up helpless Jews to take away, but did not. Instead, she listened carefully while taking small bites of her sandwich on a still queasy stomach. He gestured at her lack of appetite, and she mentioned how she felt ill.

He frowned. "You should have told me. I would have suggested another time to meet."

"It doesn't matter. You went through the trouble

of contacting me." Helen bit her lip, wishing the words didn't sound so eager. In fact, she hoped to be driving the conversation to a point where she could tell him about her engagement. But she had no idea what such news might trigger. Like an investigation of the farm or worse. *God, help me.*

"I will let you return home to rest." The captain stood to his feet. "Do you need help getting home?"

"Oh no, I can drive. It isn't far at all."

He offered her his arm, but she ignored it and fumbled instead with her purse. He strolled beside her, sharing more of his boyhood memories but leaving out anything of his adult life. Helen hoped maybe he would become guilt-ridden over his actions in her homeland. What the Germans were doing was an evil thing to be a part of, and she dearly wanted to tell him so.

When they arrived at the car, the captain opened the door for her. "Are you certain you're all right?"

"Yes. Thank you for a pleasant time."

"Will I see you again?"

The question caught her off guard. "Well . . . I—I don't know. Auntie has so much work for me to do on the farm. Visits put us so behind. I will need to ask."

He nodded and backed away, saying no more. Helen breathed a sigh of relief when she started the engine and rumbled down the street. For an instant, she felt a flicker of guilt over not telling him of her engagement, but the timing wasn't right. She hoped she hadn't left the door open. She did mention how busy she was, and he had his military duties after all. Perhaps this would be the end of it. But in her heart, she feared the worst. The captain would return.

Erik tried to keep busy wrapping new cheese in cloth for the aging process, but all he could think about was Helen. He often stole away to look past the main house and down the road for any sign of the automobile she had borrowed. The longer she stayed, the more his thoughts ran away with him. What if this captain had taken her against her will? What if he found out they had brought Jewish children out of Amsterdam? What if he arrested her? Until he knew what had transpired, he ordered the children to remain in the dugout. The few times Erik checked on them, they were busy working on the lessons Helen had given them the evening before. At the last check, they were dutifully coloring pictures when David piped up.

"Where did Miss Helen go today?"

Erik wished he could calm the trembling he felt inside. "She had to meet someone in town."

David turned to Josiah and whispered loud enough for Erik to hear. "I bet she went to see the soldier. The one who came here." He straightened then and looked wide-eyed at Erik. "She told us to stay in the closet, but I got out of the closet to listen. She and Mrs. Visser and the soldier were friendly. They were speaking strange words too."

"You do understand why Miss Helen and Mrs. Visser did what they did. Sometimes we have to play a game with the enemy and make them think we're someone that we're not. This way they will leave us alone."

"Is that what Miss Helen went to do today?"

Erik nodded. She had taken a big risk, but so did they when they brought these three youngsters out of Amsterdam. All of this though was wearing him down, as was the entire conflict— now entering its fourth year with no end in sight.

At last Erik heard the rumble of the car. He hurried to the main house, expecting to see a shivering and emotional mess of a woman needing comfort and reassurance. Instead, she bounced out of the car, smiling big and waving. Delia joined Erik on the porch with some refreshments.

"The captain was actually an interesting man," Helen told them, eating a cookie and indulging in a fine fruit drink. "Thank you for this, Delia. I'm afraid I didn't eat much today."

Erik disliked her praise of the man. "I'm hoping this will be the end of him."

"I don't think he will come back for a while. I

told him I was ill and that we were busy with the farm." Helen took another bite of the cookie. "It was not a lie either. Last night I was terribly sick to my stomach."

"Dear me, are you all right?" Delia asked.

"I'm better now, thank you. I think it was just nerves over the meeting. But thankfully it went well."

"What do you mean by that?" Erik wondered, not sure he wanted to know.

"The conversation was pleasant, without difficulty or a sense of warning. I discovered that not all Germans are full of evil and hatred. Some were forced to join the army out of a sense of duty. Werner did what his family ordered. I think he would have been content to remain in Germany, living at home by a big castle. He grew up near it and often played there. He did scoff at religion, but I think I was able to plant some good seeds."

Erik exhaled a loud sigh. Never had he imagined Helen might actually enjoy the meeting. He wanted to be a comfort and tell her everything would be all right, and if needed he would come to the rescue. "He's still the enemy, you know," he said slowly, trying to maintain his composure.

"I know. But how are we supposed to treat an enemy? Feed them, help them."

Like Erik, Delia also sighed. "But you do know if he finds out about the children . . ."

"He won't. If it happens again, I will only meet him in town."

Erik stood up. "You're not going to meet him again, are you? Helen!"

"I never agreed to meet him again. I'm hoping he will forget about me and move on. He works by the North Sea with its defenses, so likely his company will be leaving."

Erik opened his mouth, wanting to spew out the multitude of concerns growing by the minute about a man who had obviously made a mark on Helen and her willingness to become his spiritual adviser. He worried she had fallen into a trap that he had no power to get her out of. Now he regretted not marrying her before they left Amsterdam.

No one said anything more in the days that followed until a courier arrived with flowers and a note for Helen. Erik pretended not to be concerned, but his anxious thoughts grew to a frenzy when he spied her admiring the flowers she had arranged in a vase in the sitting room. "From the captain?" Erik asked.

"Yes. He wrote in the note that if I'm feeling better, he has another day of leave coming soon."

Erik chewed on his lower lip before saying, "Why are you doing this, Helen? I don't understand."

"What do you mean? I'm doing this because I have to. Don't you see? I dare not refuse."

"This is a dangerous game you're playing. You realize by continuing with this charade, you're only encouraging him. " He saw tense lines crease her face. "But of course you told him we are engaged."

She looked away. "I was going to, but then we started talking about my illness and—"

Erik slapped his forehead in exasperation. "Helen! You were supposed to tell him. Now he thinks the door is wide open to woo you and date you and who knows what else. No wonder he sent the flowers and asked to see you again. A German officer!"

Helen turned away and folded her arms. "I couldn't say anything right away. We were just talking like acquaintances. I didn't know if I said anything if he would get angry and send his soldiers here to cause problems. And by the end of the meeting, it was too late." She shook her head and stared down at the wooden floor. "And what if they come here and discover the children? I couldn't take that kind of guilt, Erik. I have to handle this the best way I know how."

He raked his hands through his hair. "This is getting out of hand."

"Let me meet him again and see where things stand."

"Helen, as long as he sees you as a willing prize, we remain in danger." A flicker of fear crossed her eyes, and her mouth opened in distress. He hated making her nervous, but she must know where things stood. Especially with that soldier. He refused to be in danger of losing her.

"Erik, if that's so . . . if it looks like he will not let me go . . . if it looks like he might do something dangerous . . . if I have no choice, I may have to make a difficult decision and—"

Erik grabbed her arm, more roughly than he intended. "No, you won't! Don't you even think it. Tell him we are engaged . . . or I will."

Helen shook her head, and her eyes glimmered with tears. "We have to keep the children safe. That's all that matters. And if it means me going with him to keep you all safe, then I will." She turned and hurried away.

Erik's arms collapsed helplessly at his sides. His head bowed. He had lost her already, and there was nothing on this earth he could do to stop it.

CHAPTER 20

"You look beautiful. The dress is very becoming."

Helen forced herself to smile. The dress was one of Delia's old ones that Delia had quickly hemmed and sewed in pleats to fit her. It did have a pretty flowered print, but right now she felt like they were flowers decorating her grave. This was her fourth meeting with the captain in as many weeks, and each encounter appeared to be growing more serious. More concerning was how distant she and Erik had become. But maybe it was for the better. She knew where this was headed and resigned herself to the fact. She'd heard of the sacrifices others had made to safeguard loved ones. And if she must take the captain's hand instead of Erik's so he and the children would remain safe, she would do it. Even if life as she knew it would cease to exist.

Werner took her hand. The day was warm with the breath of spring chasing away the frigid winter. Though for Helen, the cold around her only seemed to grow more intense. He brought her hand to his lips and kissed it, then sat back, her hand still gripped in his. "Where did you get such a magnificent ring?"

Helen saw the emerald Erik had given her as a symbol of their betrothal. Her mind began to race.

If only he had seen it at their first outing or she had thought to show it to him. She could have told him of her engagement long ago. But now, having seen him many times, to tell him at this point would be disastrous. "A—A man gave it to me."

"Who?" He stared with icy blue eyes that seemed to probe for an answer.

"It was a long time ago. War changes everything. But I kept it because it's worth something. I don't have many worldly possessions left."

To her relief, he nodded. "That will not be true for you any longer. If you will allow me." He took a box from his pocket.

Helen nearly fainted when she saw it. She began to shake so much, she feared she might stumble and fall to the pavement below. "Why, Werner. Wh–What are you doing?"

"I found it in a shop. It reminded me of you."

She took the box and opened it to reveal a pin in the shape of flowers. Relief washed over her that it was not an engagement ring. "Why, it's lovely. Thank you."

He lifted it out for her to see, but she took it from his hand and pinned it on herself. He smiled and picked up her hand again. "I think you know that I'm finding you more interesting as the days pass. I hope you feel the same way."

Helen managed to slowly withdraw from his grasp and tucked the sweater she wore closer around her shoulders. The chill she felt was not from anything weather related but something much worse. "Now, you never did tell me of the women you knew in Germany."

Werner laughed. "There were a few," he admitted. "I haven't seen any of them in many years. Since I joined the army."

"Do you really hail your führer?" she suddenly asked. "I've heard it on the radio. It sounds like honoring him as if he's some kind of god."

His happy countenance deteriorated into a scowl. "We do not hail the führer. He is our leader. *Seig Heil* means 'On to victory.'"

Helen glanced upward to the clear sky. "My Champion is in heaven."

"Oh, your religion."

"It's more than just religion. For me, it's a way of life. My victory. Christ in me, the hope of glory."

He placed his arms behind his back, and in that gesture she saw a military man controlled by human power. "If so, it's a poor life that leaves you all so vulnerable and easily conquered in a few days."

Her muscles tensed. She tried hard to remain passive and not to react in anger to this announcement of victory over her poor country. "Israel fell into similar circumstances. They had enemies corner them and overrun their lands. They were even taken to live in Persia as captives. Is that what you're doing here?"

"No." He turned back to her. "We want our fellow Aryan people to live together in peace and goodwill."

"And those who aren't Aryan? Werner, you can hardly say that all this is goodwill and peace. When the—" She stopped herself when she saw his face turn bright red and realized if she overstepped her bounds, he could wreak unknown havoc if he chose. He had the power to do whatever he wanted. "I'm sorry. I'm trying to understand. But this is my country, so naturally I still have patriotic feelings."

"You wouldn't be a Dutchman if you didn't. Just be careful where it leads you, Margaret. The Netherlands is no longer the way it once was. It is time to embrace the new society." They walked on, not holding hands, much to Helen's relief, until they came to the edge of town. She tensed as a German patrol passed them by. Several nodded at Werner as if they knew him, but since he was not in uniform, they did not salute. Just the sight of them left her with that same nauseous feeling. It made her realize she could never be with this man. She wouldn't survive it emotionally or mentally. *God, there must be another way! Please. Send him away. A military relocation. Or back to Germany.*

"I see you're now quiet," he remarked.

"Oh, it's this same sickness. I think it's my nerves again."

"We should not speak politics when we're together. It's not *gut* for you or anyone." He paused and swept back a bit of her hair from her face. "I'm sorry if I made you upset."

In that moment, she saw Erik doing the same, just before he kissed her. Suddenly she drew back and shook her head. "I'm feeling very ill. I'm sorry."

Werner said nothing more but walked with her back to town. He insisted that he take her back to the farm and she not drive herself in this condition. The mere thought of the man visiting the farm again and encountering Erik fed another wave of nausea. She feared she might be sick in front of him. "I just need to rest for a bit," she told him, gesturing to a bench overlooking the canal. "Besides, Uncle will be furious if I don't bring back his car. And he never allows strangers to drive it."

Werner frowned and sat with her. They watched a few ducks paddling along the canal and passersby carrying parcels. It appeared a serene moment, but for Helen nothing was peaceful about it. She had dug herself a grave and now only needed dirt tossed on it for it to be complete. *I'm sorry, Lord. I'm so inadequate for these tasks. The spirit is willing but the flesh is weak.* After a time, she stood and proclaimed herself much better and commented again on the lovely pin and nice afternoon. He glanced at the pin before refocusing on her face with the same ice-cold blue of the eyes that reminded her of a never-ending winter.

"Goodbye then, Margaret."

"Wh–When shall we see each other again?" Not that she desired any such meeting. But if she didn't say it, he might suspect something. How she hated the bondage of this relationship.

"I will let you know." He lifted his cap and moved off. She watched until he disappeared around a bend in the road. A full breath of air released from her lungs. She hurried to the car and entered the driver's seat, looking in the mirror for anyone who might be following her. Helen knew as she drove through the fields of northern Holland, taking the long way back, that she could not endure much more of this charade. It had all but unseated both her heart and her soul. Something had to change, and soon.

Erik walked out of the milking barn, pails in hand, to find Ephraim's car parked out front. He dropped the pails off in the cheese barn and immediately headed for the house. When he opened the front door, Delia was sitting with the children, reading a book. There was no sign of Helen. Delia gestured toward the stairs. He climbed two stairs at a time and paused before the closed door to hear soft weeping. The pitiful sound melted his heart. He gently knocked. "Helen? It's Erik."

"Please go away," came her tremulous voice.

"I just want to make sure you're all right."

She blew her nose and answered in a scratchy voice, "I'm fine."

"No, you're not. We should talk. Please."

"I don't have anything to say." The words were barely audible. Erik stepped back, his thoughts spinning. Had she done what she said she would do? Was it truly over for them? He listened a bit longer but only heard muffled sounds and then nothing. His heart thumped madly as his fingers closed around the doorknob. He wanted to make sure the man hadn't hurt her or something else dreadful. Slowly he opened the door and peeked in to find her prostrate on the bed, her face buried, the dress she wore spilling like a colorful arc across the bedspread. He considered what to say, but no words came to mind. Slowly he closed the door and returned downstairs to the expectant faces of Delia and the children.

"She's worn out," he finally said, plunking down in a chair. "I hope she isn't sick again."

"I'll go check on her in a bit," Delia said. "Give her time, Erik."

He shook his head. "There is no time. Not when the enemy is breathing down our necks." But he said no more, not wanting to scare the children. Delia instructed them to go find the candy she had hidden in secret places in her sewing room. Laughing in glee, they took off to begin the scavenger hunt.

"You're so good to them," Erik said with a smile.

"Why not? They are my grandchildren." She sat back and looked at him expectantly. "But it's clear something's not right between you and Helen."

"I'm afraid this German soldier has stolen her heart."

Delia chuckled. "A German soldier stealing Helen's heart? Never."

"I don't know. She alluded to the fact a few weeks back that if she had to, she would leave with him."

Now it was Delia's turn to stare at him with wide eyes. "Helen would never do that."

"She said she would if it meant keeping me and the children safe. Which is why I think she's upstairs crying. She has made her decision." The final words came out in a gasp of despair.

Delia came to her feet, and for a moment Erik was glad the older woman felt as he did, stunned and confused. He continued on, telling her what Helen believed. There was no alternative to outwit the enemy. She thought running away with the man would be the saving grace and keep the Germans at bay. Sacrifice was required to keep everyone safe.

Delia shook her head. "I don't believe for a moment Helen would run off with this fellow unless she felt she had no choice. I know she loves you very much. If that is the case . . . that she feels there is no way out, we must find another place for the children to hide and you both to be set free from this burden. This is not worth seeing your relationship fall apart."

Erik stared. "You would take the children from us?"

"I want to keep them safe and you both as well. I can see what this is doing to you. Helen has been sick. Your relationship is on the brink of failure. Something must change."

Erik burst to his feet. First Helen might be on the brink of leaving with some German soldier. Now the children. It was too much to bear, and his heart felt like it was shredding under the blade of a knife. "Am I supposed to be alone, then?"

"Erik, dear, we need to consider these youngsters here. None of this is their fault. When you took them from Amsterdam to come here, you took on a responsibility for their safety. Nothing is more important than that. I think Helen is finding herself forced to fulfill a vow she made to keep the young ones safe, no matter the cost. Maybe that's why she feels there is no way out with this captain. She believes if she says yes to him, and dear God I pray she never does, the children will be safe. But if we find another home for them, you are both free to marry and live your lives."

Erik paused to consider this. What would a drastic move do to the children? They'd been through so much. But he realized if it meant Helen would be spared a terrible life as a German officer's wife and it would keep their commitment sound, then they would have no choice but to part with the children. Finally, he said in a quiet voice, "Do you know of anyone who could take them in?"

"We know a trusted pastor who may have an answer. I will have Ephraim speak to him."

Erik could not believe how life was turning from bad to worse. The children taken away. Helen's heart lost in an emotional wave created by a German soldier. His family not knowing if he was alive or dead. Living as a wanted man for taking Jewish children, with the unending fear of discovery, and without peace. This couldn't be God's will for his life. Jesus said that He gives peace. But how could he find peace when everything precious in his life was being taken away?

Unless these were the sacrifices Helen said they each must be willing to make. He thought of those before him. The man who destroyed little Josiah's card at the schouwburg. The mother who let go of Lida, her precious daughter. Those like the Vissers who took fugitives into their homes to keep them safe, even as others were dragged away in trucks and trains. In all this, God said *"Peace."* Peace in the storm, no matter what might happen.

Helen finally emerged from her room, her face red, her cheeks still damp as she pushed back strings of blond hair hanging in her face. She would always be the lovely bride of his heart.

"I'm sorry I couldn't speak to you until now," she said in a flat voice, her eyes glazed.

Erik decided not to push but to wait for her to speak of her own accord about what happened. He stifled any emotional reaction. But he did notice the flash of a fancy pin on her dress. "That's pretty. Is it Delia's?"

Helen looked down, grabbed hold of it, and ripped it off, tearing the dress. He stared in confusion as she set the pin, with a bit of ripped fabric still attached, on the table. "He gave it to me. I hate it. I don't know what to do."

Erik slowly approached her, and she tumbled into his arms like one of the children.

"I'm afraid I will lose you, Erik. And the children."

His heart stirred. She voiced the same fears he was experiencing. The same doubt. The same worry. "Helen, we will pray for a solution. God will not give us anything more than we can handle." He added, "Delia told me she and Ephraim have a good pastor friend who may be able to find a new hiding place for the children."

She pulled back and looked at him. "You mean take them away from us?"

"It's always been about the children. You know that. To help them hide and stay alive. If the pastor can find a new home, then you and I can go back to Amsterdam and—"

Her eyes widened in shock. "But—"

Suddenly they heard a cry. David stood there, holding one of his trucks. "You're going to send us away? You—You can't! You can't do that!"

The other two children came running. All three stared at Erik and Helen with large eyes and trembling lips.

"You can't leave us!" David said again.

Lida wrapped her arms around Helen's waist. "Please, please don't leave me, Mama."

"Erik," Helen murmured, searching his face, "there has to be another way for us to remain together. We are a family now."

He agreed and asked the children to join them. When they did, he gave them each a hug. "We will ask God right now to help us find a way to stay together as a family. If it's His will. But if not and He chooses another family for you, they will be good too. We must believe it."

Later that evening, Helen and Erik gathered with the Vissers after the children were tucked in for the night. It had been a somber time as each child gazed in wonder and concern, asking if they would be leaving soon. Erik didn't say much except to reassure them that God was watching over them and they would do whatever was right to keep them from harm. Lida nestled under the covers and was soon asleep with her doll by her side. David stayed awake the longest, opinionated as ever for a now nine-year-old when he declared he liked it at the Visser farm and would not go. Erik explained that they would leave only if there was no other choice and that David must continue to be brave. The boy relented and, like his adopted siblings, drifted off to sleep. Erik prayed the boy's dreams were filled with comfort and peace.

Now in the sitting room with the Vissers, he saw Helen as fidgety as he had ever seen her, crossing and uncrossing her legs, winding a length of golden braid around one finger. She had just explained to Delia about the rip in the dress, with red eyes and trembling lips, and with her usual grace, Delia dismissed it all. No longer did Helen appear confident, and Erik grieved. He remembered well the time in the classroom at the college when she informed him they must take children into hiding. Now he wished for that spark of defiance to return, for her to believe a miracle could happen even if everything looked bleak. To keep fighting, no matter what.

"Delia has told me your concerns," Ephraim said. "I will say that since the captain and his soldiers came that one day, I worried they would return and conduct a search of the farm. There have been raids in many places as the Germans' grip tightens. And the captain's obvious interest in Helen also makes for additional worry." He glanced at Delia and sighed. "Because of this, you may well need to find another place to hide. At least for the children."

Erik saw Helen stir and glance out the window. "Delia said you might have a contact to help us."

"Pastor de Windt. A good and godly man. He has been in touch with those in the underground, and they may have a solution for you."

Helen turned back. "I wonder if they know Lars," she said softly. "My brother worked in the underground."

Ephraim nodded. "A noble task. But understand, you can't return to Amsterdam. The SS are emptying the city and this country as we speak. Truckloads of Jews and others are going to Westerbork and on to Auschwitz. If you are caught there, it would be very bad."

Helen glanced at Erik. She must feel as he did—weak and tired against such evil. "Find this pastor, then," she said suddenly. "We will do what we must. Whatever it is." She bent her head, her fingers intertwining. "I never had intentions toward that captain, you understand. I was only doing what I felt I must."

"My dear, you don't have to explain anything to us," Ephraim said. "Delia told me how you've acted most heroically. We do whatever we can to safeguard those we love. And now we must go forward with a new plan to keep you all safe."

"But what about you?" Erik asked. "Won't you be in trouble?"

"Since no one knows that we have sheltered you and three Jewish children from Amsterdam, I think not. We have food that people need. But we will make plans nevertheless, just as you must." Ephraim stood. "I will let you know what the pastor discovers. For now, I suggest you keep to the outlying areas of the dugout and rear barn and avoid the main house." Ephraim leveled his gaze on Helen. "Will that captain call again?"

"I don't know. Probably."

"Very well. We will take things as they come. It's all we can do."

Helen and Erik bade the Vissers good night and headed for their sleeping areas. Suddenly Erik caught her arm. "Helen, I love you deeply. More than you could know."

"I know." She managed a crooked smile. "Thank you for praying for me."

"How did you know?"

She chuckled. "I always know."

"And thank you for doing all you can to see us safe. God will reward you."

Helen sighed. "I would love it if my reward was to see this whole terrible ordeal done with, once and for all."

"Amen."

CHAPTER 21

Erik could not work or do much of anything as he paced back and forth in the barn. Helen tried to read to the children, pausing on occasion to watch him in his jittery state. He wished he could calm himself while awaiting the news from this pastor that Ephraim knew. The pastor had gone out of town and was not expected back for several days. In expectation, however, Erik instructed everyone to pack up their few essential belongings and pile the rest of their goods together to store in the dugout, including the toys. "These are very dangerous times," he told the children. "The bad men could come here at any time. Because they have been here before, we must be ready to leave at a moment's notice. We can't take extra things with us like toys. They are safe here with Mr. and Mrs. Visser, who will keep them until we return."

"Will they be safe?" David asked. "I wish I could take my truck." He held it up before reluctantly setting it in the pile of toys.

Erik reassured them. "They will take good care of everything. I hope and pray we aren't gone long. The war can't go on for much longer."

He sighed, remembering when the Vissers heard the news on their radio of the British conducting more bombing raids to try and weaken

Germany's ability to wage war. At one point, when Helen had left to gather eggs at the henhouse, Ephraim told Erik that North Amsterdam had been mistakenly bombed by the British. "I think I recall that you came from Amsterdam Noord."

"Helen's family lives there," Erik said, looking around, expecting Helen to appear at any moment. If she heard the news, without a doubt she would insist on returning to check on her family. The Germans were fighting to maintain their hold on the annexed territories, and revenge was fierce. There was no telling what might happen. "We can't tell her. Please don't. Not until it's the right time."

Ephraim promised. He went on to say that many of his Jewish friends had been rounded up in Edam. Raids were occurring everywhere. "It's a dangerous time to be leaving to go to a new hiding place," he noted somberly. "But there's little choice."

Erik continued to pace about the barn with all these thoughts bombarding his mind. He was responsible for the safety of them all, and not knowing the future left him all the more anxious. Helen left the children with the book she had been reading to them to go to him. "Are you all right?" she asked. "What's wrong?"

He wanted to tell her outright that she may have lost her family in a rogue bombing, raids were occurring everywhere, and there was untold danger no matter what they did, whether staying or leaving. Keeping all the worry bottled up inside only magnified his own. Yet he only said, "I hope we have news from the pastor soon."

Helen stepped away to look out toward the home in the distance, with the evening shadows of summer dancing across the land. "I'm sure we will." At least Helen's captain had not paid a visit or even called on her. Perhaps he had been transferred to other duties, and therein remained the only bright spot in all this turmoil. Erik took her hand and held it tight. At least he had a renewed confidence that she was his.

Suddenly there came a distant rumble of a vehicle. Erik told Helen to remain with the children while he went to talk to Ephraim. When he approached the main house, it was not Ephraim's car but a German jeep bearing the prominent black cross. His body went numb as he hid behind a large oak tree. He peeked out a few times. A man exited, dressed smartly in his uniform and helmet. *Oh God. Is that him?* Delia gave a friendly greeting and informed him in Dutch that Helen had gone on an errand. *It's him!* The man answered in German and English— neither of which was understood well. But the captain must have understood Delia's meaning enough because he returned to his jeep. Erik tensed, his hand balling into a fist, desiring to get rid of the captain with every part of his being.

One thing was clear. This man was not going away as Erik had hoped.

Once the jeep drove off, Erik made his way to the main house where Delia was finishing dinner. "I'm afraid you will have to take the food back to the barn tonight," she told him. "I don't dare have you at the house for dinner after the captain was here."

"Did he want to see Helen?"

"Yes. I think I was able to tell him that she wasn't here. But I don't know. The last time we spoke, Helen translated in Engels for him."

Erik sensed it as she did. Time was running out. "What about Ephraim? When do you expect him back?"

"He said that he will be late. I'm sorry."

Erik heaved a sigh, worried that Ephraim had still been unable to make contact with the pastor. And now on the heels of this came the German captain wanting to be with Helen. He felt like he had been dropped into a bottomless pit. *Oh God, I know You must be very tired of my requests. Every day I come with more dire issues needing Your help. We have to escape again. Help get us to safety. Especially for Helen, before it's too late.*

Erik ate little for dinner that night despite his favorite meal of fragrant gehaktballen over noodles. He stirred the meatballs and gravy around in the bowl before David leaned over and snatched a meatball. Helen reprimanded him, but Erik waved it off. "Let him eat it if he wants. He's going to need it." Erik surrendered his bowl to the hungry boy. Helen tried to engage Erik in conversation, but he felt as if a stone had lodged in his throat. He hated keeping everything from her. First the bombing of her hometown and now the captain's visit. He knew if he told her though, she would be gone before he could even blink. But if he said nothing and the captain decided to return to have a look around for himself, it could put them in even greater danger.

Just then Helen grabbed his hand and led him to an old stall filled with musty hay. She turned to face him. "Erik, what's happening? I can see it in your face. It's bad news, isn't it?"

He sighed. "Remember when I went to check on Ephraim's arrival from town earlier today? When I got there, that captain had arrived in his jeep." In the dimness, he could see her blue eyes reflecting the lantern light.

"He was looking for me?"

"Delia told him you were on an errand. But she spoke in Nederland and he in *Duits* and Engels, and I don't think they understood each other well. He might return."

Helen whirled. "I must go see him then."

He grabbed her arm. "Nee! You can't! What if he demands you leave with him?"

324

"Erik, you must trust me. Or God working in me. But I have to communicate, and if he wants to see me, I have to go. He and his soldiers will search this place if he suspects anything. Everything must appear normal to his eyes."

Erik knew she was right and reluctantly let her go. She hurried to the small suitcase, knelt, and took out the only other dress she had—the one Delia had altered for her after she tore the flowered dress. It appeared ragged and creased, and a part of him was glad. The more haggard she looked, the better chance the captain would reject her. He hoped. When she turned to leave, he only wanted to grab her hand and hold it tight. But God had given her confidence in the situation. She told him to move to the dugout with the children just in case. He let her go, and she made her way into the deepening twilight until it swallowed her.

Erik gathered the three children, along with their possessions and what remained of dinner, to head for the dugout they had converted into a hiding place. Just the idea of being there magnified the fear. Even the children were unusually quiet, clinging to a few toys and his arms as if never wanting to let go. When he heard noises outside, he whispered that they must be like mice, never seen and making no noise either, until it was safe. He waited what felt like an eternity, uncertain of what was happening. Wondering if he would even see Helen again. And while they waited, he made a vow to himself. Before they escaped again, he would marry her. Even if the ceremony took place in the dark and damp dugout, he would not let another day pass by without making Helen his wife. The time was now.

After what seemed like hours in the cramped and cold place, waiting and wondering, he heard a soft knock on the door of the dugout. Erik froze and pressed a finger to his lips to still the children. He waited.

"Erik, it is I, Ephraim. Are you in there?"

He slowly opened the heavy wood door covered in vines and moss to see the friendly face shining in the light from a lantern. "Did you see Helen?" Erik asked.

"No, I'm sorry, I didn't. She must have left before I came home. Delia told me about the visit today by the German officer."

"She left to be with him. What if she never comes back?"

"We trust God. It's all any of us can do. But I have news. I saw Pastor de Windt. He knows the Dutch-Belgium resistance in Maastricht. As soon as Helen returns, he will take you there, and they will help you find a place to stay."

"Tonight?"

"Yes, tonight. It's too dangerous to remain any longer. The pastor believes this is the best choice for you with the Dutch countryside being overrun and house-to-house raids being conducted. So far Helen's meetings with the captain seem to have prevented such raids in this area. Perhaps the distraction of it all. When she returns though, you all must leave."

At that moment, Erik saw a vision of Helen among the tulips, accepting his emerald ring and expressing her happiness over their engagement. The wedding would not wait any longer. "Ephraim, is it possible this pastor could marry us before we leave?"

Ephraim stared at him in silence for a moment. "I don't know. If he can spare the time, maybe."

"We are indebted to him for all he is doing. But this must be done. It cannot be put off any longer."

Ephraim nodded. "We will make the necessary preparations. I wish I had a suit that fits you." He laughed, acknowledging his rather plump stomach. It was a strange sound to hear in the midst of this upheaval. But for Erik, it lent comfort and healing to these desperate times.

"Thank you for everything." Erik shook the man's hand and watched him walk off into the night shadows. He wished he could keep the door open and await Helen's return. Instead, he bit his lip and closed the door. He dared not think of anything but seeing her bright blue eyes and honey-colored hair, feeling her arms in his, and their lips saying to each other, *I do*. If God would only bring her safely back to him.

He turned to see David looking at him. Lida and Josiah lay in a mass of blankets, already asleep. "We are leaving tonight," he told the boy. "Another adventure."

"I'm tired of adventures," David said solemnly. "I want to go home."

Erik couldn't help but agree.

Helen stared at the sight of the glittering diamond ring wavering before her as the tears pooled in her eyes. She had done it. She'd agreed to marry the relentless captain in exchange for safety. She had no choice. All she knew in life was over. She had done what others had done when faced by superior odds. Capitulated. In the pocket of her dress rested the ring Erik had given her. She had kissed Werner Vogt after she accepted the ring on her finger as a final act of her submission. Why she ever agreed to marry a German captain went beyond all reason. Reasoning had been abandoned to fear. Like everyone else in the Netherlands, she had raised the white flag of surrender and told the enemy to occupy her life. There was nothing left.

Helen wiped her eyes with one hand and sat up straighter in the driver's seat as she tried to negotiate the road to the farm. This was indeed the longest drive of her life. She'd asked Werner if she could gather a few of her belongings and say farewell to those she loved. He agreed and said he would pick her up at ten o'clock the next morning and they would leave for Germany. He had obtained a leave for three days so they could wed. Everything was set.

The mere thought of what was about to happen made her eyes burn. She could barely see the road before her that appeared like shimmers of water in the headlights. It felt like she was driving into the sea, and right now that might not be such a bad idea. Werner told her he was in love with her, that he would give her a good home in Germany, that his family would love her, and that the two of them would raise a fine family. And she would be proud of him in all he did. For Helen, all she could think of was Erik and the children. At least they would be safe. They would go on without her. It might be painful, but they would live. And that was all that mattered, even if her life had ended by agreeing to this engagement.

When the farmhouse appeared, Helen inhaled a deep breath. She saw a strange vehicle parked in front of the main house and the windows glowing gold from the lights. Had Werner come to take her away tonight? He had agreed she would have time to pack. She stepped out to find the Vissers, Erik, and a man she didn't recognize all gathered on the porch, waiting.

"Erik . . . ," she began. He took her hand and

hurried her into the house. "What is going on?"

"Pastor de Windt is taking us to Maastricht tonight," he said in a husky voice. "He knows people there who can help us."

"But Erik—"

"Before we leave, we are going to be married. Right now."

Married? She stared at him as he picked up her ring hand and saw the glimmer of a diamond. "What is that?"

"N–Nothing," she told him. "I–I'll be right back." She went upstairs and twisted the ring off her finger. She felt for the emerald in the pocket of her dress and placed it back on her hand, then paused before the mirror and drew in a deep breath. *All things work together for good, Helen.* When she returned, she said to Erik, "Let's do this quickly. Very quickly."

Ephraim motioned them to the sitting room. Delia pressed a few of her wooden tulips into Helen's hands. They stood a few feet apart, gazing into each other's eyes as Pastor de Windt performed the brief ceremony. When he proclaimed them man and wife, Erik embraced her, whispered that they would be safe, and kissed her to the clapping of the Vissers.

"Please, can you give us a moment?" Erik asked. He sat down with Helen as the others quietly conversed in the dining room.

Helen knew she must tell Erik what had transpired tonight. How this had been a last-minute miracle. She showed him her hand that held his emerald. "I have to tell you something. What you saw earlier on my hand was a diamond ring. Werner gave it to me tonight. I put it on and agreed to marry him."

"What?"

"I thought there was no way out. I—I told him to come back tomorrow morning, and we would leave for Germany. I wanted you all safe." She crumpled into his arms. "Now we must leave tonight. We have no choice."

"We *are* leaving." He smoothed back her blond hair. "God heard our prayers and saw your sacrifice. He said we will be safe. And we will be. We are married. Now we will get the children and be off with Pastor de Windt. He found a new place for us to hide."

She breathed a sigh. "Erik, no matter what happens, I'm glad we're married. So very glad."

They sealed the moment with a kiss, lengthening the encounter as they drew close, seeking strength in the embrace and a soothing of frayed nerves that would rise again with the next escape thrust before them. Once more, in faith, they would have to leap off the precipice and into the unknown, with three young children who only wanted stability and a place to call home. Now they had a chance of making it come true through their vows to one another.

They looked up as the Vissers and Pastor de Windt entered the room. "We must leave now," the pastor said. "It's several hours' drive to Maastricht. I must have you there on time to meet the guide."

Ephraim stepped forward, a paper rattling in his hand. "Before you leave, we have something to share with the both of you." He paused. "Delia and I thought it over and prayed. We don't know what the future holds, but we've come to a decision about our worldly goods. We are deeding the farm and all its contents and livestock to you upon our passing."

Helen released Erik's arm and covered her mouth with her hand. "I . . . I don't understand."

Delia, always a cheerful soul, smiled broadly. "It's very simple. If something happens to us, we want to know that the farm is in safe hands."

Helen shook her head. "Nothing is going to happen to you."

"You can no more predict the future than we could have predicted anything that has come upon us," Ephraim said. "With such uncertainty, we have peace knowing our possessions and land will not be scattered to the wind. It will be managed by a fine fellow who has some knowledge of the farm and cheese making and running a shop." Ephraim's wrinkled hand trembled as he gave Erik a folded paper. Erik opened it to see the bequeathment to Erik and Helen Minger. "We know there is danger having this on your person with your false identities, so we will give it to the pastor for safekeeping. But we wanted you to see it before you leave."

Helen had tears in her eyes, and Delia did also. She embraced the older woman. "Please be safe," Helen mourned. "Please."

Delia smiled. "You realize we are always safe in the Master's hands. No matter what happens." She stepped back and stared unflinchingly into Helen's eyes. "No matter what happens," she repeated.

Erik shook Ephraim's hand before stepping forward and embracing him.

"Thank you for being the son I have dearly missed," the man murmured. "This has been such a comfort to me and Delia."

Erik looked at Helen, who returned his gaze with a readiness to depart. He picked up her hand that glimmered with the emerald.

"Just a minute." Helen hastened upstairs and snatched up the diamond ring. Inhaling a breath, she looked around to see a piece of paper and a pencil from the children's schooling and scribbled out a note, praying Werner would accept her decision and disappear as quickly as he appeared. She returned to the sitting room and pressed the note and ring into Delia's hand. "He will be here tomorrow at ten. Give this to him."

Delia nodded before coming forward and giving Helen a kiss. "God be with you."

Erik took Helen's hand, and together they followed the pastor to the car. Once inside they drove to the rear of the farm where he and Helen fetched the sleepy children from the dugout along with the leather knapsacks and a suitcase. Once more they were escaping into the hand of God.

"Erik . . . ," Helen said, unable to speak the words of another long and dark unknown.

"I know."

CHAPTER 22

Helen listened to Erik chatter away with the pastor—everything from his church to his family to his thoughts about the German occupation. She sat between them in the cramped front seat with the children crowded in the back seat, occasionally glancing back to see them falling over each other, fast asleep, and praying they were having good dreams of playing or sailing a toy boat in a canal. The final thought reminded her of the first day she met Erik on the road and him taking Hans in a cart to sail a handmade boat in a canal race. How long ago that seemed, but how expertly Erik had taken each challenge with wisdom and grace—from fixing her bike to the moment of this escape yet again out of the enemy's clutches. She felt for the emerald ring, reminding herself she was now married to him, for better or for worse. It didn't feel like it as they drove across the dark countryside. Would she and Erik ever have a normal life together?

But what was normal anyway? She used to think it was college and work and waiting for love and marriage and raising children, along with all their complexities. She could clearly say none of her current circumstances were normal in the least, but she still yearned for peace and laughter and good times again.

Thankfully, the road they traveled was absent of any traffic, being well after midnight. Pastor de Windt said they should arrive about two thirty in the morning to greet their guide. She hoped the children wouldn't be too exhausted with a harrowing journey on little sleep. But they had no choice. The German forces were closing in. She prayed they wouldn't run into any SS or other patrols sent out by the captain when word came down in the morning. How she prayed the Vissers would be all right when Werner arrived and found her gone. Knowing Delia, she would serve him biscuits and coffee and then give him the note she had written. Helen closed her eyes, praying everything would be all right. There was nothing else she could do.

Just then Erik grabbed her hand as if he too wrestled with a myriad of thoughts as the car rushed along the dark road. He had to be wondering what awaited them in the dead of night with their three young charges. Did he also consider their marriage, the fate of their country, their families, and what the future held? How she wanted to spend hours talking to him about it all, as well as their future. Instead, she stayed silent as Erik asked the pastor about their guide.

"I've had several dealings with Marc. He helped several of my parishioners leave the country. He knows the Belgian resistance well."

Helen finally found her voice in the conversation. "But will we be safe there? Belgium borders the Netherlands and—"

"There is far less German infiltration in Belgium than in the Netherlands. The townspeople also fight back. It's been very difficult seeing our people so willingly accept mandates from the Nazis with little resistance. If every nation fought back, the Germans could not control any of us."

"But so many would die," Helen said softly.

"Many are dead anyway. What is happening goes beyond words." The pastor sighed long and loud before glancing in his rearview mirror at the sleeping children. "I will tell you right now, if you had not done what you did with those children, they would be dead. The Germans are killing thousands of Jewish men, women, and children. Gassing them at the camps. No child under fifteen survives."

Helen gripped Erik's hand. She thanked God, but tears of shock rose when she thought of those left behind—the happy children in the crèche playing with their toys or reading books, unaware of their fate. She buried her head in Erik's shoulder and tried not to think for the pain of it. But it made her realize too that God had used them. If only they would see an end to this madness.

The pastor glanced at her. "I'm sorry to have caused you distress. I thought it would do your heart good to know that your work in the Lord was not in vain."

"I wish now I had taken another child with us. Just one more. We could have done it." She sniffed with the tears filling her eyes and felt around in her pocket for a handkerchief.

"Don't you dare carry such a burden," the pastor gently reprimanded. "We know in our hearts that the children who left this world are in the presence of Jezus. It is better to be absent from the body and at home with the Lord. Whether in life or death, we can rest in Him. As can the children."

Helen blew her nose. Just then she felt a tiny hand on the back of her neck and turned to see Lida, shifting her doll from one arm to the other, her small mouth breaking open in a yawn. "Mama, are you crying?" she asked in a sleepy voice.

"Go back to sleep, darling. I'm fine." But her heart swelled at the title Lida gave her. Just twenty-three years of age and a mother of three. Who would have thought this would be her calling? Her journey began in college to become a teacher, and now she was a refugee in the darkness, escaping with her husband and three children. But the memory that came next, of nearly succumbing to a life with a German soldier, his face over hers as he kissed her and gave her the ring, made her shudder. She gripped Erik's arm and prayed they would soon arrive safely in Maastricht.

They drove by a wooden shack set up beside the road. The pastor continued on but kept frequent watch in the rearview mirror. He sighed and wiped his forehead. "This is what I was afraid of. The Germans have set up checkpoints along the roads. Do you have your papers?"

"Yes, but only for us and two of the children," Erik told him. "We took Josiah at the last minute, and there wasn't time to get papers for him."

Just then a jeep pulled out from behind the shack. Bright headlights blinked on and off as it bore down with increasing speed. Helen shook. If it was Werner Vogt, they were as good as dead. And they might still be as they pulled off the road and waited. Never had she felt so close to death, seeing the German soldier march up to the driver's window, carrying a large rifle. Thankfully, the children remained asleep.

"Let me see your papers," he barked in German, shining a flashlight full in their faces before scanning the sleeping faces in the back seat.

Erik handed papers over to the pastor, who handed them out the window. The pastor chit-chatted in German.

The soldier looked at the papers, then the children once more. "You have two IDs, but there are three children."

"Where is the third ID?" the pastor asked Erik. He reached across Helen and began pulling at Erik's pockets. "*Dummkopf.*"

Helen sat still and silent. Erik searched each pocket and shrugged.

The soldier sighed loudly as the pastor continued to speak to him. He then stepped back, hesitated, and waved them on. Helen could not believe it as the pastor thanked him and drove back onto the road.

"Will he follow us?" Erik asked.

Pastor de Windt shook his head. "No. We are all right." He swiped a hand across his face. "Praise Jezus."

"What did you say to him?" Erik asked.

"I said you were a terrible assistant and I should fire you. But we just came from a prayer meeting and you had given your heart to Jezus. I told him I'm praying things will get better." He paused. "The name of Jezus sends the demons fleeing, and I don't think the soldier wanted to stay and hear any more about it."

Helen marveled at the man who gripped the steering wheel. She wanted to hug him out of pure relief. Instead, she clung to Erik's arm. "Thank you," she whispered. God had parted the sea before them to the promised land.

Erik rested on the damp and cold stone floor, cradling Helen in his arms, the softly snoring children arrayed around them. In the distance he could hear water dripping while he watched the lantern light flicker off the figure of the guide perusing a map. Never in his wildest imagination would he have thought they would be delivered to Maastricht like this—and find themselves waiting out the few remaining hours of the night inside a cave. But here they were, none the worse. When they arrived at Maastricht and met the guide, Marc, the children could hardly be pushed to stay awake, let alone walk the two-mile distance to Belgium. Marc suggested that they rest in this stony alcove before continuing on their way. It was safe, the man assured them, as many from Maastricht had hidden here during the fiercest bombings when the Luftwaffe flew over the country in the initial invasion. Which for Erik seemed like another lifetime.

Helen's breathing turned soft and rhythmic, and he knew she had finally drifted off into a more sound sleep. What a nerve-wracking time for all of them, from the captain's interest in Helen to the soldier who stopped them tonight on a dark country road as they entered Limburg province. He didn't dare tell her, but the grip of Helen's hand encircling his arm nearly pinched off the blood flow. Pastor de Windt had been a marvel, and Erik wished he had half the man's wisdom and courage for the perilous times that remained.

Erik gently eased Helen to the cave floor, using

another folded blanket to rest her head. He then cautiously approached their guide. Marc wore a ripped coat, wool cap, and dirty trousers. Erik had prayed that Marc would prove reliable and would lead them to safety. But after tonight, he had no cause whatsoever to doubt the godly pastor who delivered them here. "Once we leave the cave, where will we go?" he asked in a low voice.

"We will walk through a cave to Belgium and from there to a family who has agreed to keep you."

"Walk through a cave to Belgium?" Erik glanced around, barely able to see the straight walls around him that showed a cave carved out by human hands long ago.

Marc showed him on a rough map the route they would take.

"I had no idea there were caves leading to Belgium."

"Oh, there's a great many here. Many miles of them. In fact, several of the caves are being used to store valuable goods, paintings and such, to keep them out of German hands. A few areas of the cave even have living quarters."

"Could we hide there?"

The man shook his head. "No. It's not good for your children. But don't worry. The family I know is very happy to have you."

Erik rubbed his hand through his hair in worry

and then willed himself to stop. He glanced beyond their murky surroundings at the dark passage leading into the unknown, wondering what the children would think. The boys would find it all fascinating, for sure. He hoped Lida wouldn't be scared of the dark. "Is Belgium safe for Jewish children?"

"Belgium has escaped a good deal of the Nazis' attention, unlike the Netherlands," Marc said, folding the map and putting it in his coat pocket. He crossed his legs in a confident posture with his hands tucked behind his head. "For one, your country shares a common border. The Germans conduct more raids in the dead of night. We help each other in Belgium and tell each other when the Germans are coming so there is time to hide. In the Netherlands, many betray each other for money. Or they simply go along with the orders of the enemy and don't hide. It's really quite sad."

Erik frowned. Never would he have thought his countrymen would betray one another. But seeing how swiftly the Dutch authorities succumbed to German command without question, meeting their decrees and heaping great harm onto their Jewish population, it grieved him all the more for his homeland. Nothing would be the same even if the Allies did liberate them. What would become of them as a country?

After a few hours, the children stirred. David

rubbed his eyes and inquired of their whereabouts in this dark and dank place. Marc rose and lit their lanterns. He gave them some bread and cheese. "Eat quickly, then we must be off. It's still a few hours before dawn and an excellent time to make our way through the cave."

Helen was still groggy but managed a smile and ate just a small piece of bread with cheese as she asked Erik about the plan. "We will walk to Belgium through a cave, Helen."

Her wide eyes reflected the light of the lantern. "I had no idea."

"Neither did I. The caves here have been very useful for protecting and concealing . . . and now for escaping." He encouraged the children to finish their meal as they were going on another adventure—this time through a cave.

"Are there animals?" Lida asked, clutching her doll close.

"No animals," Marc assured her. "Some bats."

The boys whooped, both eager to see a bat.

Erik rounded the children up along with their possessions, and they followed Marc through the dark interiors. Water dripped from the ceiling above. Puddles on the cavern floor reflected the glow of the lantern light. Helen held Lida's hand, helping the girl along. Suddenly Helen stopped short and stared. "Look! A painting on the cave wall!"

"There are quite a few drawings in the cave,"

Marc said. "Some are very elaborate. When one is caught here for many days or even weeks, there's plenty of time to create some beautiful works."

"I want to draw on the cave wall," David announced.

"We must keep going," Erik told him. "Our new family is anxious to see us, and we must get there before we see any more bad men."

They marched on through the darkness that began to narrow and grow even wetter. Lida complained about her wet feet. In a few places, Erik hefted her into his arms and carried her through the water that soaked his ankles. The boys fared better in the murky, dank conditions with water to their knees.

"We are walking under a river," Marc explained.

The boys talked about being underwater like fish, and Erik used the journey to tell them they were like the Israelites passing through the Red Sea to escape Pharaoh's army. The boys soaked it in like water to a sponge and grew even more excited, not caring in the least about their soggy shoes and wet trousers. Erik caught sight of a myriad of reddish hues, growing as they continued.

"Belgium," Marc announced with a smile. Slowly they emerged out of a hole in the ground to see a dark blue horizon colored bright red and orange with the coming dawn. "We have less than an hour before the sun rises. I have an auto parked not far away."

"I have some money, sir," Erik said. "You have done so much."

"Save it for the children. They are all that matters. And it is no less than what you are doing. The pastor told me how you left everything behind in Amsterdam to care for them. And God is watching it all."

Erik heard a sniff and saw Helen wipe a tear from her cheek. He wrapped his arm around her and gave her a kiss, tasting the saltiness the tear left behind. "We'll be all right."

"Yes," she agreed.

Not long after, they were safely in the car, speeding along as the skies slowly brightened. When they arrived at their place of safety that looked much like the Visser farm they had just left, with a main house and outlying barns, Erik felt at ease at once. The Offerman family greeted them with open arms and a hot breakfast.

While the family went inside, Erik followed Marc back to his automobile. "Echt heel erg bedankt," he said, offering grateful thanks.

"It won't be long," Marc assured him and placed his cap firmly on his head. "The Allies are massing in England. The invasion is coming. We will win. Wait and see."

Erik wished he could believe him, but after

so many years and with a war-weary mind and spirit, he had to wonder. But he offered a smile of hope anyway and returned to see the family gathered at the table and hear Mrs. Offerman telling the children about the wonderful animals on their farm and the good things they would do.

"I know how to milk and make cheese," Erik announced.

Mr. Offerman laughed. "I have gained a new helper, and we have children to brighten our lives. All will be well. Very soon."

Erik glanced at Helen over a bountiful serving of eggs and good ham, smiled at the happy but tired faces of his family, and thanked the Lord for so many blessings. They added a prayer that their loved ones were safe, no matter where they were. His joyful heart stilled. May this soon be over, as Marc said, so they could be reunited once again.

PART FOUR

Liberation
1945

CHAPTER 23

Helen could hardly believe it was true. The war had ended at last, and they were going home. The Offermans had kept them close to two years until the Allies came. They rejoiced when the Allies landed in Normandy. As the troops advanced, liberating countries one by one, the cheers grew louder. When the troops finally made it to Belgium, Mr. Offerman suggested they all pile into his automobile and join the celebration in the streets of Liege. Allied forces marched through, soldiers nodding and smiling as the townspeople cheered. Erik motioned for Lida to stand on some stairs to a house so she could see the soldiers and wave her little Belgian flag. Belgian flag. Helen dearly wanted to return home then, but it was many months later and another hard winter before Holland was liberated. When the time finally came, hugs turned into tears as they prepared to return home. Helen thanked the Offerman family for all they had done. So many had aided their escape from Amsterdam, and she was grateful for their sacrifice.

"Please let us know how you are and come visit again," Mrs. Offerman said and then gave them all her famous chocolate covered sugar cookies. Helen enjoyed greatly the Belgian chocolate the

Offermans were able to procure, making the time much more pleasant. But when they offered her and Erik a cottage to stay in for a short and sweet honeymoon while the Offermans cared for the children, the time meant the most to Helen and Erik.

Now they made their way back to Maastricht through a friend of the Offermans to where Ephraim Visser promised to pick them up. They waited patiently until Helen recognized the familiar car that she had used many times to see Werner in Edam. She refused to dwell on that time and only thought now of the strength of the man by her side. They were Mr. and Mrs. Minger, and all had been made right.

Ephraim slowly rose out of the car, his smile weak, his clothing hanging on his emaciated form. He wore a long silvery beard. Helen would not have recognized him but for his voice. She put away her concern to embrace him. "It's so good to see you. How I've missed you and Delia."

"You all look well," he said. "I missed you on the farm."

"I'm looking forward to helping," Erik said.

"If only there was more work to do," he said somberly. On the drive back he told them the German army had taken most of his animals and crops. He used the dugout to hide whatever he could, including seed to replant the crops, plus money and valuables. Still, without a good herd of cows, he had to close the cheese shop. But he made do with what they had, and another worker helped out when he could. "I was recently able to buy a few cows, but there aren't many since the hard winter, and they are very expensive." He paused. "The Germans cut off our food supply when they heard the Allies were coming. There was no food in many towns. People starved to death."

Helen glanced Erik's way to see the seriousness of his face, and the joy she felt at their return was muted by this sad news. Ephraim drove past piles of rubble and blackened pits of earth from exploding ordnance. "We got bombed, especially as the Allies advanced," he explained.

"We had bombs go off too," David said from the back seat. "In Belgium."

"I didn't like them," Lida added. "They were so loud."

"So, tell me about your time in Belgium," Ephraim asked.

Erik explained how Ephraim's careful tutelage helped with the farming at the Offermans. Helen confessed how much she loved Belgian chocolate, and the children talked about the animals, all they learned, and the parades when the good guys came marching across the land and big tanks came rolling down the street.

"And how is Delia?" Helen wondered. "I've missed her so much."

Ephraim's bony fingers tightened around the wheel and a tinge of pink entered his pale cheeks. "Well, let me tell you, Helen. God decided He needed her to be with Johan, our boy. She left me a few months ago, and they had a big reunion in heaven."

Helen felt as if she had been tossed into an icebox. She began to tremble. "What?" she said weakly as Erik reached for her hand.

"One morning she just didn't wake up." He sniffed, but a smile crept across his wrinkled face. "She was wearing a big grin, she was. She saw heaven and all its glory. My Delia."

Tears invaded Helen's eyes and she quickly wiped them away. "I'm so sorry."

"No need to be sorry. She is happy. When the tulips bloomed, I gathered a bunch for her resting place and put the rest in the sitting room on the mantel where she used to put out those wooden ones, you know? I'm sure she liked seeing the house all fixed up like that. And she is happy to know you are safe."

Helen sat numbed by the news. Erik expounded on Delia's giving and loving heart, but the words lay frozen in Helen's throat.

Just then Josiah piped up from the rear seat. "What does it mean Delia went to see God?"

"It's like this," Ephraim said in a gravelly voice. "Delia went to sleep one night and woke up in heaven with all the beautiful birds and big trees. And she saw the Lord on His throne and our own little boy, Johan."

"You mean she's not here?"

"Ja," Erik said to the three children who stared with large eyes.

Helen wanted to cry aloud but stifled her tears. She remembered what Delia emphatically told her before she left to hide in Belgium. *"You realize we are always safe in the Master's hands. No matter what happens."* It was like Delia knew she would not be here for long, and her faith still shone through, despite everything.

Ephraim's voice suddenly rang out in the solemn atmosphere prevailing inside the car. "Now I don't want you to be sad for her. She's rejoicing. I am too, even though I miss her. And you know why? Because you gave her such joy during the time you spent with us at our farm. You gave us a purpose and a reason to live."

Helen reflected on his words as they arrived at the farm. A little while later, she saw Delia's simple grave in a quiet field not far from the dugout. Erik found her hand and gripped it tightly as they saw Delia's name carved on the stone. Now Helen worried who else might have died that she didn't know about. Like her family. "Erik, I must know what happened to our families."

He removed his hand from hers and tucked it into his pocket. "I worry too," he confessed. "We heard over the radio some time ago that Noord was bombed."

Noord was bombed? Helen tensed. "What? When?"

"We were in the middle of the predicament with the captain and working to escape to Belgium. I'm sorry, Helen. I—I couldn't tell you at that time. I knew what you would do if I did. I couldn't risk you going back."

A raw fury filled her. Helen opened her mouth, ready to spew out angry words, until she realized he was right. If she had known, she would have returned to the house and possibly jeopardized everything. But to think her family may have died and she never told them goodbye. They could have died not knowing her whereabouts or even if she was alive. Distress filled her. She hurried away from Erik and to the main house.

"Helen, wait!"

"I'm going right now to Noord. I must know what happened. And don't you dare try to stop me."

"I'm coming too."

He held out his hand. Helen grasped it, and they walked quickly to the house to ask Ephraim for the car keys. Helen bit back the awful fear at the thought of losing the ones they loved. As they had during every other time in their lives, they would let God's strength carry them through.

• • •

Helen's sight blurred from emotion when they entered the outskirts of Noord to see the heavily damaged buildings. Only a few people could be found walking about, appearing like corpses with bleak faces, dark eyes, and emaciated bodies. With debris scattered about the area, they parked the car and walked to Helen's street. She could not believe what she saw in this once-beautiful neighborhood in northern Amsterdam. Piles of rubble met their gaze where gabled brick and wood structures once proudly stood. Several cars had caught on fire, and their black metallic shells were all that was left. She entered the street, and her heart began to beat furiously. She wanted to close her eyes and pray this was all a dream. Her feet slowed. And then she saw it. Her home still stood, but the windows were boarded up and part of the porch had collapsed. The stately oak had lost most of its branches. She ran up and banged on the door. *Oh, please answer! Please!*

The door opened to reveal a thin figure wearing a tangled beard and looking out with bloodshot eyes. "Helen? Helen!" The bony arms of her father wrapped around her and hugged her close. "You're alive. Oh, dear God, you're alive."

"Oh Papa." His tears dampened her blouse. From the doorway came her mother and Simon, who had grown so tall his head nearly touched the ceiling. They surrounded her and embraced her with tears of joy. The feel of bony prominences poking through their clothing told her life must have been a nightmare for them. Above her the ceiling had many cracks and bowed in dangerously. They talked for a while about their lives since Helen had left. She told them of the children and her marriage to Erik, and her family told of living in a few back rooms since the bombardment, worried the house might collapse. Food had run out. At one point, Papa had dug up all Mama's prized tulips to harvest the bulbs for food. But they had survived. God had helped them.

"Have you heard from Lars?"

"He is safe the last we heard. He checked on us after the bombing and was able to get us some supplies before returning to the underground."

Helen glanced again at the crumbling structure. "You cannot stay here. It's far too dangerous. We have a farm outside of Edam that belongs to a very nice gentleman, Ephraim Visser. They kept us safe for many months. Come back and stay with us. We will be a family again."

She glanced over at Erik and saw pain flicker across his face. He too must see to his family. She told him to go and check on his loved ones while she helped her family sort through what belongings they needed. Erik buried his hands in his pockets and left. How she wished she could go with him, but her family needed help. She prayed a quick prayer for his circumstances, that God would be with him.

After Erik left, Mama took Helen to one of the back rooms and gave her a treasured item she had left behind. The camera. Helen took it as if it were a revered piece, intact and undamaged. Happy memories were still inscribed on film within it. Now she could fill it with pictures of the liberation and her new family.

A few hours later, Erik returned. Seeing his somber face, Helen feared the worst. "My family is safe," he said quickly, accepting her embrace of comfort. "So is their house. There was little bombardment in central Amsterdam itself. Hans was so happy to see me. He's grown taller than me. I hardly recognized him. They said if any of your family needs to stay in Amsterdam, they would be most welcome. They knew Noord received heavy bombardment and were worried for your family."

"But something is wrong, isn't it?"

Lines of tension crisscrossed Erik's face. He nodded slowly. "My boss, Mr. Baas, didn't survive. The store is boarded up. Helen, I also went to Plantage Middenlaan. There's no one at the crèche. Or the college. I don't know what happened, but both places are deserted."

Helen inhaled a sharp breath. It seemed like ages ago since she and Erik rescued the children from the crèche that dreadful day. "Do we have any way of knowing if the children's parents might have survived?"

"From what I've heard, lists will be posted soon. Many are asking. But Helen, it's not good. We have to assume few survived. No one who left the schouwburg on the trucks has returned alive. That's what some people told me. Tens of thousands from all over were deported with no word of their condition. The Jewish Quarter is empty and the apartments all ransacked."

Helen closed her eyes, trying to comprehend the horror of this news. The Cohens. Mrs. Brinn. So many others she had seen in the streets or knew in college or the crèche.

Mama came up then and laid a hand on her arm. "I know it's terrible news, Helen. But look what you did for the sweet children you were telling me about. They would not be alive if it weren't for you. As hard as it was not knowing if you were alive or dead, what you did with our son-in-law here is beautiful. Those children will be our grandchildren, and I will love them with all that is in me."

"Dank je wel, Mama," Helen said with a sniff, resting her head on her mother's shoulder.

The next morning, Erik and Helen drove back to the farm with her parents. They met Ephraim and the children, and they all sat together in the sitting room, drinking out of Delia's delftware that survived the war. How happy Delia would be to see this scene. Maybe even now she was looking down from heaven and watching it all. Afterward Mama and Papa entertained the children, and soon they trooped off together to investigate the farm and their new home.

Helen felt Erik's hand pull hers and beckon her to the front porch. The sun had begun its journey westward to the horizon, casting a fiery orange glaze across the fields. He nuzzled her neck and kissed her. "Helen, the war is finally over."

She turned to him. His dark blue eyes stared into hers, conveying what she felt inside. A great relief it was over but knowing too the great task of rebuilding. "It's over. Thank You, God. Now we must learn to live again."

AUTHOR'S NOTE

Dear Reader:

Thank you for journeying through the eyes of Helen and Erik during a devastating time for the Netherlands during World War II. The German occupation in the 1940s was particularly cruel, and because of it, only thirty-five thousand of the roughly one hundred forty thousand Jews in the Netherlands survived. Even with this horrific statistic, there is good to be found. Helen and Erik's experience and the danger of hiding children memorializes the true stories of those who hid, some living in attics, closets, under the floorboards of a house, or as Anne Frank's family did, in a secret annex, for the duration of the war. It commemorates the untold sacrifice of those who rescued and assisted the Jews, risking betrayal, imprisonment, and death. Because of this effort, nearly 70 percent of those who went into hiding survived.

Professor Johan van Hulst of the Reformed Teacher's Training College and Miss Henriëtte Pimentel of the central Amsterdam crèche were both real people. Through their combined efforts, a thousand children were saved from certain death in the gas chambers of Auschwitz and Sobibór. Sadly, Miss Pimentel was arrested for her efforts at the crèche to help the children. She and her staff were sent to Auschwitz, where they perished. Professor van Hulst used his college to hide children, and because the institution's backyard bordered the crèche, children were spirited over the wall and into his college for safekeeping. When the Germans were alerted to their efforts, Professor van Hulst had to flee Amsterdam with his own set of children. During that painful moment in time, Professor van Hulst said, "Try to imagine seventy, eighty, or a hundred children standing there and you have to decide which to take with you. That was the most difficult day of my life. You know for a fact the children you leave behind are going to die. I took twelve with me. Later I asked myself, 'Why not thirteen?' "

Professor van Hulst survived the war and was awarded the Yad Vashem distinction of Righteous Among the Nations—a title given to Gentiles who risked their lives to save Jews from the Holocaust. He died in 2018 at the age of 107.

My prayer is that you will rejoice in the efforts of those who saved others and find times and places in your lives to help those in need, as difficult and sacrificial as that can be.

God bless you,
Lauralee Bliss

Lauralee Bliss is a published author of many romance novels and novellas, both historical and contemporary. Lauralee's prayer is that readers will come away with both an entertaining story and a lesson that speaks to the heart and soul. When not writing, Lauralee can often be found on the trails where the author has logged over 10,000 miles of hiking. She makes her home in the Blue Ridge mountains with her family. Visit Lauraleebliss.com for more information about the author and her adventures.